He moves, his feet slapping the thin carpet, and a moment later I hear the bang of his door as it slams shut. I stand, poised and ready, the knife tight in my hand, my mind counting the seconds, waiting for what is coming. The click of my lock, the swing of my door, the stab of my knife, the gasp of his breath. Finally. Blood spurting, covering my hands. Pain in his eyes, control in my grip. A life in my hands. 72 seconds.

124 seconds.

648 seconds. I slide to the floor, rolling my wrists as I watch the knife flash in the darkness.

793 seconds. I press my ear to the door, straining for some sound, some clue as to what is happening.

921 seconds.

1,122 seconds. My knife falls to the ground and I feel tears drip down my cheeks.

1,400 seconds. I fall asleep, my bare skin curled against the door, my head drooping at an uncomfortable angle.

Alessandra Torre is the *New York Times* bestselling author of Amazon chart-toppers *Black Lies, Blindfolded Innocence* and erotic thriller, *The Girl in 6E*. From her home near the warm waters of the Emerald Coast in Florida, Alessandra devotes several hours each day to various writing projects and interacting with her fans on Facebook, Twitter and Pinterest. Happily married with one son, she loves watching SEC football games, horseback riding, reading and watching movies. To find out more, visit her website at www.alessandratorre.com

BY A. R. TORRE

The Girl in 6E

AS ALESSANDRA TORRE

Black Lies
Blindfolded Innocence
Masked Innocence
The Diary of Brad De Luca
End of the Innocence
The Dumont Diaries
Sex Love Repeat

THE GIRL IN 6E

A R TORRE

An Orion Paperback

First published in Great Britain in 2014
by Orion Books
This paperback edition published in 2015
by Orion Books,
an imprint of The Orion Publishing Group Ltd,
Orion House, 5 Upper St Martin's Lane,
London WC2H 9EA

An Hachette UK company

3 5 7 9 10 8 6 4 2

Copyright © A. R. Torre 2014

A different version of this book was published
as *On Me, In Me, Dead Beneath Me*

A CIP catalogue record for this book
is available from the British Library.

ISBN 978-1-4091-5350-4

Printed and bound by CPI Group (UK) Ltd, Croydon, CR0 4YY

The Orion Publishing Group's policy is to use papers that
are natural, renewable and recyclable products and made
from wood grown in sustainable forests. The logging and
manufacturing processes are expected to conform to the
environmental regulations of the country of origin.

www.orionbooks.co.uk

This book is dedicated to Terezia, a sister who understands the beauty of a great book, Dr Pepper, naps, and puppy breath.

I HAVE IMAGINED him in my mind for so long, my imagination creating a monster of grotesque features and proportions. But standing before me, his head tilted and eyes sharp, is just a man. Slightly balding, twenty pounds too heavy, whose mouth is turning into a sneer. Whose eyes are narrowing, stance strong, the combined effect sinister. This man, this balding, thick man, has whispered in my ear, poured out the disgusting thoughts in his soul, showed me the dark evil in his heart. And now he is stepping closer, the excitement radiating from his body like a foul smell.

He thinks I am weak. He thinks he can manipulate and subdue me. Kill me. He has no idea that my small frame and delicate features contain an evil that rivals his own. I finger the knife in my pocket and fight to keep a grin off my face.

This is it. This is my time.

Wait

> The mind is its own place, and in itself can make
> a Heaven of Hell, a Hell of Heaven.
>
> —John Milton, *Paradise Lost*

UNDRESSING IS AN everyday occurrence. Most women do it mindlessly—automatic motions that accomplish an end result. But if done correctly, stripping can be the ultimate foreplay, a sexual seduction that can wipe clear any rational thoughts and leave a man totally and utterly at your mercy. I have mastered the art.

I kneel on the bed and trail my fingers over my skin—light, teasing caresses designed to heighten my senses and stimulate my body. I exhale slow, trembling breaths as my hands travel near sensitive areas, the dip in my neckline, the lace over my breasts. I keep my eyes down, subservient to him, and wait for the command. One always comes.

"Take off your top. Slowly." The voice is foreign, English words dipped in culture and dialect. I comply, lifting my eyes and biting my bottom lip gently, my tongue darting out, and hear his gasp in response. I run my hands down my neck, grazing the top of my collarbone and dipping under the silk of my negligee. I slide down one strap, then two, the silk bunching over my breasts, the fabric clinging to my nipples.

Then I rise to my knees, crossing my arms, sliding the fabric higher, letting it reveal inch by slow inch of skin until it unveils the curve of breasts, dip of throat, and pout of pink lips.

"Good," he groans. "Very good. I like you, Jessica."

Jessica. Not my real name. He thinks he knows me. They all think they know me. After all, they've seen my Facebook page, seen the Photoshopped photos that construct my manufactured life. They believe what they see, because they want to believe. They want to believe that I am normal. And for the brief moments I am with them, I fool myself into thinking the same thing.

I turn to the wall and stand, dragging my expensive thong down over toned hips, bending over and exposing my most private area to his hungry eyes. The embroidered lace slides the rest of the way down my legs and drops around my ankles, snagging on the Italian stilettos that encase perfectly pedicured feet. I am naked now and slide down to lie on my side in front of him, propped up on one elbow, his eyes feasting hungrily on my body. The lights, bright and hot, illuminate my bare skin, causing it to glow. He speaks, the arousal present in his voice, in the slight thickening of his accent.

"Touch yourself. Just your fingers. I want to see you come."

He wants my fingers, a seductive performance of gasps, moans, and slick foreplay. Eventually, fingers won't be enough. The next visit he'll want more, something bigger, deeper—my moans to be louder, my orgasm stronger. There will be no secrets anymore, no boundaries, no requests he won't be comfortable giving. At this moment I am his, to do with as he pleases. And right now, he wants fingers.

I angle my body so that he can see my parted legs, my completely bare sex, wet, opened and closed with experienced movements. I dip one finger, then two, inside of me, moving them in and out with slow, seductive strokes, my eyes closed, head tilted back. I hear his gasp, the rustle of clothing, a zipper, and a moan as his hand finds his cock. Unintelligible words, a brief slip into a foreign tongue, the meaning clear despite the language. I increase the speed of my fingers, then pause, spreading my lips and exposing the sensitive bud that holds the power over my ecstasy. I moan softly, a breathy sigh that speaks of want and need, spreading wetness over my swollen clit, the change in pace causing a groan from him.

"Jessica…" He whispers my name, longing and need filling every syllable. "Please. I need to see you come."

I open my eyes, staring forward into the bright lights, a thin sheen of moisture on my skin. I bite my bottom lip, widening my eyes when my fingers again plunge into my core, quick, fast darts of movement, skin on skin, every thrust placing the heel of my hand over my clit with a delicious friction that moves me in the general direction of an orgasm.

I won't come. An actual orgasm is an occasional occurrence, one that my tortured body spits out in exhausted exasperation, one of those "here, take it!" gifts. But for the most part, I am severely oversexed, and my body, my pussy, has grown immune to stimulation. But he doesn't know that. All he knows is that ten minutes after my fingers make their first dip into the wet folds of my sanctum, my back arches, my eyes close, and I have a full-body, toe-curling best-orgasm-of-my-life. I shudder, I gasp; I own the shit out of that fake orgasm. As I always do.

He groans at my climax, his hand creating slick sounds at an impossible speed, and a strangled sound meets my ears, a shuddering moan that disappears into thick gasps.

Then, pure silence. No breaths, no fabric rustling, no sated sighs.

An electronic beep sounds, a tone that I've heard thousands of times. I stretch, grab my lingerie and roll over, hop off the bed, and walk carefully across soft carpet in four-inch heels until I reach my computer's keyboard. I press a key, exiting the website.

The lights go out.

CHAPTER I

I HAVEN'T TOUCHED another person in three years. That seems like a difficult task, but it's not. Not anymore, thanks to the Internet. The Internet, which makes my income possible and provides anything I could possibly want in exchange for my credit card number. I've had to go into the underground world for a few things, and once in that world, I decided to stock up on a few fun items, like a new identity. I am now, when necessary, Jessica Beth Reilly. I use my alias to prevent others from finding out my past. Pity is a bitch I'd like to avoid. The underground provides a plethora of temptations, but so far, with one notable exception, I've stayed away from illegal arms and unregistered guns. I know my limits.

The UPS man knows me by now—knows to leave my boxes in the hall and to scrawl my name on his signature pad. His name is Jeremy. About a year ago he was sick, and a stranger came to my door. He refused to leave the package without seeing me. I almost opened the door and went for his box cutters. They almost always carry box cutters. That's one of the things I love about deliverymen. I stayed fast, refusing to open the door, and he stayed stubborn, arguing with me until he grew tired and left, taking the damn package with him. Jeremy hasn't been sick since then. I don't know what I'll ever do if he quits. I like Jeremy, and from my warped peephole view, there is a lot about him to like. Muscular build, short dark hair, and a smile that stretches quickly and easily over his face, even when there isn't a damn thing to smile about.

The first shrink I had said I have anthropophobia, which is fear of human interaction. Anthropophobia, mixed with an unhealthy dose of dacnomania, which is obsession with murder. He told me that via Skype. In exchange for his psychological opinions, I watched him jack off. He had a little cock. I think he was right on the second half of that diagnosis. But I don't fear human interaction. I fear what will happen when I get close enough to a human to interact. Let's just say I don't play well with others.

While I may go out of my way to avoid physical human interaction, virtual human interaction is what I spend all day doing. To the people I cam with, I am JessReilly19, a bubbly nineteen-year-old college student—a hospitality major—who enjoys pop music, underage drinking, and shopping. None of them really know the true me. I am who they want me to be, and they like it like that. So do I.

Knowing the real me would be a bit of a buzzkill. The real me is Deanna Madden, whose mother killed her entire family, then committed suicide. At the time it was big news, the "tragedy strikes perfect family" story of the summer. My name was attached to sympathy, notoriety. But then other tragedies occurred and my family dropped off the grid. I inherited a lot from my mother, including delicate features, long legs, and dark hair, but the biggest genetic inheritance has been her homicidal tendencies. *That's* the reason I stay away from people. Because I want to kill. Constantly. It's almost all I think about.

My inner demons have driven me here, to apartment 6E, my world for the last three years, all I need contained in nine hundred square feet. I've learned, from inside these walls, how to generate and optimize my income. From eight a.m. to three p.m. I work on a website called Sexnow.com, which has a clientele of mostly Asians, Europeans, and Australians. From six p.m. to eleven p.m. I'm on American turf, Cams.com. In between shifts, I eat, work out, shower, and return e-mails—always in that order. I spend my days on a strict schedule. It helps to tell my brain when to behave a certain way and helps to keep my impulses and fantasies under control.

Whenever possible, I try to get clients to bypass the camsites and use my personal website to book an appointment and pay. If they go through my website, I make 96.5 percent of their payout, plus I can hide the income from Uncle Sam. The camsites pay me only 28 percent, which officially constitutes highway robbery. I charge $6.99 a minute. On a good month, I make around $55,000 from camming—on a bad one, about $30,000.

That income makes up about 70 percent of my total dough; the rest comes from my website's subscription memberships, which allow men to watch a live video feed of my different cam sessions. I broadcast at least four hours a day and charge subscribers twenty bucks a month. I wouldn't pay ten cents to watch me masturbate online, but apparently 350 subscribers feel differently.

The $6.99 a minute grants clients the ability to bare their sexual secrets and fantasize to their heart's content, without fear of exposure or criticism. I don't judge the men and women who chat with me and reveal their secrets and perversions. How can I? My secret, my obsession, is worse than any of theirs. To contain it, I do the only thing I can: I lock myself up. And in doing so, I keep myself, and everyone else, safe.

It is, in simple terms, a shitload of money. Money that I have no earthly idea what to do with. I can spend only so much on sex toys and lube. But thinking about the money makes me think about life outside of this apartment, so I don't. The funds go in my account and are ignored. Maybe they will be used one day, maybe they won't. But I'd rather have the cash than not. I feel protected having it there. I feel like at least one part of my life is going right.

I try to sleep at least eight hours a night. Nighttime is when I typically struggle the most. It is when I thirst for blood, for gore. So Simon Evans and I have an agreement. Simon lives three doors down from me in this shithole that we all call an apartment complex. Over the last three years, he has developed a strong addiction to prescription pain-killers. I keep his medicine bottle filled, and he locks me up at night. Without a doubt, my door is the only one in the complex without a dead-bolt switch on the inside.

I used to have Marilyn do it. She's a grandmotherly type who struggles by on the pittance that is her Social Security.

She lives across from Simon. But Marilyn stressed out too much; she was always worried that I would have some personal emergency, or fire, or something, and would need to get out. I had to find someone else. Because I knew what was coming. At night, my fingers would start to itch, and I would come close to picking up that phone, to asking her to unlock my door. And then I would wait beside it, wait for the tumblers to move and my door to be unlocked. And when I opened it, when I saw Marilyn's lined and tired face, I would kill her. Not immediately. I would stab her a few times, leaving some life in her, and wait for her to run, to scream. I like the sound of screams—real screams, not the pathetic excuse that most movies try to pass off as the sound of terror. Then I would chase her down and finish the job, as slowly as I could. Dragging out her pain, her agony, her realization that she had caused her own death. I had gotten to the point where I had picked out a knife, started to keep it in the cardboard box that sits by the door and holds my outgoing mail and various crap. That was when I knew I was getting too close. That was when I picked Simon instead. Simon's addiction supersedes any concern he has for my well-being.

I know what you think. That I'm being dramatic. That I saw a Stephen King movie once and got excited at the thought of blood. But you don't know the depravity of my mind. You don't know the thoughts I struggle with, what I fight to contain. Simon certainly doesn't know. He thinks I'm a hermit with night terrors—that I sleepwalk. I'm sure he thinks my steadfast dedication to the lock is ridiculous, the unyielding nature of my strict demands extreme. My threats always heighten when he is late, but that doesn't happen often. It takes only a mention of cutting his supply and he snaps to attention. The most reliable thing on earth is a druggie's cravings. I think they are worse than mine. But the only person Simon is hurting with his addiction is himself. I have a whole world of victims outside these walls.

CHAPTER 2

HIS FANTASIES ARE getting stronger. It has been almost three years since the last girl, and his need has overtaken the rational part of his mind. The invitation didn't help. The announcement, like a huge glowing sign, that she is turning six. It had come in the mail, pink construction paper with handwritten details in a childish script that could only be hers.

He had hoped that a scratch wouldn't be needed, that the itch could be minimized and held at a level that was bearable, controllable. But he can feel himself weakening, feel a break in his streak coming. He hopes role-playing will be enough to satisfy his itch, his enjoyment of the sessions giving him hope.

But just in case, he needs to prepare. If he is going to stumble, if he is going to fall, things must be in place. This time he will keep the girl around longer. Create enough memories to tide him over for a longer period. His hands shake and he stuffs them in his pockets, moving through the grass to the front of the trailer, pulling out the creased envelope that holds the key. He glances around the empty yard, the wind rustling through quiet brush, isolation surrounding him. Ripping the paper, he ignores the landlord's letter and palms the key.

Preparation. Just to be safe. Maybe he won't need this place. But just in case, better make sure that everything is ready. Preparation has always paid off in the past.

CHAPTER 3

I HAVE EXCEPTIONAL hearing in my left ear and enjoy sitting against my sixth-floor apartment door, listening to the activities going on in the hall. It's amazing how much people give away on their way from the elevator to their apartment. Sometimes people step out of their apartment for "privacy," a fact I find hilarious. From my doorside seat, I hear the fights, the secret phone conversations, and the everyday normalcy that gives away so much about a person.

Simon was, for a long time, "the Brown-Haired Smoker." I keep a notebook next to the door, in the cardboard box. In it, I have a page dedicated to every resident on our floor, including me. There are fifteen "Sixers," as I like to refer to us, and when Simon moved in, "the Brown-Haired Smoker" is what I wrote on the top of the page.

He moved in with a girl who, as best I could tell from my peephole, was one step above trailer trash. They were arguing, carrying black trash bags full of crap, and her voice interrupted his twice between the elevator and their door. I started a page for her and titled it "Trailer Trash Tonya."

I later found out her name was Beth, and she worked at Applebee's. Two weeks after moving in, they got in a fight, she moved out, and I threw away her page. From the words of their parting, she would not be coming back.

Simon's current girlfriend is Vicodin. In return for my containment, I keep his girlfriend coming. From his level of dependence, Vicodin is one demanding bitch, reducing him to a sniveling, whiny submissive in the days leading to the first of the month, when his next order arrives. Simon understands that if he ever unlocks me, ever releases me before morning, his prescriptions will stop and his addiction will go hungry. He doesn't realize he might die at my hand.

CHAPTER 4
ANNIE

ANNIE SITS ON one of the high stools in her kitchen, kicking the baseboard of the bar top, which causes her stool to slowly spin, right and then left. Her book bag, the edges frayed from three years of use, slumps against the bar, exhausted from a day of reading, writing, and riding the bus.

"Stop that," her mother says—not turning—the sound from Annie's kicks grating on her nerves. She lays out two pieces of bread, then spreads peanut butter onto one side. Letting out a deep breath, she screws on the lid, then opens the jelly jar and glances at Annie with a warning look.

Annie stops, using her hands instead to spin her stool, and looks at the digital display of the old microwave above the stove: 3:49 p.m. Only two more days till her party. She pushes off the stool, and the worn soles of her sneakers smack against the kitchen's clean linoleum floor as she heads to the round table pushed into one corner of the kitchen. Rounding the table slowly, she runs her hands over the tops of the bright and sparkly packaged plastic bags, stuffed with candy, markers, and packets of stickers. Ten favors in all, for her ten best friends. Hearing her father's call, she turns from the table and runs, following the sound of his voice until she reaches his chair, set up in the living room.

Her father wants company, so Annie sits in the living room with him, her feet tucked under her, curled into the corner of the couch. Their dog, a mutt that had scratched at the trailer door for two weeks before her mother finally relented and welcomed him in, jumps up beside her, circling twice before settling in, snug against her body. His wire-bristle black-and-gray hair scratches her bare leg, and she reaches out and pats his head. His tail thumps, slow and steady, and he opens one eye to look at her contentedly. He is a good dog, but what she really wants is a kitten—one with soft fur and big eyes, who will curl up in bed with her at night.

"How was school?" Her father's voice creaks, roughened by too many years of cigarettes and coughing. He reaches for his tea, and drops of condensation drip down the side, landing with a soft splat on the worn surface of the table.

"It was good, Daddy."

"You like first grade?"

A soda commercial comes on TV, and Annie watches a bejeweled pop star singing and dancing through a crowded street. "I guess."

"How's your teacher? Miss Parakeet, is that her name?"

She dissolves into giggles and reaches out and pinches his arm. "It's Miss *Sparrow*, Daddy. I've told you that, like *eight* times."

"Oh, I'm sorry. I get confused." He tousles the top of her blond head playfully. "Excited about your party?"

She nods enthusiastically. "Super excited, Daddy."

CHAPTER 5

MALE ASS PLAY: Many men find anal sex pleasurable, and some may reach orgasm through anal penetration — by stimulation of the prostate in men. Pegging is the term for the sexual practice in which a woman penetrates a man's anus with a strap-on dildo.[1] The National Institutes of Health, with information published in the *British Medical Journal*, states, "There are little published data on how many heterosexual men would like their anus to be sexually stimulated in a hetero-sexual relationship. Anecdotally, it is a substantial number. What data we do have almost all relate to penetrative sexual acts, and the superficial contact of the anal ring with fingers or the tongue is even less well documented but may be assumed to be a common sexual activity for men of all sexual orientations."[2]

A CLIENT'S USERNAME can tell me a lot about the person. With descriptive usernames, like DoctorPat92 or 1HotLawyer, it is often who they are or who they wish they were. Numbers in a username typically stand for a birth year, their graduation year, or their age. I have a lot of "doctors" that pass through my chat room, but DoctorPat is, for once, an actual doctor. And as you might guess, I occasionally have a need for one.

DoctorPat92's real name is Dr. Patrick Henton. He is a fifty-five-year-old general practitioner in a little town in Maine called Buckfield. According to reviews on Google, he is well liked and competent, though I don't know how competent the sole doctor in a town of nineteen hundred people needs to be. He is more than adequate for my basic needs. A sequestered individual, with no access to the outside world, has to work pretty hard to get sick or injured. My basic needs revolve around one thing—drugs. Not for me, but for Simon. I'm sure DoctorPat thinks *I* am the painkiller addict. I don't really care what DoctorPat thinks. He writes me prescriptions, and I watch him take eight-inch dildos. It's a win-win for both of us.

Our chat sessions started out normal enough, and in the way that most relationships do.

DoctorPat92: hey

"Hi, Doc. My name is Jessica. What's yours?"

DoctorPat92: Pat. Patrick, if you want to be formal.

I laughed, cross-legged on the bed, a wide grin on my face. "I'm not formal. So, Pat. *Are* you a doctor?"

DoctorPat92: yes

"Wow! I always fantasized about being with a doctor." I widened my eyes and moved to my knees. "And what are you interested in tonight?"

DoctorPat92: you. can u take off your clothes?

"Of course. All of them?"

DoctorPat92: u r beautiful

DoctorPat92: yes. slowly please.

DoctorPat92: slower

DoctorPat92: thx. now lay, just like that, and tell me about yourself.

I stopped physically typing my responses a long time ago. Most camgirls type and don't speak. I don't know if it's because their English sucks or if it's because they are in a camming sweatshop of sorts, where if all of the girls were talking, it'd sound like a Russian call center. Men don't want to know that they are one of many. They want to imagine a girl in her bedroom, no one else around, wanting to talk only to them. I think the fact that I talk adds to my popularity. The fact that I am American, an oddity in itself, is also a big draw. So the client experience is one reason I don't type. The other reason is that it's really hard to type and masturbate at the same time, at least for me. The men don't seem to have a problem with it.

We were eight chats in before DoctorPat hooked up a webcam. I like when I can see the clients. It's funny how your mind will create an image of a person and how wrong your mind almost always is. My mind wasn't too far off with DoctorPat. He was utterly nondescript, a typical adult male in his fifties, with a head of thick salt-and-pepper hair, average build, and average looks. What I found more surprising from DoctorPat's streaming video was that he was dressed, wire-rimmed glasses perched on his nose, looking as innocent as if he were sitting down to Skype with his grandchildren. The second time he displayed his cam, I asked him about it.

DoctorPat92: can you see me?

"Yes. The video just came up. Hey!" I waved excitedly, as though I'd been waiting all day to see him.

DoctorPat92: good. Sorry, can't use audio. My wife is downstairs.

"It's okay. Is that why you are dressed?"

DoctorPat92: yes

He seemed as if he was going to type more, so I waited.

DoctorPat92: plus

DoctorPat92: I'm not ready for u to see what I like to do

"Why?"

DoctorPat92: it's weird

I laughed. "I assure you, it's not weird. And weird isn't necessarily a bad thing. I like weird."

DoctorPat92: maybe another time

"Do you normally...touch yourself when we chat?" I ran my hand slowly down my naked body. I was lying on my side, atop my pink bedspread, the pattern picked out specifically because it looked young, innocent. Virginal. Men like that.

DoctorPat92: sometimes. if no one is around. i like to watch you. sometimes I think of you later.

"When you're with your wife?"

DoctorPat92: yes. or when I'm pleasuring myself.

"Have you ever been with a patient?"

DoctorPat92: no.

His expression didn't encourage that line of questioning, so I dropped it. "I know you aren't ready to show me what you like, but will you tell me?"

He reached up and turned off the webcam. I waited, my expression relaxed. He was either about to end the chat or about to tell me more. For some reason, men feel more comfortable divulging their secrets when they are invisible.

DoctorPat92: don't think I'm weird.

I laughed. "I promise, I won't think you're weird. I swear."

DoctorPat92: I like to put things inside of me.

I lowered my voice and used my you-are-a-bad-boy-but-I-think-it's-hot voice. "You mean you like to get fucked?"

A long pause. I bit my bottom lip and kept my eyes on the webcam.

DoctorPat92: yes

"That's not weird. I think it's hot. I like it when a man is kinky." I slid my hand lower, until it grazed my bikini line.

DoctorPat92: do u think I'm gay?

What's so hard about reading typed words is not knowing how some questions are asked. I didn't know if he was trying to figure out himself if he was gay, or if he wanted me to think he was gay, or if this was a test of my reaction.

I tilted my head. "I guess it would depend on what you think about when you are being penetrated. You like chatting with me, right?"

DoctorPat92: yes

"You know this site has men, gay men, who wouldn't blink twice at you being fucked. Why aren't you chatting with them?"

DoctorPat92: b/c I like you. You are funny and sweet. I think about you when I put things inside of me.

DoctorPat92: I think about you watching me.

I giggled. "Then let's do it! Let's set an appointment for some time when you will be alone…" I moved my hand farther, gently running my fingers along my sensitive lips.

"And I can watch you. I want to watch you. I've never seen anything like that before."

DoctorPat92: really?

"Yes!"

It was a lie. It's actually quite common for men to ask me to watch them fuck themselves. I don't understand it, but then again, I have a pussy that is perfect for a toy. If they had a pussy, they probably wouldn't be sticking anything up that hole either. I also don't have a prostate. If I did, maybe I would understand the draw to anal sex. According to my sex therapist, some of the men who want to fuck toys *are* homosexuals—they just refuse to admit it to themselves. They think that having a girl watch them take a ten-inch black cock makes it less gay. But, my therapist warned me, there is a flip side to it. Just because a guy wants to bend over and shove something up his ass doesn't make him gay. There are straight men who get off on that form of stimulation yet have no interest in the touch of another man.

So I didn't jump to conclusions, I didn't assume that DoctorPat was gay, straight, or any combination of the two. To be utterly honest, I didn't give a shit what he was. All I cared about was that the clock on the upper right-hand corner of my screen was ticking, turning over minute by minute, earning me dollar by dollar.

That was the beginning of our relationship. I waited for two months before I brought up the prescriptions, wanting to see if he would stick around as a regular first. He stuck around, I proposed an arrangement, and he accepted. We are now two years into that arrangement. An arrangement where I have watched this utterly average doctor ride thick plastic dildos, use anal beads, and once—on one random Thursday—make a Budweiser beer bottle his personal ass toy. One webchat every other week for one prescription a month. I think half the reason DoctorPat writes me illegal prescriptions is that he worries about me blackmailing him. He has a wife and three teenage kids, a fact easily discovered after four minutes on Google. He doesn't need to worry. What turns him on is his business, not mine or anyone else's.

CHAPTER 6

THE LIGHTS SHUT off, an automatic setting that occurs at the end of a chat. I roll over and lie still for a moment, allowing my naked body to cool now that the heat from the lamps is gone. I stare up at the vaulted ceilings, my eyes following the lines of the exposed ductwork.

My apartment is one large, open space. I have a strong suspicion that the entire sixth floor was an afterthought — attic space closed up in some last-minute decision. Half of my space is unusable, the slant of ceiling making entire sections of wall only three feet tall. The kitchen, composed of one short row of cabinets and appliances, lies in the middle of the back wall. I use it as a divider mark, keeping half of the apartment as my personal living space and half the apartment as my cam studio. The layout is funky, the roofline guarantees me one knock on the head monthly, but it was one of the few units with a washer/dryer, and for that reason alone, I jumped all over it. Late night laundry sessions in the complex's community laundry room would have pretty much guaranteed a break in my I-haven't-killed-anyone-in-years streak.

I understand that for the normal individual, my life is strange. But I have accepted it as it is. I am okay with this life because I know that there is not another option available. If I want to keep others safe, I need to be contained. Would I like to run free through life, have friends, fall in love, feel the sun on my face? Yes. But that is no longer an option for me; there is no point in dwelling on and torturing myself over it.

I used to keep a scrapbook of my future life. I subscribed to magazines and cut and pasted onto square pages all of the elements that would make up my future life. It was *my* Pinterest, before Pinterest. My shrink said it was detrimental to my progress and happiness, and in retrospect, I think he was right. It wasn't healthy, how I pored over those pages, my daydreams before sleep involving girls' nights and romance. I didn't want to throw away the scrapbook, I held on to it like an alcoholic's last drink, my conversations with Dr. Derek leading to arguments that ended with me slamming down the phone, my fingers running with reverence over my scrapbook, my obsession growing stronger with every order from him to let it go.

I spent over a year with that book before I stacked it, and all of my magazines, into a big black trash bag and set it into the hall. Then I sat, with my back against the front door, listening for Simon's steps, fighting the urge to open the door and reclaim my hopes and dreams.

He came, he took, and my scrapbook joined a tangle of life's castoffs in the dumpster behind our complex. I envisioned it lying alongside old banana peels, baby diapers, and condoms, my treasured future dying a pauper's death.

It took a few days, a few days where I didn't speak to my

shrink and didn't cam, days where I lay in bed and mourned the life I didn't have. But then time marched on. Deliveries arrived, bills needed paying, and my in-box cluttered with e-mails. I called Dr. Derek and, for the first time in months, really listened to what he had to say. That was the day I stopped thinking about the life I don't have. That was the turning point that allowed me to recognize my situation as what it was. This is my reality, and that was the day I finally accepted it.

CHAPTER 7
ANNIE

THERE ARE THREE presents wrapped on the table. Annie already knows what two of them are. Last Sunday, after church, she snuck into her mother's room, pulled back her winter coats, and looked for presents. Her mother always hid her presents there. Behind the big, fluffy black coat with the hole in the bottom hem was a plastic bag. She reached in the bag as quietly as possible and pulled out the two items inside. One was a dark gray My Little Pony horse, the plastic package slightly dented, the cardboard colors faded. The other was a zippered pouch with sixty-four colored pencils. She squealed excitedly—before remembering where she was—quickly stuffed the items back inside the bag, and left the room before she was caught and punished.

She now examines the third brightly wrapped package with interest: poking, lifting, and shaking it to try to figure out what is inside. It is a box, large and square, about the size of a basketball. It feels heavier than a basketball. Her mind burns through the possibilities, the thought of waiting an entire day to open it torturous. She hears her mother call and turns, quickly setting down the wrapped gift and sprinting through the house, her tennis shoes making squeaking sounds on the cheap floor.

CHAPTER 8

I, OR RATHER JessReilly19, am currently the number three model on Cams.com. Number one is Tonya222, a forty-year-old semiattractive woman with ginormous fake titties who talks in a baby voice all day. Number two is JuneGirl, a Russian chick with an insane grasp of the English language, who can fit a Monster Energy drink can into pretty much any hole in her body. Behind the three of us are about two million cam models, mostly Europeans, every shape, size, and sexual perversion represented. For every 110-pound she-male with a ten-inch cock, there are one hundred paying clients ready to part with their hard-earned money.

I have decided my popularity is based on a number of things, the first being my workload. The more you work, the more clients you will meet, therefore the more money you will make. *Duh.* Second, my nationality plays a huge role. American girls seem to be living under a rock with regard to camming. Any town out there can wrangle up thirty strippers or forty Hooters waitresses, but there are fewer than a thousand American camgirls online. The fact that I am American, speak English, have a toll-free number, and know who the Yankees are guarantees me about nine legs up on the other models. Or two legs up if you want to be witty about it. The third reason I am popular? I'm hot, sexually adventurous, and *always* horny.

I have exploited my God-given talents to the nth degree in order to sell minutes, memberships, and gifts. But what's funny is the one attribute that I have never used—a serious ace in the hole that could guarantee me a whole new following of rabid fans: the fact that I, the self-described horniest girl in America, am, in fact, a virgin.

I didn't set out to be a virgin. It wasn't due to my Christian upbringing or the ridiculous chastity vow that my six best friends and I made back when WWJD was all the rage. It just sort of happened, thanks in large part to Francis Anderson.

Francis Anderson should have taken his parents outside and shot them, about three minutes before they made the ridiculous decision to name him something that would guarantee him ridicule and pain for the duration of his doomed-to-be-dorky life. Unfortunately, he didn't have the ability to time travel and therefore got stuck with the name Francis. His parents also gifted him with a ridiculously high IQ and a random assortment of features that, in the right light, made him look fairly handsome.

I fell in and out of love with Francis three times during my high school career. During the "out" phase, I would wonder what the hell I had ever found attractive about the boy. His feet were ridiculously big, he took out his retainer during lunch, and no matter what he wore or how he wore it, he couldn't erase the GEEK vibe from seeping out every pore of his body. During the "in love" phases, I would be certain that we were destined to be together—would find his quirks and stutters amusing, and would steadfastly decide that he was my one true love and I would never, ever, look at another man. Unluckily for Francis, a football jock, or a homecoming king, or the hot flavor-of-the-week would invariably swoop in and snatch me away. And I'd always go, with barely a second glance back. And he would always wait.

When we were dating, it was something my mother would have approved of: intellectual dates with a chaste kiss at the end of the night. He never pushed, there was no tongue, his hands never traveled, and he always "respected" me.

Nice guys occasionally *do* win. Francis is now in grad school at Harvard and holds a patent for some refrigeration chip thingy that all the restaurants are using. I stalk him online and get Google alerts every time something about him is written. He's worth about $200 million and is engaged to some perfect blue-blooded blonde who probably sucks his cock three times a day. God, was I stupid.

Despite my stupidity, the one thing that I *did* get out of my Francis infatuation was my virginity. His steadfast dedication to me, coupled with his constant presence as a friend when he wasn't my boyfriend, allowed me to be firm with my dates and gave me the confidence to not be swayed or pressured by insistent hands or smooth words.

At first, my virginity was a hindrance when it came to camming. My familiarity with fucking and masturbation was elementary at best. I had given head in high school, was anatomically familiar enough with a cock, balls, and the process of a hand job, but I had serious homework in front of me when I decided to pursue camming as a full-time occupation.

Porn ended up being my education: Jenna Jameson, Nina Hartley, and Peter North were my professors. For a two-week period, I watched ten to twelve hours of fucking a day, read how-to seduction books, and let Carmen Electra teach me the art of the striptease. I was a dedicated student, and after more than a hundred hours of study, I felt ready.

My first session was a disaster: uncomfortable dialogue followed by a lot of nervous giggling on my part. I looked uncoordinated on camera, arching my body into odd angles, my limbs moving awkwardly in ways they shouldn't, my own vagina scaring the crap out of me when displayed in high-definition on-screen. But things eventually clicked, with patient clients holding my virtual hand until I became the virginal Internet vixen I am today.

But am I still a virgin? What is the technical definition? If I've had a seven-inch dildo inside of me, is that any different from a real cock?

At the rate I'm going, physical sex doesn't seem to be in the cards for me, not unless I develop an affection for necrophilia. So I don't think my sexual classification really matters anymore. The only people who seem to care are potential suitors, and I don't have any of them lurking in the crowded corners of my apartment.

A virgin is defined as someone pure, innocent. It is also described as "not yet explored or exploited by man." By those definitions, I am mostly definitely not a virgin. And even if you got technical, divided my body into quadrants and analyzed them separately, whether or not my vagina is "pure" is of small consequence when the rest of me is anything but.

CHAPTER 9

THE MAN WATCHES the girls play. Their happy smiles, their youthful innocence. He moves from his place at the window, walking to the cashier, pulling out his wallet, and fighting the urge to glance backward. This is a small town, a town where people notice things and odd behavior stands out. A town where everyone knows and has known everyone else, since the day that they themselves were kids. A shriek of pleasure hits his ears and he focuses on the woman before him, on her lips, which are forming words he should respond to.

"That it?"

He swallows. "Yes, ma'am. Thank you, Ethel."

"No problem at all. I'll see you on Tuesday, and will let Bud know you stopped in." She beams at him, passing him the bag of groceries, and then turns to the next person in line.

He breathes hard, walking past the girls, his eyes locked forward on the handle of his truck. One step before another, three steps away, now two, now one. *Don't look over, don't listen to their laughter, don't think about what lies under the thin cotton of their dresses.* Then he is inside the truck, the radio turned to loud, and puts the truck in drive, the tires skipping slightly as he gives the truck more gas than is necessary.

He needs to get home. To get in front of the computer and find a girl. Just for a quick release. Without a release, his thoughts will wander, and lately they are wandering to the place they shouldn't go. To the one little girl that he should stay away from more than any of the rest, the one who is too close to home, the connection too strong—the chance of capture too great. He shakes his head, focusing on the road, focusing on step one.

Step 1: Get Home.
Step 2: Get Online.

CHAPTER 10

JEREMY DELIVERS A package midmorning, one I ignore until lunch, when I sit down to eat. I examine the package before opening it, the bright bubble-wrapper mailer and mail-forwarding sticker indicating that it is from a client. While I wait for the microwave to heat vegetarian lasagna, I shake it, trying to guess what is inside. No rattle, and the package is soft. Probably clothing—a sexy outfit of some sort.

The return address will normally tell me if the client is married. Married men don't put a return address or use a work address. Married men skip over the hearts drawn next to my name or smiley faces on the box. Married men don't want a returned package biting them in the ass. This package, with its pink mailer and a Maine return address, is probably from a single guy. One who has high hopes of stealing my heart and convincing me to be his, forever and ever.

The microwave dings and I press the button, stopping the timer from shrieking incessantly at me. I open a drawer, pull out children's scissors, and cut open the package.

Hand towels. That's different. I hold them up, my eyes examining the embroidered roses on the front, something that is more appropriate for an elderly woman than for me, but pretty just the same. I dig through the tissue paper for a card, find a white envelope, and pull it out.

Hand towels are not normal gifts. Jewelry, lingerie, pajamas, stationery, porn videos, personal porn videos, sex toys, costumes...those are the norm. I rip open the envelope and pull out a card with a golden retriever on the front, then open it to find handwriting in a neat script.

Jessica,
   I just got a new machine and wanted to try it out. Thought you would like this design, as I have noticed you like pink.

With love,
Lillian

Lillian. I look at the return address, which has "L. Baker" as the sender. The hand towels suddenly make more sense.

I don't have many female clients, but they are there, and they do—in some ways—take up more time than my male clientele. Women require more nurturing, personal attention. They write longer e-mails, spend more time chatting and less time masturbating, ask personal questions, and expect me to remember personal details about their preferences, life, and stories.

For women, our chats are more relationship building. Some are established lesbians, some are bisexual, some are curious. Some just seem to be lonely, while others want the physical exploration that can occur via cam. Some, like Lillian, are old enough to be my grandmother, while others are college students looking to experiment.

I've "known" Lillian for about a year now. We chat about once a month, a friendly conversation where she occasionally asks me to remove my shirt or pull up my dress and show her the lace of my panties. We have never done sexually explicit activities, but she subscribes to my website and I have watched her web traffic. The older woman watches at least an hour of my feed per day.

She is a very kind woman, always pleasant and curious about my day, my life, my general happiness level. Hand towels seem right up her alley, as does embroidery. I pull out some stationery and write her a quick thank-you card, the smell of lasagna reminding me of my lunch.

After sealing the envelope, I address the front and stick it into the large envelope that gets sent back to the mail-forwarding company. Then I rip the plastic off my lunch and dig in.

CHAPTER 11
ANNIE

AT FIVE THIRTY P.M., relatives start arriving to the party. Uncle Frank is the first, taking off his worn baseball cap in the front doorway, smiling shyly at Annie, and holding out a small, yellow-wrapped present, which looks as if it has been wrapped with half a roll of tape. She jumps excitedly, wrapping her small arms around his waist, inhaling the cigarette and earth smells that always follow him. She beams up at him, grabbing the present and shaking it excitedly. "Thank you, Uncle Frank." He squeezes the back of her neck and grins down at her.

"You're welcome, sweetie." He crouches down so they are eye to eye. "You want to open it now?"

Her eyes widen. "Can I?" she whispers.

"Sure. Let's sit on the back step, and get out of everyone's way." He straightens, holding his hand out, and she slides her tiny one into his and tugs, pulling him through the small living room to the worn-out back door.

They sit close, heads together, legs touching, on the small concrete step of the back stoop. She leans against his shoulder, pulling at the paper with anxious hands, her frustration with the tape eliciting a laugh from him. He takes the package gently and works the tape loose. "There," he says, passing it back to her. "Now you can rip it to shreds."

Inside the house, the front door is opened to another young girl, her father holding on to her small hand until they cross the threshold. The girl runs, heading to the table of favors, her feet pounding the thin floors of the trailer. "Where's Annie?" the man asks, watching his daughter streak through the house.

"She'll be in in a minute," Carolyn Thompson says, setting down a pitcher of tea and flashing a smile. "I know she'll be excited to see Dana. It's been too long since you brought her over."

The man grimaces, wiping his forehead with the sleeve of his shirt. "You know how it goes, Carolyn. Too many other temptations on our time."

The woman nods as she sets out a stack of cups, then turns to head back into the kitchen. On the way she stops at the back door, watching the step, seeing her brother lean down and whisper something into Annie's ear.

CHAPTER 12

I HAVE TWO shrinks. I don't really know why, except that I can't seem to tell one of them things that I can tell the other, and vice versa. I actually pay both shrinks, which is an oddity for me since I normally try to exchange goods for services. Sex, even Internet sex, seems to be a universal currency. I tried using a client as a shrink once, and it was disastrous. Of course, with a username like QuackAttack, I probably should have known from the beginning that it wouldn't work out. That was the guy with the little dick.

Dr. Brian Russell is my first shrink, my sex doctor. He is a sex therapist who is basically my gossip buddy. His website shows a thin, bald white man whose photos absolutely *shriek* gay, even though he is doing nothing but smiling into a camera with a business suit on. I wanted a gay shrink so I wouldn't have to worry about turning him on when I describe my sessions. I talk to him about my customers, and he tells me their sexual motivations and how I can best connect with them. That is the official description of our relationship, but mostly we just giggle about what goes on during my cam sessions. I have no one else to talk to about this, and due to our doctor/patient relationship, he is a vault.

Dr. Derek Vanderbilt is my second shrink and has been on the payroll for eighteen months. He's the closest thing to a friend I have had in the last three years. I can't find a photo of him online, which irks me no end. For some reason, knowing what the person on the other end of the line looks like makes me feel I have the upper hand...at least in my mind. We talk once a week, on Wednesdays at two p.m. He has strongly suggested that I increase my sessions to twice weekly, but I have ignored that suggestion. He doesn't know I have a second shrink. If he did, he might not worry about my psychological health so much. I talk to Derek about my murderous inclinations and the effects of my isolation. I don't mind being killer-crazy, but I don't want to be loony-bin-crazy. That would probably be bad for business—a bit of a turnoff.

"Tell me about your most recent fantasy." Derek's voice is smooth, deep, and masculine. I could listen to it all day long, though at $150 an hour, I limit myself to hour-long sessions.

"I enter a house at night. It's quiet. All I can hear is the occasional chirp of a smoke alarm. The sound drives me crazy. I can't find anyone downstairs, and as I climb the stairs, my heart is pounding. I am wet."

"Wet—from rain?" Derek inquires.

"No. Wet, as in aroused," I clarify.

"Are you often aroused in your fantasies?"

This takes us off topic, and I want to finish telling him my damn fantasy. He often does this, jumping on a random thing I've said and chasing it down till we've exhausted the poor little subject to death.

"Sometimes." I know he wants more, but I plunge on. "I start to go upstairs, and the third step squeaks—loudly. A dog from above me whines, and I know I must kill him to keep him quiet. I don't want to kill him, so I almost turn around. But the need has taken me over, and is drumming so loudly in my head, along with the damn smoke alarm, that I have to satisfy it."

I pause, but thankfully Derek stays quiet, and I continue. "The top of the stairs is lit by a small Santa Claus night-light. I am confused, because it is not winter. I stare at it for a moment, before I hear a scratch on a door. It's the dog. I reach for the handle, and suddenly I have a knife in my hand. I open the door slowly; the room is dark inside. The dog looks up at me. It is an old golden retriever. His back is swayed, and he is looking up at me with eyes of cloudy blue. His tail wags, and I start to cry. Not sob, just small streams of tears that leak from my eyes. I don't kill the dog, but my thirst for blood is angry at me for my weakness."

I shift, the memory of the dream filling me with renewed urges. "The pounding in my head increases. It's like that feeling when you are really aroused; when your body is consumed with the need for release—you would do anything, and are in such a blind fervor that you lose all rational thought. The need overtakes my rational, compassionate side, and I rush into the room, worried that they are awake and that I have lost the advantage of surprise. I stop by the bedside, and wait for my eyes to adjust. I am mad at myself for leaving the dog alone, and I hear the soft pad of his old feet on the carpet as he walks over to me. He sits at my side and pants up at me. The soft pants of his happy breath increase the maddening chorus of my mind, and I know the only way to shut it up."

I stop for a moment—breathing hard—the description of the fantasy making me excited, making the need stronger. It's a double-edged sword, talking to Derek. He helps me to calm the urges, but getting to that point often gives the urges strength.

"My eyes have adjusted and I see the room: a master bedroom. There are two bodies on the bed. The man has thrown the sheet off and is lying on his back. The woman is on her side, facing away from me. I go around to her side of the bed and do her first. Then I—"

"How do you kill her?"

I pause, clenching my hands, trying to stop the flow of excitement that is building in strength. "I use a knife. I stab her neck. She struggles but can't speak. I watch her die."

"And how did you feel as she died?"

"Empowered." I close my eyes as I say the word, knowing that it is not the answer he wants. He keeps thinking that something is going to change. That the emotion of regret will start to enter my fantasies.

"Then what happens?"

"I go to him. I take more time with him and start with his chest. I stab him there, which instantly wakes him up. I wait for him to see her, then I finish him quickly."

"Why wait for him to see her?"

I rub my forehead. "I don't know. Because I'm psychotic."

"You don't seem happy with this fantasy."

"Do I ever seem happy about my fantasies? It's just so

fucked up. I hate that I enjoy the thought of this disgusting shit. Lately, it's been depressing me more than usual."

"Do you want me to prescribe you something?" There is something in his voice, in his question, but I can't tell what it is.

"*Fuck*, no. I want you to find the magic key that will make me normal."

"No one is normal. Everyone is just pretending to be normal."

"Don't give me that shit. I used to be normal, and I liked it just fine."

"Did your mother seem normal?"

I sigh, blowing out a huge *whoosh* of air, and close my eyes. I had been wandering around the loft, my cell to my ear, so I plop down on my real bed, staring up at the ceiling. "Yeah, Mom seemed normal. It's not like I had a second mother to compare her to, but she was great. She had fresh homemade cookies every Wednesday when we'd get home from school. And she loved coupons. Dad made more than enough money, but Mom was obsessed with couponing; she did it every night after the dishes were washed, while we did homework. She seemed happy, maybe a little detached from Summer and Trent, but as normal as anyone else."

"Detached? Explain."

"She was always hugging me, wanting to talk about my day, coming up to my room to spend time with me. With Summer and Trent, there wasn't that show of affection, she didn't seem eager or interested in spending time with them. It was almost like she was afraid of getting close to them."

"Think back, Deanna. Was there any hint of what was to come?"

I close my eyes, concentrating on the question, flipping back through the past. But I already know the answer; it's a question I've asked myself for four years. "There were times she was moody or quiet, and times when we knew to give her space, but that's ordinary behavior for any person, right? And sometimes she would fly off the handle for no reason—just go ballistic on us over some little thing."

I roll over, playing with a seam on my comforter. "Something happened in the past, when I was young. I overheard Mom and Dad talking about it one day, something that caused Mom to be sent away for a bit. I asked Dad about it one day, and he just said she was sick, and I dismissed it as nothing. Honestly, even if she did fly off the handle at times, what happened seemed to come completely out of left field. The only clue I can think of, looking back on it, was that she had sent me away that day."

❖

I climbed the steps of our big white Colonial-style home, an impressive structure that screamed upper middle class, and threw open the red front door. Dropping my book bag at the base of the stairs with a heavy thud of educational oppression, I hollered, "Mom!" trying to find her in the big house.

"I'm up here, sweetie."

Her voice had come from upstairs, and I bounded up the steps two at a time, out of breath by the time I reached the second-floor landing. I trotted down the hall, glancing in bedrooms till I saw her in mine. I blew in the open door.

"You would not believe what happened today." I stopped in my tracks, looking at my bed. "What are you doing?"

She had my suitcase open on the bed—a purple suitcase I hadn't seen since last summer when I had made the horrid decision to go to volleyball camp. She must have pulled it from the attic. She had stacks of folded clothes on the bed and was in the midst of packing a pair of jeans when I asked the question.

She glanced at me, smiling. "You're going to your grandparents' for the weekend."

"What? Why? Jennifer has a party at her parents' lake house this weekend—you already said I could go!"

"I know, sweetie, and I'm sorry. But you haven't seen them in ages, and when they called and asked, I couldn't say no."

I frowned at her. This was so completely out of character. "Are Trent and Summer going?"

She hesitated, folding a gray cardigan. "No. I don't want to burden your grandparents with all three of you. Plus, it will be good for you to get one-on-one time with Papa and Nana. Once you go off to college, you won't be seeing them as often."

I walked over, looking at the clothes she had picked out. It was way too many clothes for two days at my grandparents'. But Mom had packed the right stuff. She knew what went with what and what was currently stylish. Missing Jennifer's party sucked, but I had a feeling that Mom had something up her sleeve. I was a month from graduation and wouldn't be surprised if she had something special planned. Mom was always big on surprises.

✦

"Why do you think she sent you away?"

"Mom and I were very similar. I was a younger clone of her; at least that's what she and Dad always called me."

He cuts off my next sentence. "Deanna, if you always considered yourself to be a clone of your mother, isn't it possible that you are projecting this fantasy of violence onto yourself because you think that is what she was struggling with?"

"Anything's possible, but I don't think that paranoia would manifest itself in urges like the ones that I have." Derek doesn't know that I have killed before. He doesn't know that I have sunk a knife into someone's stomach and watched them die. That I left that experience and wanted more. More bloodshed, more death. I don't trust the bonds of patient-doctor confidentiality that much. I move on before he can latch on to this theory and analyze it to death. "Anyway, I don't know that she planned what happened, but I think she might have known something was coming. Killing me would have been like killing herself."

"But she did kill herself."

I pause. "Yeah, but maybe that was unexpected. Maybe after she did what she did, she couldn't live with herself anymore."

"Is that really what you believe?"

I stiffen on the soft bed. "What do you mean?"

"I mean, don't spout off bullshit to make my questions go away."

"It's not bullshit; it's the truth. And if I wanted your questions to go away, I'd just hang up the phone."

"Maybe."

That does it. I hang up out of spite, and then, giving in to my sophomoric tendencies, I stick my tongue out at my cell.

Derek doesn't think that I am a killer. He says that my urges are strictly fantasies, that I don't manifest other traits of a killer. He thinks I'm bipolar, that the dark side of me is just one facet of my personality, not the real me. He thinks we can compartmentalize it, kill it off altogether with "proper medication."

What he doesn't realize is that just because I call it "an urge" or "the other side of me" doesn't mean it is a separate personality of mine. I used to call it Demon, because it was a lot easier for me to refer to it by name than call it dacnomania. Plus, when I was pissed at it, it was a lot easier to trash talk it if it had a moniker. But Demon was just a name, not a separate entity. I *am* Demon. There's never nice Deanna, then evil Demon. I'm always evil. Demon is Deanna. So I finally just dropped the nickname and accepted anthropophobia, dacnomania, psychosis...all of it is who I am.

My many diagnoses would help in a murder trial. And technically, since I am a murderess, I should be in prison. But you have to realize that while prison would be a good thing for me, it'd be a very bad thing for my obsession. See, there are a lot of people in prison. And they wouldn't be able to run far.

CHAPTER 13
JEREMY

HIS BROWN UNIFORM pressed, his name tag straightened, Jeremy Bryant rides the old metal elevator up to the sixth floor. The delivery isn't scheduled until tomorrow, but seeing the address, he added it to his truck for today, wanting the excuse to get on this damn elevator, ride up to the sixth floor, and go through the same routine he has for the last three years. Ring, wait, sign, and leave. Not exciting enough to waste fifteen minutes on a day already jam-packed with deliveries. Yet here he is.

The package is a small manila envelope with "Jessica Reilly" written on the front. Most deliveries to this address are for Deanna Madden, but occasionally the names on the packages change, Jessica Reilly being a frequent recipient. He'd originally assumed she had roommates, but after sharing an elevator with the apartment complex superintendent, he had discovered she lived alone, paid for her rent a year at a time, and—according to the overweight, unwashed man—was "smokin' hot."

"Really," Jeremy said. "Hot?" It had crossed his mind. The

mystery of not being able to see her had sent his imagination into overdrive—one day convinced she was gorgeous, the next day envisioning one of those gargantuan women who have to be forklifted from the couch.

"*Smokin'* hot. Beautiful face with a body that I jacked off to for days." *Hmmm. Not a forklift woman.*

"How often do you see her?"

The man laughed. "She's the mystery of this building, man. She's hiding from *someone*. She hasn't left that apartment since the day she moved in. I mean that *literally*. The door closed, and that was it. One guy pulled the fire alarm a couple of years ago, just to see if she'd come out. We all stood outside in the freezing-ass cold at two in the morning, but she didn't budge." The elevator came to a shuddering stop and the man nodded at Jeremy, moving laboriously ahead of him through the filthy opening. "See you later."

Her delivery habits corroborated the super's statements. The volume of packages she received was staggering, at least for a normal person who didn't run a retail operation out of her house. They were frequent enough that he made almost daily deliveries to this ancient apartment complex and had become accustomed to and unaffected by the dark elevator that barely made the climb to her floor. And she had consistently, for three years, refused to open her door; his first delivery had been a disastrous standoff that ended in her favor.

He hadn't given a second thought to the box, other than the fact that it was incredibly heavy, more than seventy pounds—a large box from an electronics superstore. He almost missed her door, starting to pass it and then stopping short, checking the apartment number before knocking.

There was movement in the apartment, steps, a small commotion, and then a breathless voice.

"Yes?"

"UPS. I have a package for a Deanna Madden."

"Just leave it at the door, please."

He glanced down at the box. "It's insured, ma'am. Needs a signature."

"So scribble my name."

"I'm sorry, I can't do that. If you need some time to dress, I can wait or come back later."

"I'm dressed, but I'm not opening the door. Leave the package and handle the signature however you want to."

Her voice was strong but had a sweet tone and enough sass that his mind begged for a look at the woman connected to it. He ground his teeth and looked at the door. "Ma'am, it's insured for eleven hundred dollars. I can't leave it without a signature. Would you prefer for me to deliver it tomorrow?"

"I'm not going to open the door tomorrow either."

He fought the urge to groan in frustration. He looked down at the heavy box. "I'm not sure of your size, but the box is pretty heavy. You will probably need help carrying it inside."

"I appreciate your concern, but I will be fine. Thank you."

Thank you. An assumptive statement that indicated her decision that he was going to leave the box. Decided before he had made up his mind. He sighed, torn between leaving a thousand-dollar package in this mildewed hallway and taking it with him to try this whole song and dance tomorrow.

He left the package, doing his best imitation of a girlish script on his scan pad and sending a long look into the dark peephole, trying to communicate his displeasure with the whole situation. Shaking his head, he headed toward the elevator, hoping that he never had to deal with her again.

That was three years ago. Three years in which he has heard her voice through that door—lugged, toted, and swung countless packages with annoying regularity down that dim hallway. The woman seems to have toilet paper delivered via two-day mail. He looks down at the manila package, for Jessica Reilly. The sender is a mail-forwarding company in Des Moines, Iowa. That is another mystery. About 10 percent of her packages are mail-forwarded, most from senders with no return address. Maybe she is a terrorist. A terrorist who has a penchant for household goods and who receives packages with hearts drawn on them.

The elevator doors open with the squeal of metal on metal and he steps onto the dark brown carpet that is the sixth floor. Stopping before her door, he leans forward and listens.

The sounds coming from her apartment often vary. Sometimes music, sometimes voices, once a cry that sounded sexual in nature. Today it is quiet. He straightens and raps on the door three times.

"Leave it. Thank you." The voice comes immediately, from below, as if she is crouched or seated on the other side of the door.

Leave it. Thank you. He grins despite himself, signing her name to the pad and gently leaning the package against the door. He raises a hand, waving to the silent door, unsure if she will see the gesture given the height her voice is coming from. "Have a nice day," he calls out, starting the walk back to the elevator. She won't open the door; she never does. He stood two doors down once and waited for fifteen minutes, but her door remained closed, the package sitting before it like a piece of delicious cheese in a rattrap. He presses the elevator button, the doors opening immediately, and steps in, his view of the sixth floor disappearing as the doors close.

CHAPTER 14

ON THE CAMMING sites, it costs clients an extra dollar per minute if they want to turn on their own webcam and let me watch them via the cam-to-cam feature. This feature, as well as allowing me to see them, a tool that exhibitionists love, allows sound—the ability for a client to speak instead of type. Every groan, every gasp, comes through loud and clear via the speakers that I have scattered throughout my cam room. Some clients don't like to type their responses, but they're too cheap to pay the extra dollar per minute just so they can talk. Those clients ask me to call them, the camsite economics circumvented with the simple dial of a number.

When I signed up for the site, I had to agree to a list of rules. One of those was that I can't establish contact directly with the clients. Phone calls break that rule. Initially I was the perfect cammer, following the rules to a T—biting the hand that fed me was scary, especially at the beginning, when my bank account was in the three digits and I wasn't sure how this whole webcamming thing would pan out financially. Now I break rules with blatant disregard. I advertise my personal site, I give out my mailing address, I perform "forbidden acts" like flashing my tits in free chat, and I allow clients to get emotionally attached to me.

Part of the reason I break the rules is my virtual way of giving them the middle finger. As my bank account balance and number of fans have risen, I have grown more and more irritated with the cam sites. Yes, they have made me rich, but I have paid them back tenfold. Literally. Last month, my cut from Cams.com was $57,000. My total revenue generated? $203,581.42. They pocketed a cool $150K that month for doing nothing but broadcasting my video feed. So I break their damn rules, and they don't say a damn thing about it.

That wasn't always the case. Once, I got a call from a nasally voiced man who sounded like one step up the food chain from the mailroom. He started in with a scripted lecture on how my account would be suspended if I continued to break the rules that I agreed to at sign-up. I let him finish his script before informing him that last year his website made more than $1 million off of my chat sessions. I told him to have his boss call me and hung up. That month I got a card in the mail with a personal apology and a check for ten grand. I'm not gonna lie, I had some warm and fuzzies for a week or so over that.

I do understand the rules, why they are in place. The majority of the rules are truly for our protection. The rest are for profiteering reasons. But the rules about contact—those are to protect us against the sickos. Which in my case is fucking hilarious.

I protect myself as best I can. Any packages clients want to send me get sent to a campus address in Delaware, which forwards my mail here. I also have a Delaware cell phone number, which rings to a phone I have dedicated to camming, my cheery voice mail message proclaiming that you have reached Jessica Reilly and sorry! I can't take your call right now because I am busy having fun! It is nauseatingly cheerful. The men love it. On a given day, I receive anywhere from twenty to forty voice mails. I don't return them and respond to text messages only if they concern appointment times.

I used to have a texting plan—clients could pay thirty bucks a month to text with me—but it got to be a full-time job and not one that paid $6.99 a minute. So that entrepreneurial venture lasted only three weeks. I've tried a few other harebrained ideas to generate income but have found that my time is best served in front of the camera. The lights, the clients. They pay the bills and help keep the crazy away.

CHAPTER 15
ANNIE

ANNIE PUSHES HER hair back and admires the plain wrapping, a single pink ribbon hanging loosely off the tape her uncle has worked loose.

"Well, go ahead," Frank prods, bumping her small body gently with his elbow. She looks over at him, her mouth spread wide in an expectant grin. Her small fingers grip and rip the paper, revealing a pink princess costume set, complete with a feather boa, plastic crown, and silk gloves. The sun glints off the crown's large pink jewels, and she throws away the wrapping and waves the set excitedly, the wind blowing the boa around. He stands, chasing the yellow paper, which jumps and skips across the grass yard, finally snagging it and crumpling it into a tight ball. Gripping the ball tightly, he walks back to her. She tugs on the cheap crown, trying to free it from the cardboard display board. The plastic curves, close to breaking with each pull of her fingers, and he reaches out as he sits back down beside her, taking the item gently from her. He turns it over, untwisting the plastic ties, and she leans closer, her breath blowing warm on his neck. Finally the crown is free, and he holds it up, setting it gently on her head and pushing the plastic teeth into her blond hair.

"How do I look, Uncle Frank?" she asks, grabbing the boa and wrapping it around her slim neck.

"Perfect, honey. You look absolutely beautiful." His gruff voice is quiet, but she hears the words and throws her arms around his neck, kissing him on the cheek.

"Thanks, Uncle Frank," she whispers.

"Annie!" Annie looks up into the strained eyes of her mother. "Annie, come inside. Uncle Michael and Aunt Becky are here."

She stands, brushing off the fabric of her dress, and grabs her uncle's hand, tugging it as she climbs a concrete step. "Come on! Come inside!"

"You go on. I'm gonna stay right here for a bit, Annie," her uncle says, a small frown on his face. Then he smiles at her. "I just need a minute, sweetie. Go inside, like your momma says."

She beams at him and reaches up, checking her crown. Then she spins, and in a blur of pink and blond is gone, the screen door snapping shut behind her.

Annie flies into the living room, running full force until she hits the waiting arms of Uncle Michael. He lifts her into the air, smiling up at her. She trills with laughter, and he sets her down gently, her kicking feet finding the ground early. Her aunt Becky holds out a perfect pink box tied with a thick white ribbon. "Here," she says shortly. "We can't stay long."

Annie grips it tightly, looking at her mother's pinched face for approval. "Go ahead, honey. You can open it in the kitchen." Annie beams, grabbing Aunt Becky's silky hand and tugging on it, skipping alongside her slow walk as they make their way the short distance into the next room.

The gift turns out to be a paint-by-numbers set, the price sticker still attached, displaying $4.99 in bright fluorescent orange. She runs her hands excitedly over the plastic-wrapped display, her eyes big and smile wide. She gives them both hugs and returns immediately to the set, pulling off the plastic and touching the paint pads gently, feeling their texture. She doesn't notice when they say their good-byes and leave, pulling the trailer door tightly shut.

CHAPTER 16

MIKE IS ONE of my few regulars that I know next to nothing about. Being a hacker, he makes sure that all of his personal information is locked behind impenetrable firewalls. I can't get past a dinky normal firewall, but that is why I've cozied up to Mike. When I need research on clients, he's my man.

Mike falls in the same category as 80 percent of my clients. He likes to jack off while he watches me touch myself. While some clients mix it up, he has a regular fantasy, and it never varies. As soon as his name pops up, I quickly undress, putting on knee-high white stockings, a plaid skirt, and a white cropped sweater. Sometimes he wants me to wear glasses or put my hair in pigtails, but traditionally I change into my schoolgirl outfit, sit back in front of the camera, and spread my legs wide. Then I slide a hand under my skirt, lifting it up for his eyes, and wait for him to type something.

HackOffMyBigCock: u want my cock?

"God, I want it so bad. I was thinking about it earlier,

when I was in the shower." I tug on my ponytail with one hand and bite my lower lip, teasing my pussy with the fingers of my other hand.

HackOffMyBigCock: ive been thinking about u 2. what do u want me to do 2 u

"I want you to make me kneel in front of your chair. Then I want to rub the outside of your pants, feeling the outline of that hard cock. I'm going to touch myself, pull up my little skirt, and plunge my fingers in and out of myself while I unzip your pants."

HackOffMyBigCock: oh yeah baby

"Oh, my God, I can't wait to see it. I love how hard you get for me, how tight your skin gets around that shaft. Are you hard for me now?" I shut my eyes, tilt my head back, and slide two fingers inside my sex, moving them slowly in and out so he can see my lips open and shut around my slick fingers.

HackOffMyBigCock: rock hard. i want 2 fuck you so bad.

"You're about to, baby. You're about to fuck me so hard that I scream. But I want to suck your cock first. I want to taste your sweet pre-cum and gag on that big meat of yours."

HackOffMyBigCock: oh yeah. pull it out.

I kneel, switching the input on my computer so that the overhead webcam, placed about five feet off the ground and affixed to the wall, is activated. Below the cam, also attached to the wall, is a female strap-on harness. It allows me to attach various RealSkin dildos and keep them in place. I grab a nude-colored seven-incher and clip it into place, then grab the shaft and look up into the cam.

"Tell me how you want it, baby—hard and fast or slow

and teasing?" I flick my tongue over the tip of the toy, the monitor above the webcam showing me the webcam feed and the chat message window. About 10 percent of my clients use a microphone; the rest type their responses. For that reason, I have five screens placed at different locations, allowing me to easily see their directives despite whatever position I might be in.

HackOffMyBigCock: h and f

I oblige, shoving the toy down my throat in one quick movement. Gagging on the depth, then pulling back off, keeping eye contact with the cam, I jack off the saliva-covered toy as I suck up and down on it, my eyes watering from the motion, my cheeks hollowing from the effort. I gag repeatedly, letting the reflex coat the toy with saliva, and occasionally spit on the toy and slap my face with it. While some men prefer a neat, clean blow job, the majority of my clients prefer a sloppy, wet one with lots of gagging and enthusiasm.

HackOffMyBigCock: fuck. u give such good head bb. i want to paint your face right now.

I glance at the timer, located in the top right corner of the video: 5min32sec. *Not long enough.* "Wait, baby, don't come yet," I beg. "I really need you inside of me. I've been waiting all day for your cock."

HackOffMyBigCock: ok

HackOffMyBigCock: sit back and touch yourself. i need to cool off a min

Good boy. I sit back, getting off of my knees so I can be spread-eagle on the floor. I change the input to the floor cam, located about three feet off the floor, and angle it so it focuses on my lower half. I have a total of seven cams, all top-of-the-line high-definition. My entire system is controlled by a home entertainment app that an Indian subcontractor reprogrammed for my purposes. I have an iTouch that runs the app and acts as my remote. The app allows me to choose and control the camera, adjust the lighting, and terminate chat sessions if I get uncomfortable. Under the floor cam is another strap-on fixture—the one I use for doggie-style fucking. I looked at purchasing a Sybian once, but my system works fine and a Sybian is a big investment.

HackOffMyBigCock: how have u been?

Typically, guys get chatty during the initial thirty seconds of a cam session and during a cool-off period. End-of-session chat is rare.

"I've been good—with the exception of midterms, which are next week. I am so far behind in my studying…" I make a face and continue moving my hands, circling my nipples, which perk up from the contact, and trace a path down to my pussy, which is wet. Gagging seems to always make me wet.

HackOffMyBigCock: been too busy partying? lol

"I wish! There are *no* cute guys at my school." I pout and spread open my shaved lips, showing him the pink wetness there.

HackOffMyBigCock: damn ur wet. i need to come there and fuck u in person.

Mike is the only guy I ever really worry about finding me. Initially, I paid a professional company to set up my website securely, promising me that I would be untraceable…but please. If hackers can crack the DOD's internal site, they can get past the $249.99 security package I paid for.

"God, if you were here right now, I'd fuck you so hard..." I press and hold a button on the remote, zooming the cam out until it shows my whole body, then close my eyes and lick my lips. I moan softly, my fingers dipping inside of me, then open my eyes and stare into the cam. "I need to fuck you," I whisper urgently. "Please."

HackOffMyBigCock: im ready for u bb. bend over, i want to give it to u from behind.

I reach up and forward to unsnap the nude toy and move it down to the lower connection, quickly clipping it into place. Then I flip over onto my knees, my back arched, and look over my shoulder at the cam, reaching one hand underneath me to spread my lips. "Please, please, I need it so bad."

HackOffMyBigCock: now. fuck me now.

I scoot back, moving slowly as the nude dick presses on the opening of my pussy. Guys love to watch the moment when "they" enter me, and I play it for all it's worth, gasping as my lips slide around the girth of it. I move, pushing back until it slides deeper, deeper, and then is buried inside of me. *Full.* I moan. "God, baby, you are so fucking deep in me. This is what I've needed."

HackOffMyBigCock: tell me to fuck u

I hear the chime of his message and look over my shoulder at the screen. I zoom the camera out a little, so that it displays my face in the background. I slide slowly off the dick and then push onto it again, gasping a little. "Please, Mike, I need it all. Please, Mike, fuck me! Fuck me with your big meaty cock!" My voice rises until I am almost screaming the words, and I rock back and forth on the dick with enthusiasm. "Fuck, fuck, fuck, Mike—God, that's what I need!" I grunt, guttural, and look over my shoulder at the cam, my face a mess of want and pleasure. Then I close my eyes, fucking the toy harder, faster, my breath coming out in ragged gasps.

HackOffMyBigCock: aww fuck bb im going to cum

I look over, read his words, and continue my barrage on the toy. "Where, Mike—where do you want it?" I keep my eyes glued to the screen, waiting for his response.

HackOffMyBigCock: swallow it

I pull abruptly off the toy, spinning around and grabbing it in my hands. The low angle causes me to lie down and I devour it, plunging it down my throat and staring up at the cam, jacking the cock off with my hand as I suck it, hard and fast. I moan encouragingly as I suck and squeeze my breasts, pulling gently on my nipples with my fingers.

There is silence for almost a minute, then a message.

HackOffMyBigCock: fuck that was hot. thx jess

------PRIVATE CHAT ENDED BY HackOffMyBigCock. 13min24sec

Thirteen minutes: $94.35, which, minus my personal website's transaction fees, is $91.06 to my bank account. It pays the bills.

I roll over and heave to my feet, walk naked across the floor, grab a glass, and fill it with water from the sink. From inside the cabinet I take out the Tylenol bottle, leaving the cabinet open as I pop two into my mouth and chase them down with tepid tap water. My eyes flicker over the cabinet and the racks of orange bottles that fill its shelves.

Dr. Derek prescribes antipsychotics for me. They come

like clockwork every thirty days in the mail. I don't bother to tell him that I stopped taking them nine months ago. While they did take away my urge to kill, they also took away every intelligent thought in my head. When I watch old webcam videos from that time, I cringe. I was a zombie, moving through mechanical sexual motions, my face slack, words dead.

So I stopped taking and started stockpiling them. On the upside, if I ever *do* decide to kill myself, I have more than seven hundred pills waiting for me in this cabinet.

CHAPTER 17

WHEN I WENT to my grandparents' house that weekend—*the* weekend—when Mom went mad and killed everyone, they were surprised to see me. That should have alerted me that something was wrong.

"Deanna?" My grandmother peered at me through the screen door, squinting as though she were having trouble seeing me. She pushed the screen door out, looking at me, then my suitcase, her expression confused. "Is everything okay?" I stepped forward, hugging her tightly, and planted a quick kiss on her soft, fragile cheek.

"Hey, Nana." I reached down, grabbed my suitcase handle, and dragged it forward, toward the front door. "Mom said I was spending the weekend with you guys."

Her face showed surprise, but she recovered quickly. "Oh! Well, come in, dear. Don't worry about that suitcase. I'll have your grandfather grab it." She ushered me inside, pulling the farmhouse door shut behind us,

*the smell of mothballs and old books hitting my senses as
I stood in the foyer and she scurried around me, turning
on lights and adjusting the thermostat.*

My family lay dead in our home for almost an entire
day before a next-door neighbor, while on a walk, saw
blood splatter on the kitchen window. The neighbor
looked in the window and saw my sister, Summer,
slumped over the kitchen table, a congealed pool of blood
around her head. My grandparents and I were at a church
dinner when the police came to notify us. They waited at
the house, and when we returned from church they sat,
two uniformed officers, on the porch, a black-and-white
car parked near the mailbox. Nana clutched her chest as
soon as we pulled in.

*The men stood as our car came to a stop, and Papa put it
in park. We opened the doors slowly, none of us wanting
to know why they were here. As soon as I saw their faces,
I knew they brought bad news. We all knew.*

*Nana held on to my grandfather's arm, and they
approached the two uniforms. I could see the weight of
uncertainty and fear on my grandparents' shoulders.
I moved past them up the steps, opened the unlocked
front door, and headed up the wide stairs to change
out of my church clothes. I wanted to put as much
distance as possible between them and me. As I
climbed the stairs, my head pounded, and I gingerly
touched the side of my eardrum, feeling the crust of
dried blood.*

My grandparents delivered the news to me after the policemen left, sitting me down in their formal living room, their voices shaking and eyes weeping. I had no reaction; I said nothing when they told me. My grandfather repeated the news, looking into my eyes to be sure I understood. I sat there in silence for a full minute, then a wail bubbled up in me, and once I started sobbing, I couldn't get myself to stop.

I stayed at my grandparents' until I graduated from high school, then I moved out. That was when I enrolled in community college, using the small amount that remained from my parents' life insurance. There wasn't much left after paying for four burials.

CHAPTER 18

PODOPHILIA: Commonly called foot fetishism, "podophilia is a pronounced sexual interest in feet" or footwear.[3] It is one of the more common fetishes, affecting at least 70 percent of men.[4] For a foot fetishist, their attraction can focus on the shape and size of the foot and toes, jewelry, treatments, state of dress, and odor, as well as sensory interaction—such as smelling the foot, licking, kissing, tickling, etc.[5] Even a preference for women with nice feet or who wear heels can be defined as podophilia.

I HEAR A knock at my door at nine a.m. and pause my cam, interrupting a bald Asian man who is asking to see my feet. I jog across the linoleum till I can see through the peephole. It is UPS Jeremy, holding a big box. "Leave it. Thank you," I call loudly, then watch him set down the package, scrawl something on his pad, wave to me, and walk away. I hold my ear to the door, waiting for the sound of the elevator, then jerk open the door, grab the huge cardboard box, and slam it shut again. I don't lock it. I never lock my door. I figure if someone is stupid enough to come inside, they have ill motives and deserve to die at my hands. It's one of my favorite fantasies, because it is one of the ones most likely to occur. I drop the heavy box on the floor and bound back to my pink bed, where the patient Asian waits. I apologize to him and hold up my feet close to the cam so he can see them better.

Foot fetishists make up a large part of my clientele. My feet were ignored for the first eighteen years of my life—the ends of limbs that slid into fashionable shoes before leaving the house. But in the webcam world, my feet are my bread and butter. The fact that this client is Asian has nothing to do with his fetish: it is a worldwide turn-on and more common than I ever imagined. Most men have a slight fetish—like a leg man—they enjoy seeing nicely shaped feet, either bare or in four-inch heels. Other men focus solely on feet as their erotica; they do nothing but stare at my toes, soles, and arches and jack off while doing so. It is my favorite type of clientele, in that all I have to do is wiggle my toes and rub my feet together seductively. The feet that I had abused for years—carelessly stubbing on doorjambs and stuffing barefoot into old sneakers—possess a high arch, symmetrical toes, and narrow ankles. I rock bare feet like Pamela Anderson filled that red swimsuit two decades ago.

The Asian is getting close, his face tight in concentration, his eyes glued to my feet. I lie back and slowly run my left arch over the top of my right foot, letting out a soft moan as my feet take him over the arc of ecstasy.

I take a fifteen-minute break at noon, cutting open the box and unpacking its contents. It's my food: two weeks' worth of Jenny Craig meals. Jenny is my current meal plan. I use diet plans because they make my life easier—shipping me a complete breakfast-lunch-dinner combination, two weeks of tasteless meat at a time. The fact that these companies ship me the food saves me from having to leave the apartment to get groceries. I've found I can typically tolerate a brand for about two months, but then I have to switch it up. This is my second shipment from Jenny Craig.

Life as a recluse is harder than one might think. In the beginning, there were so many details I had to figure out. The Internet has been my salvation. Not just a source of income, it is my lifeline to the world, my source for necessities. I end up buying a lot of items in bulk. It is difficult to buy some items in single quantity. Take, for example, hand soap. I have four years' worth stored underneath my kitchen counter. My diet of TV dinners eliminates the need for plates, but I do have normal silverware and an eight-piece set of glassware. Walmart.com now ships to personal addresses, but some idiot in corporate seems to have gone through their website and cherry-picked which items they will bless with home delivery. Something as important as tampons? Nope—you can choose only in-store pickup for that. Like anyone wants to trot down to their local Walmart and stand in line at customer service to pick up a reserved box of superabsorbency tampons.

My personal side of the apartment is used mostly for storing all of my excess shit. That's where I stack the lifetime supply of toilet paper, tampons, and bottled water. Think it sucks to pay for bottled water? Try paying to *ship* fucking bottled water. I physically cursed every digit of my credit card number when entering that order in. That was pre–Amazon Prime. Now, with their free two-day shipping, I've eliminated 90 percent of my shipping costs. I won't be surprised if I single-handedly cause them to stop that entire program. They've covered at least two grand of shipping for me so far this year, well worth the eighty bucks I paid to join the program.

It looks, when one is standing in the kitchen and surveying that side of the room, as if I'm a hoarder. A well-organized, cardboard-box-addicted hoarder. With the exception of food, I have enough supplies to tide me over for at least nine months. I just need the Apocalypse to come the day after my food delivery.

Popping a barbecue chicken with rice into the microwave, I think about killing myself. It's a frequent daydream of mine—a rational thought process, and one that seems to solve the threat of me causing harm to others. I have yet to walk too far down that path. I could blame it on fear, say that I am too cowardly to do it or too selfish to take my own life. But it's not that. For some reason, I can't. Can't bring myself to take the only life worth taking. Whenever I go there, consider the act, there is a word spoken as clearly as if God were standing in front of me, saying it Himself. *Wait.* I don't know what I am waiting for, but I do. I wait.

The bell dings. I open the microwave door and get out my steaming hot dish. *Bon appétit.*

❖

I killed once, a long time ago. That was one of the reasons I decided to lock myself up. Someday, someone will figure it out, and they will come for me.

When I killed that first time, I fooled myself into thinking it was a onetime thing. That while I had acted in that moment and taken that life, it wasn't who I was, but rather what I had become in that one horrific instance.

The dark obsession with killing came when my family died. It left me alone long enough to grieve, to spend hours curled in bed, sobbing for my own situation: loneliness and despair over the loss of my family taking over any other thought process. But eventually I had to recover, leave my bed, and reenter the rat race known as life. But soon *it* came a-calling, searching me out in moments of unguarded weakness. In the shower, I would be struck with a vision of slicing a throat open and letting the blood fill the drain. In class, I'd find myself focusing on my science teacher's neck, fantasizing about wrapping my small hands around it and squeezing until the life was gone from his body.

When the urge got too great—consuming every spare breath and thought that came into my mind—I tried to satisfy it in other ways. Ways that I hate to think about, ways that fill me with embarrassment and dread. *Nothing* worked. And when I started making serious plans, started picking out victims and sharpening knives, that was when I knew I had to do something. *That* was when I decided to lock myself up.

I finished the fall semester at the community college, packed up my dorm, quit my I-spray-crap-perfume-on-you-at-Abercrombie job, and moved into the shithole that I now call home. Settled in, turned on utilities, and locked the door.

I haven't seen a live person since.

CHAPTER 19

HE DISCOVERED HER on a Wednesday night. Late, at a time when normal society was asleep. He entered and left half a dozen chat rooms, each girl wrong for different reasons. Too fat. Too sexual. Too slutty. Too aggressive. And then he found her, her username familiar, one of the ones heavily promoted on the website, the girl regularly present, her commitment to working impressive in its continuity. These girls typically came and went. Pulled from one world to the next, most likely by a man. But she had stayed. And on that Wednesday night, he decided to give her a chance, despite the $6.99-per-minute price tag, a hefty chunk of change compared with what most of the other girls charged.

But she was different. He saw that the moment her smile lit up his screen. She had the same shine as Annie, a pure goodness beaming from her happy face. She blushed into the camera, reaching up with one hand to tuck her hair behind her ear, and he could see the innocence. His hand moved without thinking and he clicked the mouse, starting the timer and the quick, fast drain on his credit card.

In 2009, Southern Methodist University did a study on homicidal ideation, which is the thought or fantasy of killing someone. They found that, of people surveyed on American university campuses, 50–91 percent admit to having a homicidal fantasy. What kind of fucked-up statistic is 50–91 percent? Did one campus have only half of their students planning death and mayhem, while another campus was crawling with psychotic coeds? The range makes me think that it was a bullshit study, performed by some doctoral candidate who invented a bunch of data and plopped it down on paper. Regardless of its validity, the alarming statistic makes me feel better. It makes me feel normal, as normal as envisioning a brain splattered open can be. On second thought, maybe I don't want to be normal—not if that's what normal is. We're all fucked if that is the case.

It's ten forty-five p.m., which means I am still camming, but my mind is starting to wander, thoughts of death intruding on my sexual role-plays. It's going to be an awkward day when my mouth moves without thought and I scream out, "I'm going to kill you!" to the poor middle-aged schmuck sitting before me in his tightey-whiteys.

Ten forty-six p.m.

I think about logging out early, brushing my teeth, and crawling into bed.

It's been a long day, full of seven- and eight-minute private sessions—the guys who have fifty bucks to spend and want to make sure to get off during that time. So they jack off until they are close and then take me to a private chat where

I do nothing but rip off my clothes, spread my legs, touch myself, and moan for the next five minutes. They don't want to chat. They don't want anything special. They just want a standard result from an unorthodox source. But that's what I get on Wednesdays. Fridays are the big-spender days, when clients just got paid and are ready for some lengthy, one-on-one personalized attention. Fridays pass quickly.

I don't log out early; my OCD won't allow for the slightest variation from my schedule. I log back into free chat and wait. Barely a minute of flirting passes, then I am taken private, this time by RalphMA35.

CHAPTER 20

MY CAM SETUP didn't use to be the elaborate production it is today. When I started I had an IBM laptop and a Logitech webcam—the laptop still stuffed with community college course work, the Logitech bought for $19.99 on eBay. I didn't know about lighting, or backdrops, or sex toys, or outfits. It was just me, on my bed, a bedside lamp creating a glare if I leaned too far to the right. I had my fingers, two pairs of sexy underwear, and an extension cord that allowed me some extra maneuverability with my laptop.

My image was grainy, the video choppy, my robotic movements occasionally blurry. But I was naked, and I was American, so the clients kept appearing and my earnings kept building. My first paycheck was $5,018 for two weeks of work. I was floored.

I paid three months of rent, a grand total of eighteen hundred bucks, banked $1,000, and invested the rest in my new career. I studied the popular girls, noted the crispness of their cameras, the glow of their skin, and I reached out to them, making friends across nine thousand miles of cyberspace. They shared the wealth of knowledge, and I started purchasing.

The first thing I bought was a new camera. Professionals don't use webcams. They use high-definition digital camcorders and connect them to their computer via a FireWire cable. I bought the best camera I could afford at the time, a Canon VIXIA HF. The cameras I have now? They make that initial cam look like a kid's toy.

But at that moment in time, when I plugged that camera in and powered it on, the perfect image that scrolled with smooth action across my screen…it was incredible. I gushed, I drooled, and the webcam community responded with gusto. My free chat began filling up quickly, users taking less time to click the "Take to Private Chat" button. And with my new sex toy in hand—a nude, eight-inch, authentic-looking cock—I started raking in the dough. My next paycheck was over ten grand. I celebrated in the only way I knew how: I kicked my feet in the air, squealed with glee, and experienced a brief moment of depression when I realized I had no one to share the news with. I logged off early that night, turning off the cam and settling into bed, one-click buying everything I had ever wanted.

A Louis Vuitton purse. Bought.

A Betsey Johnson dress. Bought.

MAC makeup, in every sheen and sparkle that fit my fancy. Bought.

My dark side piped up and I switched websites.

A Dark Ops Stratofighter Stiletto Tactical Knife. Bought.

A Spyderco Embassy aluminum switchblade. Bought.

At two in the morning, I left the fun stuff and started

researching computers, finally deciding on and ordering a MacBook Pro laptop, fully loaded and promised to be delivered in the next four to six business days. I finalized my order, then closed the laptop with a satisfied smile and went to bed.

❖

I quickly learned the pointlessness of spending money on purses, shoes, and dresses. Those items are worthless if there is no one around to see them worn. They actually worked against my happiness, their designer lines and beauty mocking me from a shelf in my empty closet, an indicator of the life I wasn't leading, places I wasn't going, people I wasn't seeing.

So I stopped wasting money and focused on the good stuff. A second bed courtesy of IKEA, mattresses delivered within forty-eight hours by 1-800-Mattress. I had discovered that lube and latex make a bed stink, and I wanted one I could dedicate to camming. Lighting: six spotlights that surround my pink bed, each holding two sets of lights, more than six hundred watts per spotlight. Proper lighting makes you glow on camera, makes cellulite and wrinkles disappear. It is also motherfucking hot. I looked at buying a cooling pad for the mattress, then realized it was a hell of a lot easier to just turn down the thermostat. My utility bills are enormous but unsurprising given my sixty-six-degree apartment.

I also have the crème de la crème of sex toys, in every different color, form, and fetish. Glass dildos? Check. A nude RealSkin cock that shoots out fake cum? Um…yeah—in white, black, and extra thick. Kegel balls, anal beads, rabbits, duckies, plugs, clamps, whips, cuffs, suctions, gags, and wands. I now have dressers full of stockings, garters, lingerie, leather, latex, heels, fishnets, and lace. Very rarely does a client request something that I don't own.

❖

I redecorated the cam bedroom the second year in this apartment. By "the cam bedroom," I mean the left side of the giant open area that is apartment 6E. The side where I have the IKEA bed that I use for camming. Where my lights and cameras and the stands that everything latches into are. It was purely functional at that point in time, just a bed and the tools of my trade. The second year, I decided more attention needed to be paid to the character I played, the nineteen-year-old college student I pretended to be. I started buying, ordering every pink, girlish, freshman-in-college item I could find, including two gallons of Rose Petal paint. It took a week for everything to arrive, my apartment filling with boxes of every size and shape. Once everything was delivered, I turned off the cameras for three days, moving everything to the center of my apartment. Then I painted, assembled cheap, particleboard furniture, and started hanging items. Calendars, posters, pictures of annoying happy coeds I printed off the Internet. I got some used textbooks off eBay and stacked them on the dresser. Unwrapped and washed pink sheets and a giant comforter. After pushing my bed back in place and surveying the final product, I decided I might have overdone it a bit in the pink department. Even now, after I've thrown away some of the girlish crap, it looks as if Pepto-Bismol threw up all over that side of the apartment.

The other half of my loft? I have, for the most part, ignored that side. It is where I sleep, where I read or shop online in an attempt to distract my mind until sleep comes. My decorating motif for that side of the room is cardboard boxes, a mattress on the floor, and books. Superfancy. I call it Crazy Girl Chic.

CHAPTER 21

AGEPLAY: A form of role-playing in which an individual acts or treats another as if they were a different age. Ageplay is between adults and involves consent from all parties. Typically, ageplay involves someone pretending to be younger than they actually are.[6] Ageplay can have sexual tones but is not considered to be pedophilia, though it can involve role-playing of a child-adult relationship (such as a daddy's girl scenario).[7]

TEN FORTY-NINE P.M. I smile brightly at the webcam on my pink bed because he hasn't yet asked me to move. He did ask me to take off my shorts, which I tossed onto the floor.

RalphMA35: do u have something else 2 wear?

I smile. "Sure. What kind of thing do you like?"

RalphMA35: maybe a tshirt. something pink, with ruffles

A pink, ruffled T-shirt isn't in my closet. Doesn't sound like anything that even exists. But I know what he wants. He wants a young look. I smile brightly at him and bounce off the bed, move to the white dresser, and pull open the top drawer.

I take out a faded pink T-shirt, one that is thin enough

to show my nipples and has a blushing Minnie Mouse on the front of it. I pull it on, exchanging the silk thongs I am wearing for a pair of white cotton panties.

It is not a frequent occurrence, but I occasionally get ageplay clients whose kink borders on pedophilia. It is an issue for me, one that I often lie in bed thinking about. Dr. Brian says that it's not always that they want a young girl; rather, they are looking for innocence. They want the initial experience—to be a girl's first. She doesn't have to be under eighteen, or under fourteen, or nine—she just has to be untouched. He urges me not to judge a client just because he wants me to act innocent: to giggle, and gasp, and tell him that I have never seen a penis.

I agree with him on part of this. Some of the clients, especially the ones who are underendowed, seem to want inexperience—for me to be "wowed" by everything they say. Some want me to be hesitant, unsure, to give them resistance at first. But differentiating among the motivations is a tricky minefield and one I hate entering.

I crawl up on the bed and sit, cross-legged, smiling at the black camera eye. "Is this okay? I don't have one with ruffles." I pull my hair into a low ponytail and chew on my bottom lip.

RalphMA35: looks great bb. can we roleplay?

I lean back, resting my weight on my hands, stretching my T-shirt tight against my chest. "Sure, Ralph. But I don't have a lot of experience, so please be patient with me." I tilt my head to the side.

RalphMA35: okay bb. whats ur name

"What do you want it to be?"

RalphMA35: annie

CHAPTER 22
JEREMY

JEREMY BRYANT KNOCKS on the door, holds up the box, and waits for the cursory response. It always takes a minute to come, a minute in which his palms sweat, and he wonders. He wonders if this is the day that the knob will turn and he will be face-to-face with her. Today isn't that day.

"Leave it. Thank you."

Always polite. Always brief. Always that beautiful, lilting voice that seems to hold so much distance in it. He signs the electronic pad, waves to the silent peephole, and walks the long hall to the elevator.

Waiting for her to open the door had never worked. He is going to try something different today.

He presses the elevator button, steps inside, presses the 1 button, then quickly steps off and allows the doors to close. He flattens against the wall, hidden from view, and waits, his eyes glued to the box in front of the door to apartment 6E.

The minute the elevator car leaves, making its empty descent, there is the click of a door opening. He tenses. The door opens, a silent movement, then a pale arm and a dark head reach out, grab the package, and pull it inside. There is another click, and the door is closed. He leans back against the wall quietly, thinking.

Brunette. Pale. It is more than he knew yesterday. He hears the elevator's exhausted ascent, and then it is opening, a black man in workout clothes getting off. He nods to the man, steps into the car, and lets it carry him back downstairs. Waiting for the car to reach the ground floor, he wonders, as he always does, why she hides. Because hiding most certainly seems to be why she keeps inside. Hiding from whom? Or what? *Hiding from something, that was for damn sure.*

CHAPTER 23

I LEAN AGAINST the front door and eat teriyaki chicken, which came with rice and some steamed-to-death green stuff they called vegetables. I used to have cable, but three months into the service something broke and the screen would display only an error message. I called the company, which walked me through four different trouble-shooting solutions (none of which worked) before they came to the conclusion that I would need a service call. *No, thank you.* I told them to disconnect the service. Television took time away from camming anyway. As far as Internet goes, Mike logged into my system remotely and set it up so I could steal Internet from my three closest neighbors. I normally use the Internet from "Team Bradley," which is the apartment to the right of me: it has the fastest connection. But in the rare instances it is offline, disconnected, or running slowly, I use one of the other two wireless networks available, courtesy of my favorite horny hacker.

With no cable, my biggest form of entertainment is eavesdropping on my neighbors. I lean back, listening to dead silence on the other side of the metal door. *Surely someone will be in the hall soon.* I hope for the bodybuilder down the hall with the bleach-blonde girlfriend. They always have drama-filled conversations. There is a noise and then the slam of a door. I can tell by the sound that the door bounces a bit, not quite shutting, but the footsteps continue, and by the shuffle of them and the speed at which they are by my door, I know that it is Simon. When his feet are flush with my door, I speak. Loudly, so he can hear me.

"Your door's not shut."

His footsteps stop, and I can tell from the light underneath my door that he has turned to face me. I also know, without getting up, that he is looking in my peephole, though he knows from every other experience that he can't see anything inside.

"You freak me out when you do that." His words are muffled, almost too quiet, but my one sensitive ear easily picks up the phrase.

"You'd hate it even more if someone went in and stole all of your crap."

"Yeah." He turns, his footsteps retreating, and I hear the final click of his door being pulled tight. Then he's back, and I can tell from his pace that he's about to ask me something. "When are you...uh...getting..."

"On the first. You know that. My order always comes on the first."

"Okay. I'm just a little low."

"Ration."

He pauses and then starts to move again.

"Simon."

"Yeah?"

"You were late last night."

"Yeah, I had, uh . . . some things—"

"Simon . . ." I speak slowly and clearly, so there is no room for him to misunderstand. "If you are late again, I will stop the orders."

"Yeah, yeah. I won't be. I promise. You know I won't. Promise."

He waits for a moment, and I don't respond, spooning a forkful of rice into my mouth. Then he moves, and I hear the plastic *swoosh* of my garbage as he picks up the bag and moves down the hall. Along with locking me in at night, Simon carries my trash and any outgoing mail downstairs. I leave it outside the door, and he takes it to the dumpster out back. I hear him at the elevator, hear the car as it starts upward toward him. Past the elevator, I can't hear much of anything. As strong as my hearing is in my left ear, it doesn't make up for the inability of my other. I am hard of hearing in my right ear. It is not a condition I was born with, but rather the sole result of an accident that happened several years ago. I've never told anyone about the defect, as it doesn't seem to affect my daily life and certainly doesn't seem worth a doctor's visit or surgery to fix it. I almost like the additional quiet. It is another layer between the outside world and me.

In the outside world, there is an entire community devoted to people like me. Not online prostitutes who fantasize about death, but those who want to kill, those who obsess over gore and screams. When I was in community college I found their forums, joined their Twitter groups, signed up for their creepy monthly newsletter. I quit that community pretty quickly. I had hoped for an AA-type group, one that would allow members to support one another in their dark moments, help them keep one another off the streets and safe from others. Instead, they fed off one another, sharing fantasies and realities, discussing along the open lines of the Internet how to properly slice a throat, fashion a garrote, or know if you have choked someone to death or just to the point of passing out. That's something you never learn from the movies. That when someone is strangled, the eyes-closing, body-slumping image that you see in the movies—they aren't dead. They are passing out from asphyxiation. In order to kill them, you need to keep squeezing, wait a good minute longer. Then they will be dead.

Being on those forums, peeking into the minds of those even more depraved than me…it wasn't good for my urges. Gave them too many ideas, gave them too much to feed off of. I closed my forum accounts, unsubscribed from the newsletter, got the hell off of Twitter. I switched to plan B: slowly starving my urges to death, cutting them off from contact with the outside world, refusing to give them food and nourishment in the form of indulgent fantasies. While Dr. Derek doesn't necessarily believe in plan B, he does approve of it, though he is quick to point out that it hasn't accomplished much in the last three years.

Dr. Derek wants a more proactive approach, thinks that the way to cure me is medication. He thinks if I take the medicine regularly, popping the proper dosage each morning with a plastic cup of water, I could rejoin society. Live a normal life. But that isn't a cure, only a Band-Aid. I've taken those drugs, and I don't want the life they would bring. To have a free body but a caged mind? To stumble through the world in a zombielike state, never feeling anything, never conscious enough to really know anyone? I'd rather live my life as it is. Where I experience everything, even the horrific fantasies of my psychotic mind.

I discard the second half of my TV dinner and check my watch. Time to get back online.

CHAPTER 24

HIS FIRST VICTIM had been Haley McDonald. Seven years old, a redhead with glasses, Haley had been an unplanned event. He had been driving cross-country, eyes heavy, head nodding, and had pulled into an interstate rest stop to sleep. He had dozed for almost an hour, awakened by a loud woman who screamed obscenities into the empty parking lot air, then stomped toward the rest stop's pavilion, tapping a box of cigarettes onto her wrist and mumbling words of nonsense. He had straightened his seatback and glanced over while reaching for his seat belt, his eyes catching on and holding the view of a tearstained little girl, her face turned to his, her small body in the front seat of the old station wagon. He didn't think, he didn't prepare, he just opened his door, stepped out, and opened hers, reaching in and pulling on her arms, stopping her questions with a quick shush. "Get in my car," he said softly. "I'll take you someplace nicer."

She didn't ask questions, she didn't cry out, she just let him pick her up and set her in his backseat, jumping slightly when he shut the door. He never knew how long her mother was in the rest stop's restroom, or how long she waited to return to the car, or how long it took a police officer to show up on the scene.

All he knew was that two miles down the highway, when he told her to crawl into the front passenger seat, she did. And thirty miles down the highway he stopped, checking into a roadside motel. And one hour later, she was dead. He strangled her so there wouldn't be blood and carried her out while the parking lot was still dark, putting her in the trunk and driving away. He ditched her body in a dumpster in Oklahoma, and—as far as he knows—no one discovered her there. Then he drove home, to an expectant wife and a warm dinner. And he realized, with shock, that he felt no guilt. That the fantasies he'd been harboring his entire life had finally been satisfied without any negative side effects. That after death he slept better that night than any night before. And for a while after that, his mind had been at peace. His soul quiet. Content.

He had been twenty-four. His next kill happened at twenty-six.

CHAPTER 25
ANNIE

THEY SAY THAT children are affected by their role in the family, only children more than others. G. Stanley Hall, a famous psychologist, referred to an only child's situation as being "a disease in itself." Only children are known to be more independent but can also be stereotyped as spoiled, egocentric, and overindulged. The Thompson family didn't have room for indulgence. Survival was the main focus of their family unit, and everyone, including Annie, was aware of their tight situation. Days like last Sunday, when frivolities like cake and presents scattered the house, were few and far between, and Annie had savored every moment of it.

❖

Before my life took a downward spiral toward horrific, I was the eldest child, one of three — our age gap so great that the twins felt like my own children. Summer and Trent were six — eleven giant years younger than me. Dad says that Mom freaked out on her thirty-ninth birthday, suddenly obsessed with having another kid after a decade of just me. Modern technology blessed her with two.

I had six and a half years with them, enough time that I fell hard: they took and held hostage two large parts of my heart. As desperate as Mom had been to conceive, once the twins had been born, Mom had emotionally checked out of the maternal role, leaving me to step in with hugs, kisses, and diaper changes. I showered them both with love, and then puberty hit. After that, Dad did most of the sweet talking and bedtime stories. I don't mean to indicate that Mom stuffed us into a corner of the house and ignored us. She was a fun, spontaneous parent, but she was just…different. As I got older, we grew closer. Her disconnect seemed to be with the younger children; the twins' tears and tantrums pushed her buttons and rattled her psyche. The older I got, the closer we grew and the less time I spent with the twins. That, I blame on hormones.

Teenage hormones turned me into a fair-weather sibling— loving when it was easy, bitchy and argumentative when I felt like it. Unfortunately, bitchy was how I most often was. I should have hugged them more, kissed their bruises, let them pick the channel on TV. They loved me, idolized me, and followed me around, begging for kisses. I would give anything to just go back and have one day with them again.

I hate my former self; hate her selfishness and her lack of appreciation for her perfect suburban life. I had everything in the palm of my perfect, lazy hand and didn't even realize it.

CHAPTER 26
JEREMY

JEREMY'S EIGHT-YEAR-OLD NIECE swings her feet as they hang off her perch on the top of the picnic table. "Maybe she's a vampire, Jermy."

"A vampire."

"Yes! You said she never leaves the 'partment during the day. I bet she's a vampire. They only come out at night." She grins up at him over the top of her ice-cream cone, her toothless grin a mess of melted chocolate.

He raises his eyebrows, considering. "That is a very good idea. Maybe she *is* a vampire."

"'Cause you said she had pale skin, right?" Her eyes are big as she licks the edge of her waffle cone and nods emphatically. "Gotta be a vampire."

"Hmmm. But she does eat food. She's always getting big boxes of food, from different diet companies."

"Is she...?" She moves her hands around her waist, in a large circle, and puffs out her cheeks dramatically.

Jeremy laughs. "Overweight?"

She dissolves into giggles, wiping her mouth with the

back of her hand. "Yeah. Mom says I'm not allowed to say 'fat.'" She widens her eyes in horror and slaps her hand over her mouth. "Oops. Don't tell her I said it."

"She's not overweight, Olivia. She seems kind of…" He sucks in his stomach and his cheeks, trying to look as emaciated as possible.

She falls over laughing, holding her side—the soggy remains of her cone dropping to the dirt. "Skinny!" she screams, pointing at him and squealing with laughter.

"Yes," he says, grinning over at her. "Though I can't say for sure. I only saw a wrist."

She sits up, suddenly solemn. "Maybe she's ano rex kick."

"Anorexic? Hmmm…I hadn't thought about that. Hey, what do you know about anorexia?"

She shrugs, her small shoulders scrunching. "I don't know. Mom says Katie is that."

Jeremy nods, focused on his cone. "You know, Katie will be fine. She is just going through a difficult time. You can help her, you know that?"

She turns to him, her intelligent eyes widening. "*Me?*"

"Sure. You can be the best little sister in the world. That will make her happy."

She thinks about that, pursing her lips and looking away from him. "So…you want me to be a good little *brother*, right?"

Sensing a shift in the conversation, Jeremy grins. "Yes. What's your point?"

"Mom says if you were a good little brother, you'd go out with Bethany."

Jeremy follows her finger, outstretched and insistent, his

eyes finding and focusing on the leggy blonde with a well-enhanced upper half. "Really? That's what your mom said?"

Eyes wide, she nods quickly. "Yep. Mom says we have to find a girl for you." She lowers her voice conspiratorially. "One who's *not* a vampire."

He laughs, trying to stifle the sound as she fixes him with a stern look. "I appreciate your concern, but *Bethany* is not really my type."

The little girl snorts, and her voice takes on an authoritative tone. "Mom says Bethany is *everybody's* type."

His eyes find the blonde again, traveling over her short shorts, the tight shirt, and the pound of makeup that covers her face. "Well, forget Bethany. That's not gonna happen."

"Is that so?" The playful voice of his sister causes Jeremy to look up, light blue eyes pinning him with a strict stare. "Pray tell, *what* is wrong with the swimsuit model that I have delivered to your doorstep?"

The little girl looks up with a frown. "This is a park, Mom. Not Jermy's doorstep."

Her observation is ignored as Lily parks herself on the bench between them. "Huh? What's wrong with her?"

"I've told you, I don't need to be set up with anyone."

"Right, because you have some girl who won't talk to you taking up all of your spare time?"

"She's interesting. A lot more interesting than a short skirt with a pound of makeup."

"Silence doesn't mean interesting. It could just mean boring. Sometimes you open the door and find out that it's a big ornate sexy door to an empty closet. Maybe the only thing you're interested in is the mystery, and you'll find yourself bored with what's inside."

He gives her a wry grin. "Don't worry, I probably won't ever see what's inside. I don't see her opening that door anytime soon."

"Exactly why you should go out with Bethany. She's been drooling all over you for the last hour. You need to step it up, before you get old and gray like me."

He throws an arm around her shoulder, bringing her tight to him. "You'll love me anyway, even if I am wrinkled and alone."

She hugs him back, smiling despite herself. "Maybe." Then she stands, shooting her daughter a firm look. "No more ice cream for you. We have dinner in two hours."

Jeremy waits until she strides off, her hands cupped around her mouth, hollering orders at different children as she moves. Once she is out of sight, he leans over. "Here, you can have the rest of mine."

He hands her the last bit of his cone and looks out at the backyard of his sister's house. "I was thinking about giving this other girl something, a present."

Her face brightens. "Like a balloon?"

"Or maybe flowers."

She frowns slightly. "I don't know if vampires like flowers."

"I don't think she's a vampire. I think she's lonely."

"Be careful, Jermy. Don't let her suck your blood."

He grins at that advice, watching as she jumps off the bench and takes off toward the jungle gym. Maybe his sister is right. Hell, he knows she is right. It was ridiculous for him to pass up Bethany for a girl who won't even open a door for him. Chances are, if she—from day one—had opened her door to him like a normal person, he probably wouldn't have ever given her a second thought, no matter how many packages she received. Normal people open their doors. People who have something to hide keep them closed.

He glances at Bethany, her canned laughter traveling across the park. She is beautiful, friendly, would probably spread her legs and give him the ride of his life. There are a thousand girls like her, girls he runs into at every turn. Girls like her had decorated his high school and dominate the bars that line the downtown streets. He has bedded more of them than he cares to remember, each time feeling dirty at the completion, none of the sex worth the weeks of emotional baggage that followed. He is now ready for a real relationship—the connection of two souls with a purpose other than mindless fucking and relationship games.

Vampire girl probably isn't the best yin to his yang if he is wanting a relationship. Physical and emotional contact seem to be a bit of a prerequisite to that. Step one, he needs to get her to open that door. After that happens, maybe he can start thinking about something more.

She has to be lonely. What kind of life can it be, with her alone in that apartment?

CHAPTER 27

MEN BRAG. THEY just can't seem to help themselves. Even when they are paying me to spend time with them, when it is guaranteed I will "like" them, they feel the need to brag. Richard, username SentfromHeaven, is like that. He is a senator, a position that does not impress me in the slightest, but something he is obviously over-the-moon proud about. He mentioned it in our second session, his voice a muted whisper, as if there were someone in his empty house, or my lonely loft, who might hear his confession. He also mentioned it on our third, fourth, and fifth sessions, just in case I forgot it or didn't catch it the first time.

For a senator, he is fucking stupid. He's on a website that requires his credit card and tracks his IP address, and he uses a webcam, flashing his face during half the chat, when it isn't zoomed in on his limp and uncooperative penis. I'm not "that girl"—I don't have any desire to record our sessions and sell the photos to the highest bidder—but it is only a matter of time before another camgirl will. I told Richard as much. He should be cautious, use my personal site, and not mention his profession to any other camgirls. I know that advice went in one hairy ear and out the other.

Richard doesn't have any particular sexual hang-ups or secret fetishes. I think his ego is why he logs on. It is the forbidden thrill. It is the need to have anything and everything he wants, one of those things being perceived worship by a naked young woman. It is just a matter of time before he is exposed, his firm stance on morality defrauded.

But not by me. Killer: yes. Exploiter of secrets: no.

CHAPTER 28

AT FOUR A.M., my eyes flip open as a thud sounds against my door. I wait, my mind catching up as my ears listen, waiting for a hint of what is outside. A series of thuds, someone pounding against the solid steel of my door. I stand, moving quickly, at the door before the pounding stops, my eyes recognizing the top of his head, the wheeze of his voice. Simon. Drunk, from the sound of his voice. It's two days before delivery, and I can pretty much guarantee you he has gone through his supply. The door handle jiggles, a stiff shake as someone twists it the limited space that is allowed. Left. Right. Left. Right.

I am fully awake, my hands flexing without thought. This will be so easy. He will open it for me. All I have to do is tell him that I have more. I have pills, and I will give them to him if he opens the door. I move quickly, yanking open my kitchen drawer, my eyes dancing over the rows of knives. They are all dull, butter knives—the only type I will allow myself to use. The rest of the knives—stilettos, switchblades, butcher knives, and the like—I keep locked up, my daytime sanity composed enough to make times like this cumbersome and slow. My hope, when I locked up the knives, was that by the time I finally get to them, I will have calmed my demons enough to step away—return to bed—literally put my demons to rest.

I hop over boxes, squeezing between two tall stacks, and shove aside books and packaged paper towels until I get to the safe. The combination chants through my mind, giddiness fueling its excitement as I hear a kick at the door. My door bangs slightly, words muffled as the knob jiggles again. *Simon.* I will slice his gut—shoving my knife in and dragging it sideways, slicing organs and tissue as I stare into his eyes and watch the pain. My hands tremble over the combination dial, and my first attempt misses, the handle doing nothing when I tug. I slow my movements, hearing the click of tumblers as I roll right to 62, left to 37, right to 95. Clunk. The handle pulls downward and the door swings open, my eyes feasting on metal, silver, and cash, my hand reaching in and moving excitedly over handles and sheaths until I find the one I want.

"Jessica..." A whine from the door, a weak thud of something that is probably a fist. I grip the knife handle, yank it from its leather sheath, and move back through the boxes, vaguely aware that I am naked as I reach the door and put my eyes to the peephole.

A peephole gives a distorted view of the world. It turns attractive people ugly, thin people fat, a short hallway rounded and curved. Simon's eye, pressed to the hole, is perfectly in focus—a hazel pupil surrounded by bloodshot eyes.

"Simon…" I speak clearly, my voice raised so he can hear me through the heavy door. My door is different from all of the others. Everyone else in this shithole has a pressed-particle door that one swift kick will break. I've sat at this peephole and watched angry exes, drunks, and up-and-coming burglars break through, hitting the door hard on the side by the knob, the door saying *fuck it* in one easy concession. Splinter. Entry granted. Early on, I had mine replaced. Paid $700 for the super to order a steel one and swap mine out. It was a rare situation that required human interaction, the superintendent's beady eyes too interested, my hand shaking as I handed over the ridiculous amount. He probably thought it was nerves. If only he knew what had really been going through my mind. His blood. His death.

Simon's head snaps back at my voice, then his eye gets closer. His words tumble out fast, tripping over themselves in their haste to be said. "Jessica. Look, I know it's Monday. I know it's Monday and the delivery doesn't come till Wednesday. It's actually Tuesday now. It's four a.m. Four a.m. on Tuesday, which is only one day before Wednesday. And I'm in pain, Jessica. Really, really fucking bad pain. And I thought you might have something, anything, I need something really bad. And the delivery doesn't come till Wednesday. It's Tuesday."

"I have pills, Simon."

He moans against the door, his eye closing, his hands fisting and pounding on the metal, the sounds dull on my side. "You gotta give 'em to me. Please open the door and give them to me."

Idiot. "I can't open the door, Simon. It's locked." I speak clearly, my hand sweating as I grip the knife. I roll it in my palm, reintroducing myself to its feel, welcoming an old friend with open arms. "I need you to unlock the door, Simon. You have the key."

He shakes his head, his jaw moving rapidly back and forth, back and forth, sawing the air and making him look, through my warped window, deranged. "No. I don't have it. Open the door. I need something, Jess. Anything, please."

"Simon. Go to your apartment, and get your keys. On your key ring, you have a key to this door. Go get it."

He moans, bending over in what looks like pain, his face tight and pinched. "No...No, I don't have my keys. That bitch Rita took them because I was drunk."

I inhale, anger burning through my veins, my mind racing with panic. "Simon, I gave you two keys. Do you remember? Two years ago, I gave you two keys. Where is the second key?"

"Two keys?" He closes his eyes tightly. "You gave me *two* keys?"

Fuck. "Yes," I say shortly. "Two fucking keys. Where is the other one?"

He looks toward his apartment. "It's Tuesday. I can't make it to Wednesday. It must be in my apartment. You got pills in there?"

I exhale, trying to calm my heart, trying to keep my voice calm. "Yes. Go get the key."

He moves, his feet slapping the thin carpet, and a moment later I hear the bang of his door as it slams shut. I stand, poised and ready, the knife tight in my hand, my mind counting the seconds, waiting for what is coming. The click of my lock, the swing of my door, the stab of my knife, the gasp of his breath. Finally. Blood spurting, covering my hands. Pain in his eyes, control in my grip. A life in my hands. 72 seconds.

124 seconds.

648 seconds. I slide to the floor, rolling my wrists as I watch the knife flash in the darkness.

793 seconds. I press my ear to the door, straining for some sound, some clue as to what is happening.

921 seconds.

1,122 seconds. My knife falls to the ground and I feel tears drip down my cheeks.

1,400 seconds. I fall asleep, my bare skin curled against the door, my head drooping at an uncomfortable angle.

CHAPTER 29

I STAND UNDER the weak spray of the cheap shower and try to wash away my day. For at least the twentieth time, I contemplate moving out of this shithole. When I decided to sequester myself, I was unsure of my financial position. I had $649 in my checking account and no clear source of income. This apartment had been cheap, with no deposit required. Now, with a bank account balance comfortably in the seven-figure range, it is ridiculous that I live in a place with occasional hot water. But moving seems an insurmountable task. And I chalk it up to a penance of sorts. I killed, so I am punished.

My last cammer of the day, RalphMA35, had been the typical "young experience" client. I should be used to creeps, should be able to brush it off and move on. Maybe it's because he had been the last of the night, but for some reason I can't let the session go. I can't forget the hoarseness of his voice, the need I heard through the speakers, or the hungry emphasis on the name he called me. *Annie.* It was my third chat with Ralph and the second time he used that name. It isn't often that clients use a specific name. It isn't often that I take the place of a specific person. When he uttered her name, spoke that sweet name in a tone that was anything but, it ripped my heart out—grabbed it, squeezed it, then yanked it out, leaving devastation in its wake.

I turn off the spray, grab the towel off the hook, and rub down my wet skin. I flip off the light and walk naked through the loft till I reach the edge of my mattress. I start to reach for the blanket to pull back the sheets and crawl in. But I stop. I stop and think—a foreign and complex push and pull of emotions battling inside of me. Then I kneel, a movement both familiar and foreign. Years of tradition pushing against years of neglect. I clasp my hands and lean on the coverlet, inhaling deeply, and try to figure out what the fuck I am doing. Then, I pray.

My prayer is short and focused. I pray for peace from my demons, that the urge to hurt others will leave my unworthy body. And I pray that if there *is* a little girl out there, a little Annie, I pray that God will keep her the fuck away from the man named Ralph.

I used to be religious, our family attending church on Sundays like clockwork. Mother was the leading force in that, my father anxious for the service to be over so that he could head back to football and weekend projects. If Mother did struggle, as I do with my demons, I often wonder if that is why she went to church. If it was in an attempt to purify her soul, to destroy the devil inside with a higher power.

I have tried everything else; Jesus is on my short list of ignored possibilities. I just can't go that route. I spoke to a pastor while living at my grandparents'. He told me that my mother was in hell and that she would be there for all eternity for her sins. He didn't understand that despite her actions toward my family, despite the fact that she took away everything good in my life, I love her. She is my mother, and one night of hell doesn't take away the seventeen years of memories. Hearing his words, spoken with so much certainty…I didn't go back to that church. It was hard enough to erase the image of my mother burning in hell *without* seeing his face again.

I understand that I shouldn't base my opinions of God on one redheaded country pastor. But my mother's blood runs through my soul. If God was how she kept straight, kept normal all of those years, what caused her fall? What if I gain control of my life, fall in love, have a family, create the perfect life, and *then* stumble—the way she did? It is better how it is now—where I have no one to hurt, no babies to nurture into future psychopaths. When I look at that possibility, at the course her life took…I don't want to be normal unless I know that I am no risk to others. I can't afford to stumble, to take away others' happiness.

So I don't turn to God. But I do believe in His existence. And I do believe that some people He can help. Maybe He can help Annie, maybe He can keep her safe from the monsters that roam our world.

He can't help me. Not in the way that I need to be helped. I don't want a salve or whatever form of support my mother received. I've seen one family destroyed. I don't plan on repeating that trend.

CHAPTER 30
JEREMY

WHEN THE PHONE rings at 4:59 a.m., Jeremy lies in bed, his body stretched across the length of it, white blankets tangled at his feet. His room is dark, the television turned off at some sleepy moment during the night. He reaches out, his hand fumbling across items until it brushes against and grabs his cell.

"Yeah."

"I don't know why you even bother with this, J." The voice of his boss rings loudly from the phone.

Jeremy sits up, running his hand through his hair as he tries to wake up. "You got one for her?"

"Yep, a small package not even worth mentioning. Why don't you let Mark take it, or I'll put it on your run for tomorrow?"

"No. I've told you before—I'll handle it."

The man's voice lowers. "You know how much trouble we could all get in if corporate knew you were running these packages off the clock?"

"I know, I know. I owe you."

"You've been owing me for three years. Enjoy your day off and deliver the thing tomorrow. I'll blame the delay on New Orleans if anyone asks."

Jeremy shook his head. "No. It's the first of the month—she'll want that package. I'll be by there around eleven to pick it up."

The man laughs. "Whatever, Jeremy. I'll see you then."

❖

Jeremy rides the elevator up, looking at the soft package in his hand. He shakes it, hearing the familiar rattle of pills. This is an old game, one he tired of early on. It is a game that, despite his irritation, she seems to find necessary. That's why he didn't push this delivery to Thursday. This package is one that has more than one recipient.

When he exits the elevator, the brown-haired kid is already there, sitting on the floor, leaning against the wall. His eyes light up at Jeremy's arrival, and he shoots to his feet, fidgeting nervously. "Hey, man." He holds his hand out for the package.

Jeremy shakes his head and knocks on the door, meeting the kid's irritated face with a calm stare.

"Come *on*, man—she always says yes."

Her voice comes through the door. "It's okay. Give it to him."

Jeremy holds out the package and the kid snatches it, ripping open the plastic and walking away, muttering to himself excitedly. Jeremy looks at the dead peephole, wanting to say something, anything, but his mind is empty.

He scrawls her signature and walks away. *Nothing is normal with this chick.*

He steps off the elevator and strides out to his truck, the sun warm on his face. He checks his watch and grins. With this errand done, the day is officially his, and he pulls out his cell phone as he merges into traffic.

An hour later, he jogs onto the field, fresh-cut grass underfoot, the afternoon sun on his bare chest. Bending over, he tightens his cleats, then stands and flashes a grin at the athletic group before him. "Sorry, guys, got here as soon as I could."

"No problem—you can just cover beers when we win," one man says, tossing a soccer ball his way. "Let's go kick some ass."

The game, against a difficult opponent, stretches late, the field lights flickering on and illuminating the play as it stretches out—a tie game that neither side backs away from. And finally it happens, a perfect shot by Jeremy toward a small window of opportunity. The ball stops, its forward momentum captured and restrained. And the game is over, won by the proper victor.

He collapses on the grass, the tickle of blades gentle against his legs, the warm night allowing a breeze to float across his hot skin, his eyes opening to find a sea of stars above him.

❖

I can't see stars from my apartment. It's one of the things I miss. The sun comes in the windows, the windows that don't open. So I can see the sun's light, feel the warmth of the glass when I press my hand to it. But the breeze is not there, and at night? The stars are blocked by the surrounding buildings. If I lie on the floor and risk neck injury by craning and twisting into some unnatural position that God never intended...then I can see a baby sliver of black night sky and occasionally a faint flicker of starlight.

But I want the whole shebang. A galaxy above me, stretching from horizon line to horizon line, one unbreaking expanse of universe that says "You are not alone." After my family died, when I lived in my grandparents' home, I would spend the evenings in the grass behind their house. No other homes as far as you could see, no sounds of traffic, no city lights. I would lie on the grass and look to the sky and relax. Let the stars take my pain, my agony. I would lie out there until my eyes grew heavy and I felt myself slipping off to sleep. Then I would move, quietly reentering the house, climbing the steps to my room, and crawl into bed, grass stains on my back, dirt between my toes. And I would sleep.

Maybe stars would help me at night. I shift on my bed, my nude skin sliding under the fabric of the sheets, and stare at the vaulted ceiling, wishing for about the hundredth time that I could cut a giant hole in it, a skylight to the world. I stare at the ceiling until my eyes droop and I fall, restless and twitching, into sleep.

CHAPTER 31
ANNIE

THE HOUSE IS clean and shiny. Annie notices the waxed wood floors, the shiny kitchen appliances, and the entire fridge full of food. For a girl without a mother, Dana has a home that seems just about perfect. Her father watches them from his place in the doorway. Annie shifts her backpack nervously, feeling out of place in the shiny home. They had ridden here in Dana's father's SUV, a shiny vehicle with power windows and leather seats that warmed when you pushed a button. He had gotten them ice cream, letting Annie pick her own flavor and add extra toppings, and hadn't gotten mad when sprinkles had fallen on the seat.

"Annie, just leave your backpack on the table. Why don't you girls swim in the pool?"

"The pool?" Annie's eyes brighten. She hasn't swum in a pool since last summer, when her mother had taken them to the YMCA on a Sunday afternoon.

The girl beside her groans. "The pool? I'd rather go upstairs and show her my toys."

Her father frowns. "We have a pool out there that you

never use. Go upstairs, find a suit for Annie, and then head out back. I'll fix some lunch."

The brunette pouts, huffing dramatically and grabbing Annie's small hand. "Fine. Let's go upstairs. I'll show you my room while we change."

"Change quickly," the man warns, an edge in his tone. "I don't want you girls up in that room all day."

They change in a room filled with dolls, frills, and pink. Dana thrusts at Annie a bathing suit that is tags-still-on-it new. She pulls on the sparkly suit carefully, not wanting to stretch the fabric, and examines herself in the mirror. With the sunny room behind her, the hot-pink suit bright in its unwashed glory, she feels transformed, as if she is living a different life, in a different world not her own. She feels momentary guilt at the surge of want, envy, the desire for this life over her worn and faded one.

They swim in crystal-clear water, eat burgers and potato chips with ice-cold Cokes, and pose for pictures poolside. It is, as best Annie can ascertain, a perfect life.

She hopes she is invited back.

CHAPTER 32

THE SHED HAS not been used in some time, cobwebs stretching across the doorway when he opens it. It is small, barely the size of a walk-in closet, a counter lining one side of it, the rest of it empty. When he first opened the shed, it held a push mower and chain saw, the large items taking up the majority of the floor space. He pulls out the mower and saw, moves them underneath the overhang, and returns to the space. In it, he stands, his feet on the concrete floor, his eyes passing carefully over the room. The walls are sturdy, the window and counter high enough to make escape unlikely, especially if he can set up a restraint system of some type. He returns to the truck and pulls out a bag of hardware, his drill, and rope. Then he walks back in the space, kneels in the corner of the room, and places a large eyehook mount against the wall, low and close to the floor. He pulls out six screws and sets the first one against the wood, placing the drill bit on its thread. As the squeal of a drill and the sound of splintering wood fill the small space, his excitement grows. *It is almost time.*

✦

You know those camming rules I mentioned? The ones I break with blatant disregard? Some rules involve sexual acts. I can't piss or defecate on camera. I can't fuck animals or men on camera. And I can't pretend to be any age under eighteen.

I've never had any trouble following those rules. I have no desire to go to the bathroom on camera or sexually assault a dog. I've certainly never wanted to pretend to be young, to engage in pedophilic chat.

My clients, even the ageplay clients, obey the rules. They don't ask me how old I am or put me in situations that are uncomfortable. But RalphMA35, he is different. He pushes the boundaries, every time taking it further, younger. I could easily end this sick game. Block him and never hear his voice again. But I can take being scared. I can take the sick words he gushes, because I am safe in my apartment, somewhere he can never touch me. And because I am not the object of his desire. My fear is that if I cut his cord, end his virtual fantasies, he will turn to reality. And that won't be good for anyone.

CHAPTER 33

"IT'S BEEN A good day. Two good days, actually." I speak into my cell while sitting cross-legged on my pink bed, my laptop open before me.

"Tell me about them."

I hope he's naked. I hope Dr. Derek is sitting at his desk, a big fat cock in his hand, and he is stroking it while talking to me. I spent twenty minutes two hours ago talking to an attorney who dispensed legal advice on the phone while watching me, his orgasm barely slowing the flow of intelligent prose. The image sticks with me, popping up when I hear Dr. Derek breathe, hear a soft sigh as he shifts in his seat. These are the kinds of thoughts I need to avoid, especially if I want to continue down the path of trying to right my axis and fix my brain. But it is hard to spend a whole day engaged in sexual activity and then pick up the phone, hear that smooth, sexy voice, and not image the cock attached to his body.

"Deanna?"

"Hmm?" I answer absentmindedly, posting a camming screenshot to Twitter.

"Tell me about your good days."

"Oh." I close the laptop screen and focus on his voice, pushing aside the image of thick meat surrounded by strong hands. "No urges, no Hannibal Lecter fantasies all day yesterday, last night, and so far today. And I was up late last night, till almost one."

"What'd you eat for dinner?"

I roll my eyes. Derek has a ridiculous obsession with my dietary choices, as if the magical solution to my problem might lie in a Lean Cuisine Herb Roasted Chicken entrée.

"Pot roast. Jenny Craig."

"Have you had that before?"

I snort. "About fifty times. Maybe more." Derek once had me cut out all meat from my diet, with a hypothesis that my animal instincts were triggered by the protein from meat. When you reduce a diet company's selection to strictly vegetarian items, you are left with about four choices, all of which suck ass. I made it through about six days before I told him I would personally leave this apartment and fly to California just to murder him. We then decided the vegetarian plan wasn't helping matters. "So, anyway, I was thinking, to celebrate, I might order Chinese tonight." I hold my breath, waiting on his response. The truth of the matter is, I'm ordering Chinese no damn matter what his response is. I've been thinking about it since seven a.m. this morning, beef and broccoli taking over and dominating my mind since then, my single-minded obsession probably helping to keep the crazy thoughts at bay. But I like to complete this little exercise in asking permission anyway. If he does approve, and the Chinese deliveryman ends up dying, then

I can always point the bloodstained finger at him. *It is his fault. He thought I could handle honey chicken and shrimp fried rice.*

"I don't think that's a good idea."

Damn. I huff into the phone. "Seriously? Didn't you hear me? No urges in twenty-four hours. Plus, I don't even open the door! They leave it in the hall."

"I don't care. The more people who approach your door, the more risk you put yourself in. They will knock. You might not be strong enough not to answer."

I grind my teeth. "I'll be strong enough." If it was up to Derek, I wouldn't even get Jeremy deliveries. He'd expect me to somehow live, without supplies or food, holed up in this shithole and starving to death. Never mind the basic necessities I need to survive. No, those weren't important. What *was* important was that no one knock on my door. Knocking equals death. Can't be too careful, Derek's liability insurance might go up.

"Better to be safe than sorry."

Wow. Those six words…they could describe my whole existence. I leave that land mine alone, looking at my watch. "Time's up, Doc."

"Don't order Chinese, Deanna. Stick to the food you have in the apartment."

"Got it. Thanks for the wisdom." I hang up before he gives me another pearl of knowledge, then scroll down my phone list and press the button for Hong Kong Chinese.

Forty-five minutes later, I don't kill the little Chinese man who scurries to my door, knocks, looks around, and knocks again.

"Just leave it on the floor," I call out irritably. They should know this. I've only been ordering from them once a month for at least two years. The place seems to have higher turnover than McDonald's, a new face bringing the same plastic bag every time.

The guy finally leaves, squishing the bag against the door and looking at it for a long time before walking away.

That's right, buddy. Keep walking. Walk away before I open up this door and kill you for taking so fucking long. I wait, listening, not budging until I hear the elevator take him back downstairs. Then I open my door and lunge for the bag.

I wish that I liked pizza. If I did, then maybe I wouldn't gorge myself on MSG-loaded fare. But I don't. I can't stand the doughy, grease-laden heart attack covered in nine layers of cheese. So Chinese is my only indulgence. I limit my ordering, recognizing the wisdom in Dr. Derek's thinking, restricting myself to a once-a-month habit, and allow myself to order only if I have something to celebrate, like today.

I ordered the usual: an extra-large Dr Pepper, an order of beef and broccoli, an order of chicken with vegetables, a large egg drop soup, and five egg rolls. I put the soup, three egg rolls, and the chicken into the fridge. The rest, I sit down to savor. The Dr Pepper is watered down, the ice having melted during the delivery, all carbonation evaporated during transport; but it is soda, and I moan as I suck down the first flat, sugary sip. Then I move on, opening containers and allowing myself full, unadulterated pleasure, all in the name of MSG fun.

CHAPTER 34

> **PSYCHOSIS:** A severe mental disorder, a derangement of personality. Some individuals experience mood swings and agitation, but emotional dampening and social withdrawal are the most common symptoms. Despite society's beliefs, psychotic individuals rarely become violent and are often at a much greater risk of causing harm to themselves than to others.[8] There are many theories as to what causes psychosis. Many current theories agree that it is caused by a combination of inherited genetic factors and external environmental factors.

THE POLICE REPORTS compare my childhood kitchen to a pig slaughterhouse. They say that blood was spattered from ceiling to floor and stained furniture, tile, and clothing. Forensics and the CSI staff figured out that my mother took my father's life first—a shotgun her weapon of choice—then turned the gun on Summer and Trent, using knives after the gun for no purpose other than to further destroy their bodies. They say my mother was decisive—that there seemed to be no hesitation in her mayhem. The only thing she wasn't strong about was taking her own life. They say those stab wounds were shallow, hesitant, and only one was deep enough to be fatal. *What if* seems to be the unspoken phrase throughout the reports. What if she hadn't killed herself? What would she have done next? Would she have left the house? Harmed someone else?

I don't need to wonder about what she would have done next. It is a waste of time and energy. I know the things I need to know. I know my murderous obsessions started the night her soul left earth. I have killed once. I only hope that I can keep myself from killing again.

Wait.

I hear that in my head. Yeah. I know. Wait. I only hope it is God telling me to wait and not my mother. Or Satan. Or both. I wonder if my mother was always crazy or if it came to her out of nowhere, the way it did to me years ago.

I have read a great deal about psychosis. Mostly from the Internet, which Derek discourages. Apparently, professional doctors frown on the awesomeness that is Wikipedia. But despite the questionable validity of the sites I visit, I read everything I can find. Maybe one day I'll read something that helps to explain it, something that offers some justifiable reason for my insanity's existence. I'd love to be able to look back and blame my murderous rage on a toxic batch of well water that only my mother and I drank. Or cancer: a tumor that pushes on part of my brain, Mother and I having similar weaknesses in our bodies that allowed the tumor to grow. Maybe it's not a tumor and it's just hereditary, like alcoholism or high blood pressure. Maybe Summer would have developed the same homicidal inclinations, only she didn't live long enough for it to develop.

I don't have shooting head pains or any other clinical symptom to enter into WebMD. Just the rush of bloodthirsty need sweeping through my body in one uncontrollable rage, driving my brain and thought processes into a tangled stew of insanity that can be calmed only by blood.

The desire typically comes at night, when there is nothing to distract me and the idle time plays hopscotch with my brain. When it comes, my mind takes over my body, causing my hands to shake and my mouth to water, hatred filling my body until I vibrate with desire, wanting, needing to expel it in a way that involves bloodshed. I calm it how Dr. Derek has taught me: closing my eyes and curling into a ball, my arms tight around my legs, the pressure of my grip giving me some sense of space. Then I picture myself, my limbs free and door unlocked, a knife in my hand, my gun in my bag, my legs making the journey outside, to freedom. I breathe, quick, fast, controlled snorts of breath, the outside air hot on my legs, my heart beating a thousand times a minute. And I ask myself, "What now?"

Then I let my mind run free, my fantasy acting out in vivid Technicolor all that lies dirty and rotten in my mind. I kill, I maim, I take life joyously, drunk on the action, my mind giddy as more and more victims fall dead beneath my hands. There is screaming the entire time—the screams of my victims, but also the scream of my soul, fighting back against my pleasure, for the deaths that I am taking so gleefully.

The goal is to avoid the hit of desire. But when I can't, when it sneaks up and grabs hold of me? Then the only thing to do is indulge it. And I'd be lying if I said I don't enjoy those times.

CHAPTER 35

HUMILIATION: Humiliation play is connected to sexual fetishism and can be associated with exhibitionism in the sense of wanting others to witness one's sexual degradation. Activities such as name-calling are a way of achieving ego reduction or getting over sexual inhibitions.[9]

I WAS CAUGHT off guard the first time a small dick entered the room. Outside of my private chat room, there is a waiting room of sorts called free chat. When I am not in a private chat, I log into that room. It is designed as a place for camgirls to meet the members and convince them to take them into a private chat. The waiting room is free, and there I'm supposed to chat with all the members at one time until one of them decides to hit the "Take to Private Chat" button, which is when everyone else is kicked out and the credit card charges begin. I am lucky in that I don't typically sit in the waiting room for more than a minute or so. I am, in terms of camgirls, a hot commodity. But one Monday things were slow, and I was lounging on my side, smiling into the cam and chatting up seventy-two different members, when threeinchpenis popped up on my screen.

threeinchpenis: hey Jessica

richone45: can u show us more skin?

OSUfreshie: hey bb how much 4 private?

I laughed, leaning forward so that my cleavage was enhanced. "Hey, Three—no, Rich, you know the rules in free chat, and it's six ninety-nine a minute, Fresh."

OSUfreshie: damn. i can't afford that

richone45: i can

allaboutpussy: do you like cunnilus Jessica?

OSUfreshie: yeah right rich - then why r u in free with the rest of us?

Jacob1982: cunni...what? *grabs the dictionary*

fantasyplayer: can you show me your feet?

threeinchpenis: Jessica, is it okay if my penis is only three inches long?

richone45: b/c i like free chat freshie. anyway, i'm about to take her private.

"Of course it's okay that your cock is three inches long. Do you want to go to private, and you can show it to me?"

Jacob1982: I can't find cunnilus in the dictionary. What does it mean?

OSUfreshie: then take her rich. We r all waiting

NFLJunkie: ur hot

---frankiedoug enters room

Assman22: LOL u r all so stupid. it's spelled cunnilingus u idiots

allaboutpussy: u should feel dorky for knowing how to spell it

BlueDog1: who says cunnilus anyway? sounds like something my grandmother would say

---Packersfan13 enters room

Jacob1982: i found it. i don't want to "orally stimulate the female genitals anyway." That sounds scary.

"Thanks, NFL. You guys, please be nice. All, I love cunnilingus, and I don't give a damn how anyone spells it. Rich, were you going to take me private?"

---richone45 left room

OSUfreshie: i knew he was full of shit.

- FREE CHAT ENDED - threeinchpenis HAS STARTED A PRIVATE CHAT

I incorrectly assumed that a guy with a small cock would want reassurance that size didn't matter, that I found him attractive regardless. threeinchpenis didn't let me get very far down that path before he set me straight. His request seemed so odd; I blinked a moment at the computer screen.

threeinchpenis: STOP. don't compliment. make fun of it. laugh.

I understood cuckold stuff. That constituted about 10 percent of my chats. Cuckold has an edge of humiliation attached, and I am comfortable with that edge. But pure humiliation and ridicule was not a fetish I was experienced or necessarily comfortable with. Those clients have their own section of the camsites, with their own dedicated models—girls who specialize in leather, insults, and degradation. I've never had to go there in a session, and I wasn't particularly comfortable with a leap in that direction.

I started hesitantly, a fumbling, disastrous attempt to point awkwardly and laugh. I sounded forced, ridiculous, and kept

waiting for the ENDED CHAT message to fill my screen.
But it didn't, and he stayed with me, patient—his grainy
image filling the screen, his small cock wedged between tan,
muscular thighs. He appeared to be, from my limited view
of his stomach and crotch, someone who took meticulous
care of himself—tan, muscular, shaven. His cock was hard,
the area hairless and smooth, the short stub thin and
uncircumcised. It was tiny, and I tried to laugh and point—
but it went against every empathetic bone in my body.

With threeinchpenis's gentle coaching, I finally got it,
falling into a rhythm that sounded natural and sincerely
cruel. I told him it was pathetic, that he would never
please a woman with that. The words caused his short stub
to bob and swell; his fingers grasped the short stalk and
jerked it. The climax came five minutes later, when I told
him I wanted to invite my friends over, show them his
webcam. They would all roll on the floor laughing at how
puny and ridiculous his tiny cock was. I almost missed
it, his hand covering it, but caught a glimpse of white
spray, and then he moved his fingers and I saw it. The
normal-sized head, dwarfing the short shaft, twitching and
gushing, a shocking amount of white cum shooting out in
quick, rapid shots.

I gasped, a standard and genuine reaction when I see
a guy finish—and hesitated, not sure what the desired
response would be. I finally smiled, a smirk that spread over
my whole face. "Wow," I gushed. "That was impressive." I
tried to maintain my snobby, condescending exterior but
added some grudging approval, and he seemed to enjoy the
reaction, rubbing his dick with a white towel and leaning

forward, giving me a brief glimpse of a tan, muscular chest before his cam went dark.

threeinchpenis: thx bb. that was great.

I opened my mouth to respond, but he was gone.

------PRIVATE CHAT ENDED BY threeinchpenis. 11min 56sec

------RETURN TO FREE CHAT?

I clicked on the "yes" button, pasted a smile on my face, and waved enthusiastically to the cam in front of me, greeting the waiting clients who filled the free chat room.

Eleven minutes. Amount charged to his credit card: $76.89. My cut from the bastards that own the camsite: $21.53.

CHAPTER 36

IT HAS BEEN a long day, full of waiting. Waiting through a long day of work. Waiting through a quiet breakfast, both of them looking at each other quietly over macaroni and cheese. Two souls in an otherwise empty house. He had watched television after dinner, waiting anxiously for the house to fall quiet, for her to fall asleep. And now he is finally free. Free to do what he has waited for all day long.

He powers up his laptop, scrolling through images until he reaches the one he wanted, the one he has cropped.

He looks at her photo, blond curls surrounding a sweet and angelic face. Full of innocence, full of hope. It is almost a shame to destroy that. The sweetness never stays long. It is destroyed quickly, replaced with tears and fear. It is sad that he now connects that fear with the experience, has grown to enjoy it on a level almost equal to the innocence.

He releases a tight breath, staring at her image, his palms sweating as he allows his mind to wander. He stands abruptly, moving the mouse until the time comes into view: 11:02 p.m. He should go to the trailer. He wants to be on the property, hear the silence of the woods, and verify that her future screams will not be heard. He can go, twenty minutes to the trailer and twenty minutes back, stay just long enough to get his fill. She will never know. She will sleep through it all, just as she has before.

CHAPTER 37
JEREMY

THERE IS NO answer when Jeremy knocks at 1:55 p.m., the first time this has ever happened. He waits patiently, a small box in his hands. *She must be in the bathroom.* A minute passes, and he shifts impatiently before he knocks again.

At 1:57 he is in full-blown panic mode, his knocks increasing in frequency and volume, visions of her lying comatose on the floor filling his head. He puts his ear to the door, listening, and can swear he hears her crying out, needing help. *What if there is someone else there? An abductor or burglar?* Visions of her gagged and tied or held at knifepoint arrest him. The knob beckons, seeming to pulse at him like a neon sign. He stares at it, the world disappearing around him. Patting his body, he finds his box cutters, the only thing remotely close to a weapon he has, and looks again at the knob. *It's probably locked.*

He reaches forward, grasps the round metal tightly, and twists. The knob turns easily in his hand and the door opens smoothly, leaving his hand and swinging inward. He gapes at the open door, caught by his action, not knowing what to do. Then he hears it—a definite moan of pain. *He didn't imagine it.* He rushes forward through the open doorway and into her apartment, his box cutters out and ready to defend her: her knight in shining armor. *This could be my chance.*

He enters the room with a burst of adrenaline and stops just inside the doorway, his eyes moving everywhere at once, his skin prickling in the sudden chill of the room. This apartment is one giant open space, something he didn't expect. His eyes flit quickly over a galley kitchen, one lone recliner, and a bedroom area—sparse and ordinary—a dark purple comforter and pillows tossed messily over a mattress and box spring on the floor. Novels are stacked everywhere: around the bed and alongside a stack of cardboard boxes that make his UPS storeroom look puny. Boxes. It is like looking at a timeline of their relationship, neat stacks of varying-size squares, white labels decorating them like erratic rectangular polka dots, easily a hundred boxes crammed into a giant hill of brown. He turns, looking to the left side of the apartment, and blinks, the strange sight foreign to his eyes.

Brightness. His eyes squint at the light, then adjust, his mind trying to understand the scene before him. It is like entering another dimension—a Barbie World–*Boogie Nights* mash-up. The walls on this side are a pale shade of white, almost pink in tone, and covered with posters, framed photos, and a wall calendar—filled with notes, arrows, and hearts. The bed, a white four-poster queen, is covered in a pink bedspread, pink pillows, and ruffles. The bed frame matches a small bedside table, which holds a hot-pink lamp and notebook. It is as if a teenage girl has been given free rein at Bed Bath & Beyond and has gone wild with her mother's credit card. The bedroom is illuminated in bright, blinding light coming from four giant stands, each holding professional-grade spotlights. Cords run around the room, thin Ethernet ones, large power strip ropes, and silver-mesh strands that seem to power and orchestrate the whole ensemble. There are computers, monitors, and cameras everywhere, all focused on the area, all on wheels or tracks, portable and easily maneuvered. *She* is in the center of the bed, and everything else suddenly disappears.

She kneels upright, her dark hair disheveled, her eyes locked with his. She is naked, her breasts heaving, pink nipples stiff, her pale skin flushed and glowing. Her brown eyes sharpen on his and flash with something he instantly recognizes as anger. *Oh shit.* He tries not to stare at her skin, her breasts, or the shaved mound between her thighs. He moves his mouth, tries to speak, but nothing comes out.

❖

He is *here*, inside my apartment. I study him openly, without the distortion of dirty glass. The width of his shoulders, the muscles in his arms, tan skin, and strong features. Whatever warped vision of good looks I've seen through the peephole, this view is infinitely better.

He is here.

Confused, I recount my recent actions, realizing that my position on the pillows must have muffled my good ear. He probably knocked. And given his flushed face and panicked eyes, he thought something was wrong.

His eyes lock on me and I hold his gaze, my brain working overtime, fury creeping into my mind. He is *here*, in my space, invading my home, for what reason? Because he thinks I need *saving*?

I feel the rush of excitement, power ripping through every vein, muscle, and pore of my body. *He is here, no door or barrier between us.* I stand, my bare feet planted on the bed, my senses on high alert; I stare with hunger at my beautiful prey. It is as if God has delivered him, on a silver platter, and the proof of it all is grasped in his hand. Box cutters. My pussy clenches, instantly aching, a drop of my liquid collecting and running down my inner thigh, evidence of my excitement. *This is my time.*

❖

He is shocked that she doesn't move to cover herself, doesn't have any shame in her nakedness. A change has come over her, and she straightens to her full height on the bed, her muscles tight, a strange smile on her lips. It is as if she is both furious and excited, all at the same time. Her eyes drop to his hand, to his "weapon," and he instinctively drops it, realizing she is on the defense, probably thinking he is there to hurt her. He raises his arms. "I'm so sorry. You didn't answer. I thought you were in danger. I'm sorry." He ducks his head, pulling his reluctant eyes from her tight body, and takes a step sideways, toward the door. A sound, like a strangled but joyous battle cry, erupts from her mouth, and he freezes. She launches herself off the bed, her naked body extending, and lands on both feet. Her eyes are bright with pleasure, her mouth curved into what can only be described as a grin. Her eyes are locked on something, not him, and he follows her gaze to his box cutters, which lie on the ground at his feet. He crouches, picking them up, and flips the blade down, bringing his hand up to put them in his pocket. There is a blur of nudity, and her body collides with his, her hands greedy and reaching, her weight catching him off-balance. They fall together onto the floor, and her hand yanks the cutters from his. She fumbles with them briefly, then flips the blade out and, straddling his body, brings both hands together above her head, wild joy in her eyes. She brings her hands down together in one quick motion, the sharp point descending toward his neck.

CHAPTER 38
JEREMY

HIS HAND SHOOTS out in defense, his mind sluggish, confused by this clusterfuck of a situation. His strong palm catches the edge of the cutter, and the sharp blade slices his skin, the pain quickly bringing reality to the situation. Suddenly his mind is clear, and he backhands her. The blow knocks her sideways, and her hands splay out, the cutters still tight in one hand. She blinks, her eyes opening, and scrambles to her feet, launching at him again. His feet slip on the floor as he tries to stand, and she is on him, the blade swiping in perfect precision through the air as he tries to shove her away and get some traction, tries to get off the damn floor. The blade catches his shoulder, slicing the fabric and dipping into his skin, hot pain searing through him for a brief moment. His hand finds her arm and grips it tightly, holding her in place, her face close to his, panting, eyes intense and full of hatred.

❖

I am furious, my anger mounting as I wrestle with the man. This isn't supposed to be how it happens; it doesn't fit the daydreams that I savor like manna from heaven. Last time it had been different. Last time had been easy—my victim distracted, caught in an unprotected moment. The thought suddenly occurs to me that I might suck at killing; maybe my first experience was only a deadly fluke. I have always envisioned myself as a killing machine, finely tuned in all things lethal. *I have massively overestimated my abilities.* The realization devastates me, and in that one, weak moment of self-awareness, he flips me, straddling my body and throwing the box cutters, *my prize*, across the room.

❖

Jeremy exhales. The weapon gone, they stare at each other, his body on top of hers, naked skin between his legs, her small breasts rising and falling with her panting breaths. She is beautiful, her eyes intelligent and large, her nose slightly imperfect, lips full and parted, high cheekbones framing her face. Dark hair surrounds her like a halo; she is exquisite in her madness. And that's what he has to remember. Despite her breathtaking looks, she is trying to hurt him.

"Get the fuck off of me." The voice is so familiar; he has cherished it for so long—soft and sweet—even when she is saying those words.

He shakes his head. "Not gonna happen."

"I will scream bloody fucking murder if you don't get up, and someone will come. You left the door wide open."

He looks at the door, standing calmly open, the dim hall exposed, the damn box still sitting innocently outside the transom. He wonders how much time has passed since he tried the knob. One minute? Two? Five? It feels like a lifetime. He reaches forward, his weight pressing down harder on her body, and she squirms beneath him, pushing on his chest with weak arms, glaring at him with eyes of death. His fingers touch the door and he heaves; the door moves from the pressure, swinging softly and then clicking into place.

He grins down at her, pleased. "What *exactly* was your plan? To kill me?"

"You entered my home. I have the right to defend myself."

"That wasn't defense. That was fucking psychopath behavior. You were one step behind Hannibal Lecter with that shit." He laughs nervously and fights a battle with his cock, willing it to soften. It ignores him, defiantly taking the other route. Her eyes flicker downward, and a slow smile crosses her face. *Shit.*

She moves slightly, her bare skin sliding against the rough cloth of his uniform, her eyes watching him. Then she arches, thrusting up against his cock, the pressure causing a groan to whisper from his lips, her eyes closing slightly as she bites her bottom lip.

A transformation, all in the course of thirty seconds. The wild, crazed look is gone, replaced with a sexual potency of the Jenna Jameson variety. She thrusts firmly beneath him, grinding her bare sex into him, driving his cock wild with need. Her eyes closed, head thrown back, small moans escaping—blissful, sweet sounds that pull him deeper into this insane rabbit hole. She reaches out, grabs his shirt, and tugs—softly, then harder when he doesn't respond. His pants are stretched almost to the point of ripping, and he struggles to breathe normally, to act rationally. She opens her eyes slowly, lazily, and licks those perfect pink lips. "I need you so badly," she whispers.

He almost does it. Almost hops off her perfect body, rips open the fly of his brown uniform, and drops back down on top of her, his cock posed at her wet opening, his hands ready to take her as his. But he waits. He watches her and tries to make sense of it all.

It is a performance that is certainly tempting, mind-blowing, three staggering times hotter than any fantasy he has ever had. But something is off, and as he watches her moan and convulse beneath him, he realizes the trap. It is staged, her deceit hidden behind one false layer of sensuality. He runs his hand lightly over the thin skin of her throat, at the sensitive place where her tendons intertwine in life-giving support. As much as he loves her flushed skin, her beautiful breasts, her moans of arousal, he wants to see behind the curtain of her performance even more. He wants to know what he is dealing with. He moves his hands closer and clenches them, squeezing tightly around her neck.

CHAPTER 39

HIS HARD-ON IS proof of it. Official proof that I suck at killing. But in the destroyed remains of my confidence, I see light. His weakness could be my opening, my body the weapon that would lead to his death. I move slightly underneath him, testing my hypothesis, having had so little experience with live, breathing men. But yes, it twitches, and my skin beneath his cock turns sensitive, my body betraying me. I use the rest of myself, those parts still loyal, and lift slightly, pressing my bare pelvis up against his stiffness, my thighs shaking slightly. I bite my bottom lip, stare into his eyes, and lift again, closing my eyes in false reverence when my skin rubs with his. It is almost laughably unfair; seduction is one thing I have fully mastered.

Except that something goes wrong. He is relaxing, responding, my own body having a tough time staying composed, my thoughts skipping away from murder and starting to think about frantic, rip-off-that-uniform, passion-ate sex. It is a battle raging in my mind, sex versus murder, and I am cataloging the different weapon possibilities within reach when he leans forward and chokes me.

Jeremy's hands tighten around my throat, cutting off oxygen, causing panic to fill me. I stop grinding against him and snap my eyes to his, searching the depths of his green eyes for understanding. I see none there—only steady, indescribable strength. My instincts take over and I scream, a long, silent, angry movement in which my vocal cords desert me. He loosens his grip slightly, and I gasp for air in a desperate, shuddering inhalation. I bare my teeth, hissing at him, frustration burning through every pore of my being, my arousal taking a nosedive off this cliff of insanity. I turn on him, using my legs, arms, and latent strength to try to knock him off-balance, to push his maddening weight off of me. It is a useless exercise; my struggles only drain my energy as I resist iron muscle and dead weight. The man is surprisingly fit, and I finally give up, exhausted. I lie limp, staring stubbornly up at the ceiling, tears of frustration leaking out of the corners of my eyes. I have met opportunity and *lost*. It is an outcome I have never contemplated.

"Don't you have a package to deliver?" I snap, refusing to meet his eyes, his face hovering above mine, the features irritating in their perfection.

He chuckles, the action causing his chest to move above mine—the pockets of his shirt to rub against the thin skin of my breasts. The friction against my nipples causes a reaction in me, an unexpected one, and I shift slightly, not wanting to lose my edge again, not wanting that heady rush of lust that just wiped clean all rational thought. I am suddenly too aware of everything: his strong arms beside my head, the smell of him, a combination of masculinity, sweat, and leather. It is the closest I have been to a human in three years and the closest I have *ever* been to a grown man.

❖

"Will you please let me up?" She turns away from him and speaks quietly, in a controlled cadence he would have expected from a schoolteacher.

"Why?" He moves slightly, pulling away from her so he can concentrate on her face, the smooth, perfect lines of it, her pink, swollen lips contrasting delicate features, her slightly upturned nose making her appear younger, more vulnerable.

She turns, anger flashing in her eyes, betraying her innocence. Her eyes, a hazel blend of milk and dark chocolate hues, penetrate his very soul, and he loses a breath somewhere when they lock with his. "Why?" she grits out, her white teeth looking less dangerous when they aren't bared at him. "Why should you, an invader in my home, get off and let me get dressed? Are you daft? You're lucky if you don't get hauled off to jail for this!"

"I'll let you up just as soon as I understand what is going on." She is gone as instantly as she had come, her head turning to the side, her eyes closing briefly, shuttering closed to conversation.

He wants to sit atop her forever, examine this strange, beautiful girl whom he has imagined for so long, but he resists. He moves his hand, turning her face to him, willing her eyes to open. But she ignores him, her eyes remaining closed, her face stiff. He moves his fingers, brushing her nude lips, trailing down her chin, neck, and collarbone. There is a slight hitch in her body beneath him, almost imperceptible, but he feels it and smiles. He spreads his fingers over her skin, feeling the life reenter her body, her nipples stiffening to full attention. Her eyes snap open when he speaks.

"If I get up, what are you going to do?"

She pauses, biting her lower lip, then shrugs, the motion causing her breasts to move. He closes his eyes involuntarily. "What exactly was your plan?"

"What do you mean?"

"The whole—Tarzan woman, whooping and jumping off the bed at me—thing you did. What was your goal in getting my box cutters?"

She laughs softly, her damn breasts heaving again, her stomach tightening beneath him. "It's really, really sad that you don't know what my intent was."

"To kill me." He tests the words on his tongue, doubting the validity of the statement.

Her eyes meet his, bright and intelligent, and she nods slowly. "Good. Smart boy."

He ignores her mocking tone and grabs her wrists, one in each hand, feeling the tiny bones in them come to life as she fights the movement. He pushes them down on either side of her head, which causes her breasts to rise as if offered to him. He looks away, swearing at himself for his damn lack of control. "Why? Why kill me?" He fixes his eyes on her lips, then her hair, and finally on her open, unashamed eyes, trying to look anywhere but at her body. His breath comes hard, like the cock that continues to surge against his pants, clamoring for freedom.

Her pink lips curve as she stares up at him. "Why not?"

"Why not? That's not a reason, that's crazy…" His voice trails off on the last word, regretting the vocalization of his earlier thought. But she hears it, and her chin juts out, eyes blazing.

"I don't really give a damn what you think about it. But I'd appreciate it if you took your fucking hands off me and left me alone." She pushes up with her pelvis, attempting to buck him off, and the pressure against his dick snaps the only thread holding him together. He dives down, letting go of her wrists and grabbing her head instead, pressing his mouth hungrily to hers. She resists, her hand pushing against his hard chest. She opens her mouth to speak, and he takes advantage of the movement, dipping his tongue inside her mouth.

❖

I am distracted. Thoughts of killing him have hopped a bus and promise to be back next week. Irritated at the man still stubbornly in my apartment, I don't see his movement until it is too late. His hands are in my hair, hot breath on my face, and he is trying to kiss me—his soft lips pressed insistently on mine. I push against his hard chest and then he is *there*—in my mouth—his tongue tangled gently with mine. My own traitorous mouth responds, and my heart rate increases as my hands move of their own accord up to his strong arms. His hands, entangled in my hair, cradle my head. The smell of him invades my senses. I have forgotten what it is like to kiss—to feel the response against my tongue, to feel his hot breath on my face when he pulls off me and stares into my eyes. His face is both tortured and confused. I don't like the searching look, the invasion into my soul, and I grab his neck, pulling him back down. Everything is so foreign: the feel of warmth beneath my hands, the smell of something other than lube, books, and food in my apartment. I taste him, greedy for every sensation, my hands roaming everywhere, grabbing at his shirt, hastily undoing the buttons. His hands move down, leaving my head, traveling hesitantly, slowly, until they reach my breasts and brush my nipples, softly caressing the curve of delicate skin. I gasp and freeze.

That frozen moment in time when his fingers touch that skin, a place where I have never had human touch—it snaps me back to the present, to my reality, and I can suddenly feel *it* coming. The desire to kill. I don't want it. I want to continue this crazy, hot chemistry that has me wet and panting. I want, with every drop of my blood, to be a normal, naked woman locked in a passionate moment with a gorgeous, strong man. But *it* is there, and *it* is getting stronger.

❖

He has gone too far—touching her perfect breasts, squeezing that soft skin. She gasps, her body stiffening. He pulls back, looks into her eyes. There is passion there, heat and need, and then something flips. A turbulent wave of indecision clouds her eyes, and she closes them tightly, face squeezed in an expression close to torment. Then her eyes snap open and are filled with panic. She shoves him hard, her eyes flaring. "Go! Now! Get out!" She scrambles, skidding with her hands and feet, crawling out from underneath him, the urgent movements pushing him into action.

He stands and freezes, unsure of what to do. Then comes her strangled cry: "*Go!*" He bolts, throwing open the door and rushing into the empty, lonely hall, feeling a burst of air hit his back. He turns as the door slams shut behind him, a loud crack of steel on wood as it hits the frame, followed by a loud click and a long, tortured scream that rips through his body, the sound shaking him to the core. After that there is total silence, a long, excruciating pause that stretches on for minutes. He stands there, helpless, facing the door, listening for anything, waiting for something, alone in the empty hall, the damn box at his feet. The door, that closed door that he has stared at for three years, a barrier to her.

His mind struggles with what just happened. He gets a familiar feeling, one that comes occasionally while in a dream—the realization that what has just happened isn't possible, that the pieces don't fit together and equal normality, the *aha!* moment when "This must be a dream" crosses his mind.

But it isn't a dream. This hallway is real, the last three years of wondering are real. He had entered the apartment and finally seen the girl in 6E. Not only seen her but touched her, kissed her, felt her bare skin beneath his body.

That annoyingly rational part of his brain enters the conversation, forcing his thoughts to turn to the dark side of his visit. The raw need in her eyes, reaching hungrily for his blade. The look of dominant satisfaction and glee as she raised his cutters high above him and brought them swiftly down, his heart the target. The look of anguish when their kiss had been interrupted by *something*, the panic at which she had thrown him out, the long howl of despair on the other side of that door.

In some ways, she had superseded his fantasies. So much hotter, certainly more sexual, her perfect face and beautiful body keeping his cock hard even now, even after all that had happened. Her fire, the energy pouring out of her in a wave of life, her entire body brimming with confidence and sensuality.

But in other ways, what had lain behind that door was so much worse. *You entered my home. I have the right to defend myself.* She isn't locked inside her apartment, hiding from someone. She is lying in wait, a contained mass of who the hell knows what.

His sister's words echo in his head: *Sometimes you open the door and find out that it's a big ornate sexy door to an empty closet. Maybe the only thing you're interested in is the mystery, and you'll find yourself bored with what's inside.* He laughs. Bored. Out of all the things the girl is, boring is not one of her problems.

He casts one final look at the closed door, then turns and walks to the elevator, pressing the down button with a heavy hand.

CHAPTER 40

I DON'T THINK my grandparents knew what to do with me. It had been twenty-five years since they had coexisted with anyone other than themselves, much less a teenage girl who had just lost her entire family. They were in mourning themselves, dealing with the loss of a daughter, a son-in-law, and two grandchildren. The fact that their flesh and blood was the one who brought the carnage was a weight too heavy for them to bear.

The large farmhouse, one that was packed with happy memories from my childhood: capturing fireflies in mason jars in the large backyard, Christmas Eves spent wrapped in afghans on the worn wood floor of their formal living room, a giant tree glittering from the corner, hot chocolate in cracked mugs, fried chicken on Sunday afternoons, and Easters spent hunting for eggs through the tall grasses in their backyard. That farmhouse died around us, a house of mourning and death, no one wanting to speak or move, worried that we might step on the crack that would cause us all to come crashing down.

They put me in the downstairs bedroom, the one right off the foyer. There were no rules, no curfews, no stern looks or discussion of my activities. They moved through the house, two silent ghosts, they in their world and I in mine. I could have thrown an orgy in my room, screaming and fucking the paint off the walls, and I don't think they would have stirred, moved from their cemented resting spots. I almost wanted to kill them just to put them out of their misery.

But I wasn't ready to kill then. I was scared to hell and back by my urges. They whispered to me in the night, catching me in unguarded moments, when I had exhausted myself with tears and loneliness and frustration. They struck me while driving, when my mind would wander from the road, taking its own direction until it ended in a bloody fantasy that had me gasping with fear and need. Fear of what I envisioned, need pulling at me to make it happen. I'm glad I didn't kill them. Despite the black hole their life turned into—I don't think I could have lived with myself if I had taken their lives. Contributed further to the tragedy that is our family.

I stumbled through the graduation ceremony, my eyes dead and cheeks wet. Everything I knew, everything I had, everything I was, had disappeared. The next week, the check from Dad's insurance policy came. The first check I ever wrote was to the funeral home, my hand shaky, my signature unpracticed. That evening, I packed up my things.

An estate company auctioned off the house and all of the contents in it. I was told, by a perky redhead in a blue suit, that the home sold for less than market value, the new paint doing little to overcome the blood that was shed in our kitchen. She wanted to know when I would be by, to pack up my room and get my belongings and the personal items in the house. I told her my time frame in two simple words. *Fuck off.*

I got an e-mail two weeks later, with the address of a storage facility, a unit number, and an invoice. I paid for six months, assuming that I would sort out my emotions by then, be able to hold an item of Summer's, look into a picture frame, or smell the scent of my mother's lilac perfume. Two months ago, after six or seven milestone checks, I sent them a rent prepayment for the next five years. The last four have done nothing to heal the pain.

CHAPTER 41

"I MET SOMEONE today."

Dr. Vanderbilt—Derek—didn't respond, obviously waiting for me to say something more. I don't, and we sit there silently while I watch the digital display of my clock change, moving forward one minute, then two. Finally, he speaks.

"Was it the Chinese guy?"

I laugh despite myself, humor not a frequent part of our sessions.

"No. It wasn't the Chinese guy. But you'll be happy to know I ignored your advice, and ordered Chinese, and didn't kill or stab or even threaten the man who delivered it."

If I expect a pat on the back, I know better, and Derek sticks to his crusty ways. "Tell me about this meeting."

"I knew him before—through the door, I mean. His name is Jeremy. He delivers my packages."

"And you invited him in?" His voice is calm, soothing, irritatingly so.

"No. He came in, on his own."

Movement caught my eye. Movement never occurs in my

*apartment. I sat up, confused, and saw him, or rather the back
of him. Then he turned and our eyes met.*

"Explain." Derek's voice is sharper, though you'd have to
know his voice well to catch it.

"I was in bed. I guess I didn't hear the knock. When I
didn't answer, he opened the door and came in."

"Do you understand that he overstepped his boundaries
by taking that course of action?" Derek's voice is almost
worked up, though he manages to keep its melodious tone.

"That's a bullshit question you should know better than to
ask. I'm not mental, for Christ's sake. I know normal social
protocols. Apparently he knocked a bunch of times, I didn't
answer, so he tried the door and came in."

"You don't lock your door?"

I sigh exasperatedly. "No, *Daddy*, I don't lock my door.
Well, you know... except for at night."

"Why not?"

"I don't know. I just don't."

"You just stated that you are, in fact, of normal intelligence and are aware of society's expectations and safety
limitations. You don't not lock your door without a reason.
What is the reason?"

"I guess I was hoping that someone might come in." I stick
my chin out defiantly, waiting for what I know is coming
next.

"So you could have a friend?" There is a bit of hope in the
sentence. Which is ridiculous, since he doesn't even trust
me to have food delivered.

"No, Derek. So I could *kill* them. If someone comes into
my house, I am allowed to protect myself."

He makes this weird noise that sounds like a cross between a groan and a sigh. "Do you think that this guy—Jeremy—came in to hurt you?"

He stood in a fighter's stance, his legs slightly spread and hands clenched at his sides, his face flushed and panicked, eyes flitting everywhere, then locking on me.

"No. I think he was worried when I didn't answer. I've always answered. I think he opened the door, and maybe heard me moan. Thought I was hurt. He rushed in like something was wrong."

"And what did you do?"

I grimace into the phone, my hand coming up to cover my face. "I tried to attack him, to get his box cutters."

"Have you fantasized about killing him before?"

"Oh yeah. Plenty of times."

"What happened when you attacked him?"

Ugh. The embarrassing moment had come. "It sucked. It was nothing like my fantasy. My attack was bad, uncoordinated." I blush, rubbing my forehead. "Let's just leave it at the fact that it didn't work. He took the cutters from me."

"Was he upset?"

"I think he was confused."

Derek chuckles. "I'm sure he was confused."

"And aroused." The words slip out before I can grab them, and they hang in the air between us. Derek waits, and I wait back—*our familiar game.*

"Why would he be aroused?"

"I don't know. I was naked. Maybe it was the whole us rolling around thing."

"Were *you* aroused?"

I close my eyes and remember the moment, the feel of his tongue against mine, of his firm but gentle hands on my skin. "Yeah. It was...different, you know? Being with a guy. It's been a long time since I've been touched."

"I don't want to make you uncomfortable, Deanna. You don't have to tell me what happened." As if speaking about arousal could make me uncomfortable. I passed that point a million chats ago.

"Nothing really happened. We kissed. And he was hard. I haven't...you know...it's just been a long time. That's all. It was nice."

"Are you attracted to him?"

"Yes. He's hot. And there was this brief moment—like when we first made eye contact—it was like a spark."

"A spark?"

"Yeah. But I don't know. That part is kind of fuzzy, because then I went all Xena Warrior Princess on his ass." I grin, forgetting for a moment that he can't see me.

"So what ended up happening?"

"We were kissing, on the floor, and I was doing good—not thinking about murder or death or anything. But then he touched me on my breast, and it was such a shock—so strange for me, just because no one has ever touched me there before. It broke the moment, and I could feel myself changing, could feel it coming..."

"What did you do, Deanna?"

"I told him to leave. Pushed him."

"And he did?"

"Yeah. I think he was a little confused."

"Why did you want him to leave?"

"Because I didn't want to hurt him. Not that I could have. Since I'm so weak and pathetic."

"This is a good step, Deanna. You had the chance to keep him there, to wait until your urges got the best of you, but you didn't. You told him to leave."

"That's stupid. I always try to *not* hurt people. That's why I'm locked away in this shithole to begin with!"

"But Deanna, you lock yourself up because you don't trust yourself to control your urges. Today, in a sense, you did control your urges. When you told him to leave."

I don't say anything in response. I don't tell him that I lay in bed for an hour after Jeremy left, systematically planning a way to lure him back inside and do a proper job of extinguishing his life. *Derek is proud of me.* It's a rare moment, and I don't want to spoil it.

CHAPTER 42

PEDOPHILIA: Defined as a psychiatric disorder typically characterized by a primary or exclusive sexual interest toward prepubescent children, pedophilia involves feelings the individual has either acted on or which cause distress or interpersonal difficulty.[10] "The experience of sexual abuse as a child was previously thought to be a strong risk factor, but research does not show a causal relationship, as the vast majority of sexually abused children do not grow up to be adult offenders, nor do the majority of adult offenders report childhood sexual abuse."[11] "Offenders are more likely to be relatives or acquaintances of their victim than strangers."[12]

MY FINGER MOVES on the mouse pad, hovering above the "block" button that all our chat rooms feature. I'm torn. I have blocked clients before—sometimes you'll get an asshole, sometimes you'll get a stalker, and once someone recognized me from high school. But this block is one I am having trouble with. During the time of my indecision, the button disappears, and my software loads the new screen. I am now in a private chat, and the object of my indecision sits in front of me. *Damn.*

RalphMA35: hey bb
I smile brightly. "Hey, Ralph."
RalphMA35: you know what I want, right?
I nod, moving to the side of the bed, out of the camera's view, and change into the outfit he has requested the last three times: a pink boa, cheap plastic crown, and pink silk gloves. *Freak-a-zoid.*

Later, I take another long, depressed shower, in which I try to figure out what to do about Ralph. The man is disturbed; his requests and role-plays are of the violent rape variety and all fixated on one individual, Annie. The worst is when he gets on his cam, when the typing stops and the speaking begins. His tone is guttural, excited. *Evil.* Every time he says her name, I cringe inside. He is definitely blocking material—the worst type of client, one that throws me into a sea of depression after every session. I have no doubt that Annie is real. That somewhere, she is a sitting duck for this sick fuck. What I can't figure out is if I am feeding his sickness or satisfying it. If I am protecting her or endangering her further.

I come to a decision and turn off the water, stopping the pathetic, tepid flow. I dry off, dress in my pajamas, and log back online, looking for HackOffMyBigCock. I log into

Skype and IM him, and his response pops up before a full minute passes.

---what's up sexy?

I need to talk to you. You free?

---let me wrap up something. Let's do voice chat in five.

Great. Thx

One ridiculous invasion of privacy that Cams.com affords us models is the IP address of any client who enters our private or free chats. I didn't write down Ralph's IP address, but I do have a key logger program installed on my computer that takes a screenshot of my screen every thirty seconds. I log into the software and find the screenshots from earlier, and RalphMA35's IP address is displayed clearly in the lower left section of the screen. I jot it on a sticky note and log back into Skype. Mike is already there, waiting for me.

"Whatcha got for me?" His voice comes through clearly, though he has turned off the camera.

"I need you to trace an IP address."

"You want just a location—address?"

"I want everything you can get me."

"Everything is a lot. You sure you want—"

"Everything. I'll have more questions for you once I get that info."

"What's in it for me?"

"What do you want?"

"Two hundred bucks. And an anal show—twenty minutes."

"How about three hundred and no anal? You know I hate that shit."

He laughs, the mike distorting the sound. "That's why

I'm asking for it. Come on. You can choose the toy. Twenty minutes and two hundred bucks."

"Ten minutes. You know I can get you off in that time period."

"Ouch. But you have a point." He pauses, and I wait, fighting the urge to bite my nails. "Okay. E-mail me the IP, and I'll send you the info later tonight."

I smile. "You're the best."

"I try. Night, baby."

"Night, Mike."

❖

Mike is as good as promised. Within two hours I have Ralph's name, address, Social Security number, and last two tax returns. I also have a complete dossier on the man, including employment records, medical reports, and a background check. I grab a Jenny Craig apple strudel from the kitchen and settle in to read the information.

Ralph Atkins, age forty-one, is a plumber. He was born in Statesboro, Georgia, and has two siblings. No dependents listed on his tax returns. Income last year was $54,029. Criminal background check is clean. Medical stats show him to be five feet nine inches tall, 190 pounds, with 30 percent body fat. He had an appendectomy six years ago and is currently prescribed 10 milligrams a day of Crestor for high cholesterol. He drives a year-old navy blue Ford Explorer with a tag number of X42FF.

He lives not in Massachusetts, as I expected from his MA moniker, but in Brooklet, Georgia—a small farming town with a population of 1,250, a tiny police force, and one local doctor. Google Maps shows Brooklet to be a thirteen-hour drive from my apartment.

What is missing from the information is if he knows a young girl named Annie. The possibilities seem endless. A small town full of neighborhood kids and a job that takes him in and out of homes in all the surrounding towns. Couple that with two siblings, unknown cousins, and unknown nieces. How could I ever find her? What if her name isn't Annie? What if she doesn't even exist?

I IM Mike back, asking for all known relatives of Ralph's siblings, as well as all neighbor kids within a five-mile radius. I also ask for the last six months of plumbing jobs that Ralph had had and any hobbies or extracurricular activities of his.

Mike's response comes too soon to be productive.

---Your pussy isn't that good bb.

How much?

---$1000

Okay. I also need to know everything he is doing online—computer history, that kind of stuff. Can you get all that from his computer?

---Why?

Can you get it? I'll go to someone else if not.

---Bitchy . . . Will he open an attachment that u send him?

Yes. If you can hide it in an image or video file.

---Ok. Then yes. Two thousand.

For both?

---No. For the computer clone. It will give you his files also.

$3K is pricey. Services exchange?

---Not for this shit. This is jail time shit.

Okay. $3500 if I can get it in the next 48 hours.
---Deal.
---Still love you babe
u2. get to work. :)

❖

I ended up wasting that initial thousand dollars. I didn't have
to do any searching for her at all. Three days later, everyone
in Georgia knew who Annie was. And everyone was hoping
she was still alive.

CHAPTER 43

FINANCIAL DOMINATION: A fetish that is rooted in deep need for a loss of control. A form of BDSM, the submissive's arousal comes from the thought or action of being swindled or manipulated into parting with money.[13] The larger the sum, the more aroused the submissive might become. Traditional "findom" acts include blackmail, tributes (monetary gifts), and the sharing of credit card and bank account information for unfettered access.[14]

TAKEITALL61 SEEMED TO be the perfect man: sweet, caring, and wanting to give me every dollar in his wallet. We chatted for almost two months before he dropped off the face of the earth. I'm assuming he finally hit rock bottom. I hope the orgasms were worth it.

Our first chat was almost six months ago.

- FREE CHAT ENDED - takeitALL61 HAS STARTED A PRIVATE CHAT

"Hey, takeit!" I smiled and reached back, unclipping my bra and sliding it off, exposing my breasts for the cam.

takeitALL61: hey babe. My name is Frank

"Hey, Frank. What are you in the mood for today?"

takeitALL61: I want you to order me to give you money.

takeitALL61 was the first financial dom client I ever had. He was patient with me, as are most clients with unusual requests, and by our third chat I understood exactly what it was he wanted.

"Don't you pull out your fucking cock, Frank—that is not what I want!" I pointed into the camera, my face fierce and angry.

takeitALL61: yes bb. sorry. what do you want?

"I want you to pull out your fucking wallet. Did you go to the bank today?"

takeitALL61: yes beautiful. I went at lunch

"Did you spend any money since then?" I knelt, a silk robe wrapped around me, all trace of compassion gone from my eyes.

takeitALL61: no! i promise.

"Good boy. I want you to open up your wallet, and then I'll let you pull out that cock. You're going to have to give me every dollar in that wallet before I let you come. Do you understand?"

takeitALL61: yes bb. i will. but I have bills that i need to pay

"Fuck that! You aren't paying the bills this month, Frank. You are going to give me your money, every last cent of it, until you are broke and living in the gutter. Do you understand me, Frank? You jack off that cock if you understand."

Frank never gave me a dollar over the preset $6.99 a

minute. He didn't even use the "tip" button that is displayed so prominently over our chat window. I could have used that as part of our play, but it seemed too cruel. Especially to a client who was already doomed to financial ruin.

CHAPTER 44

Four years earlier

Jennifer Blake. She was that girl at school—the one everyone wanted to be friends with and whose friends were in constant fear of getting kicked to the curb. The queen bee: beautiful, ruthless, with everything going for her. Money, power, and Josh Martin—the most gorgeous, perfect guy any of us had ever met. Jennifer's parents had a lake house about ten miles out of town, and it was there that Jennifer hosted her annual party. No parents, free alcohol, and enough bedrooms for a hundred high school seniors to have one hell of a good time. I was only one step above goody-goody, so I wouldn't be having sex or doing drugs. But I wasn't above drinking a few Smirnoff Ices and making out on a couch. And I desperately wanted to go to that party. I hadn't been invited the previous year and had spent the whole night feeling sorry for myself in my bedroom. This year I had gotten the coveted invite, passed on casually by Jennifer as she walked by my locker one remarkable Wednesday. I was finally "in," and I'd be damned if I missed the party by sleeping at my grandparents'.

So Saturday night I decided—sometime between Nana's apple pie and Papa's evening news, once I realized that there was, in fact, no graduation surprise planned—that I would go. I'd wait till they both fell asleep, sneak out the back, and then drive to the lake house. I'd be back and sound asleep in bed by the time they woke up for church the next morning. Easy peasy.

I sat through three Seinfeld episodes before I kissed them both good night and headed upstairs, locking the door behind me and unzipping my suitcase. I quickly realized, after flipping through the folded piles, that Mom had not packed a single party outfit that would be Jennifer Blake acceptable. The worst thing was that I knew the perfect outfit—pictured it as clearly as if it hung before me. The green sundress—fitted enough to be sexy, but casual enough that I didn't look like I was trying too hard. I had purchased it just two days ago, the shopping bag tossed carelessly in the backseat of Mom's car, where it no doubt still sat. I chewed my thumbnail and thought, weighing my options: Skip the party; attend the party in the wrong outfit; or swing by my house on the way. I checked my watch. Fuck it. I'd stop by home, sneak into the garage, grab the dress, and change in the car. That late at night, everyone would be inside or asleep anyway.

When there is evil in someone, it grows, unattended by all and fielded by its harborer. I know this; I feel it each and every day, growing stronger inside of me till one day— *snap*—it will take control, and every logical thought process, every thought of survival and preservation, will disappear, and I will be a loose cannon, fired and on my path of destruction, with nothing but my own doom ahead of me and the demise of whoever lay in my final path.

RalphMA35 hasn't snapped yet. But I can see his path as clearly as I can see my own. And it is coming. His demented evil is growing, and I am undoubtedly fanning the flame. I promise you, that is not my intention. My intention is only to save her.

CHAPTER 45
JEREMY

JEREMY COULDN'T STOP thinking about her. Part of it was the fucked-up-ness of it all; part of it was the image of her, naked beneath him. Part of it was the infatuation that had kept his mind and heart occupied for the last three years. Two long days had passed without any packages for her. Today, salvation had come in the form of an overnight express package from Instruct DVDs, the parcel addressed to "Jessica Reilly." Twice he stopped to buy her flowers and both times idled at the florist's curb for a few minutes before he ultimately talked himself out of it and pulled away.

Now there is nothing to do but knock. He had spent all day trying to figure out what to say and had come up with absolutely zilch. He hesitates, then lifts his hand and knocks.

There is a pause—a long pause—during which he has to remind himself to breathe. He fantasizes for a second that today would be a repeat of last time; that she would not respond, wanting him to burst in, and she would be naked and waiting. Then she speaks, and the fantasy evaporates.

"Leave it. Thank you."

The same short response he had heard for weeks… months…years. The same tone, inflection, and utter lack of connection. It is as if it had never happened, as if she had never been naked beneath him, as if they had never kissed, caressed, thought about doing more. He stands there, tongue-tied, the small package in his hand.

"I thought maybe—" His sentence dies abruptly, and he wets his lips and tries again. "I—"

"Leave it. Thank you." Same tone. Same inflection.

He sets down the package, scrawls her name with slow strokes, and tries to think. Then he turns and walks to the elevator, glancing back twice at her closed door.

❖

I stand at the door, my eye to the peephole, watching his strong profile as it turns, pauses, and then continues. My body twitches, a battle raging. Need driving my core. Need for interaction, for his touch, and for his blood. My hand shaking, I loosen my grip, and the knife drops harmlessly to the floor, the sound loud in my empty apartment.

I sob, the cry bursting uncontrollably out of me, and sink to the floor. There, against the hard door, I allow myself one brief moment of tears. Tears for the missed opportunity, for the life I am missing outside these walls, and for the utter waste at letting that beautiful man walk away alone.

Self-pity. Millicent Fenwick describes it as a terrible squirrel cage of self. For me, it is a futile waste of time. I breathe, suck it up, and stand, wiping tears and heading back to my pink bed of distraction.

snap

CHAPTER 46
ANNIE

ANNIE LIES IN bed and looks at the ceiling, plastic glow-in-the-dark stars glued to its surface. The stars don't glow anymore, but they still sit there—stuck on and forgotten about. The room is hot, but her momma doesn't believe in turning on the air-conditioning until at least June. There is a slight breeze from the open window, and she turns her body so that more of it hits her skin. The trailer creaks and settles, and after a few minutes, her eyes close.

❖

Two hours later, the man walks silently down the side of the trailer, the dead ground quiet beneath his feet. He reaches the open window and waits, still, listening to the sounds of the fields surrounding him. Bending, he sets the stool on the ground and then climbs onto it, the additional height allowing him to lean his torso directly into the window. He reaches into his back pocket and pulls out the long silver flashlight he has stuck there. Leaning forward, he switches it on, moving the beam through the girl's room, illuminating clothes, a plastic drawer set, and the bed. He slows the light's movement, playing it over pale legs, pink cloth, until finally it rests on a face, pale and slack with sleep, yellow hair framing it against the white sheets.

❖

Something is bright, hurting her eyes. She squints, moving a hand, and the light disappears and then reappears. Then it is gone, and she opens her eyes to darkness. Out of the darkness, there is a voice.

"Annie."

"Yes?" She sits up, confused.

"It's me. See? Come to the window."

She yawns, sits up slowly, and rubs her eyes, her limbs uncooperative, her mind sluggish and confused. Why is he here? In the middle of the night? At her window? She pads to the opening, the plastic blinds pulled up by her mother last night, the small window barely accommodating his big size. "What?" she whispers.

"I have a surprise for you—out in the car. Be quiet, sweetie, and go unlock the front door. Meet me on the front steps. Don't wake your mommy, she'll make me take it back."

Every part of Annie is instantly awake, trembling with excitement. "Is it a kitten? You know I've been wanting a kitty—"

"Shhh!" The sound is harsh, mad, and she quickly stops talking, the next words stuck in her throat. "Go to the front.

Be extra quiet and wait on the step." She nods quietly and turns, tiptoeing out of her room and past her parents' closed bedroom door.

The man breathes a sigh of relief when he sees her pink-clad body sitting on the step, arms wrapped around her little knees. He is close, so close. He holds out his hand and she stands, rushing forward and grabbing it, her small hand slipping into his. They turn as one, walking past her bike, turned over in the dirt, and on to his car, which sits at the outside corner of their lot, dark and silent in the night.

She realizes something is wrong earlier than he expected. She had believed him when he said that the kitten was down the road in a box. She had gotten in, fastened the seat belt, and leaned forward expectantly—scanning the fields and approaching roads for a sign of it. But now, six miles down the road, she is silent, her questions less frequent, her face tighter.

"How long before we get there?"

"About fifteen minutes, sweetie. I forgot, I decided to take the kitten to our house instead. It's there, drinking some milk."

"But what about my mommy and daddy seeing it? Aren't I going to get to keep it at my house?"

He reaches over, rubbing her knee. "Of course, Annie. We're just going to make a quick stop at my house first." He reaches for the cupholder and lifts out an opened bottle of Coke. "Here, Annie. Drink this."

She reaches for the soda, her eyes wide. Soda is a luxury not allowed in her home; the few sips she's had were taken at others' birthday parties and friends' homes. She grips the cold bottle carefully and lifts it with both hands to her mouth, the bubbly taste of the soda foreign on her tongue.

He watches her, his mouth curving into a smile. "That's good, Annie. It's a hot night. Go ahead and finish it all."

CHAPTER 47

I WAIT AT the door until I hear the elevator open, Jeremy step on, and the car move downward. Then I open the door and grab the large cardboard box marked FRAGILE. *Lightbulbs for my cam spotlights.* I carry the box in; swinging the door shut with my foot, I look down at the top of it, at the foreign object stuffed halfway into the pocket of the label.

It is a card, the envelope pink and the words on the front painstakingly neat: "To the Girl Who Lives in Apt. 6E." I smile at the title, understanding the meaning behind it, its reference to my many aliases. I open the unsealed flap and slide out the plain white card. Inside, the message is short, block writing in blue ink:

> *I don't know what's going on with you, with your whole "I don't talk to people, I kill them" act. But I know what's going on with me, and that's that I can't get you out of my mind. Please let me in.*
>
> *Sincerely,*
> *Jeremy*

I read it twice before setting it on the desk in front of me. I sit and stare at it, thinking. Then I pick up the phone and call Derek.

He answers on the second ring. "What's wrong?"

"Nothing. I can't call a friend to chat?"

"We're not friends, and we don't have an appointment. You never call without an appointment."

"Are you busy?" I feel a flash of jealousy, quick and green, but then it's gone.

"No. What's up?" I hear a creak and envision him leaning back in his chair, relaxing.

"Nothing. I mean, something happened, and I need advice."

"Another episode?"

"No—nothing about that. It's Jeremy...you know, the guy who—"

"You've had one human interaction in three years, I know who you're talking about. What happened?"

"He left me a note. Outside. With my package." I read him the note, trying not to add inflections that probably don't exist. When I finish, there is silence—silence that stretches out so long, I find myself fidgeting.

"What do you want from me, Deanna?"

"I want you to tell me what to do! I don't know how to handle this shit."

"What do you want to do?"

"I—I don't know what I want. I just need you to tell me what to do."

"What was it like when you were with him?"

I stand, pacing the expanse between my two bedrooms.

Crossing and recrossing the division of space feels like moving between my two selves—sex kitten to lonely woman. JessReilly19 to scheming murderess. *I pushed against his hard chest, and then he was there, in my mouth, his tongue pressed gently against mine, and my own traitorous mouth responded, my heart rate increased, my hands moved of their own accord to his strong arms.* Shoving the blade of the box cutters deep into his skin, the blood bursting from the movement, spraying gently upon my hand. *I tasted him, greedy for everything; my hands roamed everywhere, grabbed at his shirt, hastily undoing the buttons.* If he came back, if he came inside, I could be more prepared, could succeed in my quest for death.

"Deanna?"

I halt, trying to focus. "I'm sorry—what was the question?"

"What was it like when you were with him? How did you feel?"

"I wanted him." *On me, in me, dead beneath me.*

"In what way?" Derek's voice is so sensual, so soothing, so male. I make a decision, moving to my pink bed, and lie back on the sheets that smell of lube and latex.

"Every way. I wanted him to continue, to touch me, to run his hands up and down my body. I wanted to feel the warmth of him against my skin. I wanted his cock, hard and firm, fucking me in and out—" I stop, my fingers inside of me, my pussy wet, my back arched—posing for the camera that isn't on me. *I have done it.* I have slipped into the Jessica role, into my habit of graphically describing sex, the habit that my clients love, the habit that makes them hard and causes them to come. *With Derek.* What the fuck is wrong with me? Is any part of me left? Or have my two egos claimed it all?

There is silence on his end. Silence and breath.

"I'm sorry," I say quickly, sitting up and trying to resume some semblance of a professional tone. "I wanted him to fuck me, but I also wanted to kill him. It was exhausting—an inner battle that, at one moment, would have the sexual side dominating, winning—but then I would lose control and want to hurt him. I don't want to go through that again."

"Then you have your decision."

"Kind of."

"Kind of?"

I glance at the clock, waiting, willing the numbers to change. They behave, dutifully changing as my eyes watched. "It's been thirty minutes. I'll talk to you next week."

"Deanna, we need to finish this—"

I hang up, pressing the "end" button longer than necessary, watching the phone dim and then go black. Then I roll, coming off the bed, and yank open my right top drawer, pulling out black leather and silver studs. Today is definitely a dominatrix day.

CHAPTER 48
CAROLYN THOMPSON

THE UTILITY BILL is due. Actually, it is overdue—by two weeks now. They owe $124.55 and can't get another extension. Carolyn Thompson walks down the narrow hall to Annie's room, trying to think of a solution. Henry's disability check won't arrive for another two weeks, and it barely covers his medication, let alone the mountain of bills. She pushes on Annie's door, and the thin wood slides open soundlessly. Annie's bed is empty, the light from the window filling the room with bright sunshine.

"Annie..." Walking forward, she speaks quietly, not wanting to wake her husband, asleep in the next room. She picks up a discarded sock and the remnants of a popped balloon off the floor, moving to the clothes hamper and then the trash. Always something. Never enough time or enough money. "Annie, I don't have time for this. We've got to get you ready for school." She returns to the hall, moves to the bathroom and opens the door, looks behind the shower curtain. "Annie!" Irritated, she gives up the attempt to be quiet, too short on time. "Annie! Come out, I've got to get you dressed! I don't have time to look for you!"

There is a noise from the back bedroom. *Great*. Her husband is awake. She opens the door to their bedroom. "Honey, Annie is hiding. Let me find her and get her dressed, then I'll come and help you." He nods from the bed, and she closes the door, then moves past the wheelchair in the hall and heads for the living room, her voice now at maximum volume. "Annie Thompson! I am not playing with you! Get out here *now*!"

❖

Annie is not in the trailer, a fact easily discovered in the five minutes her mother spends searching. It is one of the few benefits of three people living in eight hundred square feet. She moves outside, her stride purposeful, the utility bill forgotten. She is not yet worried.

Henry Thompson sits upright in bed, cursing his useless legs. He heard Carolyn search the home, heard her calls to Annie, saw her come in the bedroom and search the small space, hoping that she hid under their bed or in their closet. Now she is outside, her calls increasing in volume and frequency. Something is wrong. Carolyn might not yet realize it, but something is definitely wrong. Annie wouldn't do this to them. She wouldn't bring worry to Carolyn, a woman who already carried too much stress. He lifts his legs, sliding his body to the edge of the bed, and reaches out for the nightstand with his hand.

Carolyn stands in Georgia dirt, cotton fields surrounding her—the plants small, in early stages of growth, too short and puny to hide a child. And she realizes, as sun warms her back and gentle wind rustles empty fields, Annie is gone.

He feels her despair, feels the moment that she comes to the same realization he does. He hears her inner wail before it leaves her lips. And in that moment, that breakage, when Carolyn sinks to her knees in the Georgia clay, his hand slips and his body tumbles to the ground, legs helpless to catch him.

Somewhere, in darkness, Annie begins to cry.

CHAPTER 49

HAP0972 IS IN love with me, or rather JessReilly19. His real name is Paul. Paul Something-or-other that is long and complicated. He lives in Alaska and works on an oil pipeline there. Either oil pipeline workers get paid really well or he uses 80 percent of his income on me. I hope it's the first possibility.

Paul is one of those nice guys destined for heartbreak—too nice to be sexy. We chat for at least an hour a day. Typically, he doesn't even watch me; he just logs into my site, starts the clock, and then wanders around his house, talking to me on his cell. It's the easiest part of my day.

I get heartburn about it sometimes. I feel like I'm stealing from him. But I know if I left him, if I refused to chat, he would find another cammer—one who might accept the gifts he always tries to push on me, the money he always offers to send. That's how I justify it in my mind. I know he used to chat with a cammer named Brooke. He mentions her sometimes; I think he still has feelings for her. Two years ago, he logged online for a preset appointment, pulled up her website, and she was gone. He looked for her for four months, signing up at every camgirl website he could find, searching through millions of profiles, desperate. And that was how he found me. And now I am his new Brooke, and he is terrified that one day I will disappear.

He seems lonely in Alaska. The pictures he sends me are of whiteness: white snow, his white dog, a polar bear that lumbered by his home one day. Out of the hundreds of photos that he has e-mailed me, I have gotten very few pictures of him. Two, to be exact. Both of them are photos that hide his looks. In one, he has a hooded jacket with thick fur around the edges, pulled tightly closed, only his eyes and part of his nose visible. I think he is part Eskimo—from what I can see, he has dark skin. Someone else took the second photo I received. It was taken in a blizzard, a faint outline of a person barely perceptible behind a wall of white flurries. Maybe he is deformed. Or maybe he is a Brad Pitt shoo-in who worries that I will love him only for his stunning good looks. Whatever he looks like, he is nice, too nice. Too nice for me to love him back. Which is good for him. Lowers his risk of death significantly.

We talk about everything, and I lie about everything. The bad thing about Paul is that he wants to know everything about me, everything about my day. Keeping up the facade to that degree is exhausting. And he doesn't just *ask* questions; he really listens to and digests my answers. I have a calendar I keep just for Paul. It is one of those big desktop types, and I have it propped up to where I can see it from my fake bed. On it I have my fake class schedule, my fake professors' names, and any fake events that I have mentioned on our calls. I am very creative when it comes to my daily activities. Sometimes I have to curb that creativity—too much detail breeds suspicion.

Paul likes to read. He has gifted at least twelve books to my Amazon account. They are all stacked beside my bed, and I am really, really trying to get through the first one, *The Alchemist*. I've been trying to read it for six months now but just can't get into it. I should probably give up on it and move to the next book in the stack. But Paul is patient. He doesn't rush my reading; he just keeps ordering me more damn books.

His dog is named Whitehorse. It's the weirdest dog name I've ever heard. I told him that and he laughed. Whitehorse is pregnant, and Paul wants to send me one of the pups. I'd love to have a dog. I need something to comfort me sometimes. I know I'm twenty-one, but at times I get homesick. Not homesick in that I wish I were at my childhood home, but homesick in that I want to crawl into someone's arms and have them comfort me. I want them to rub my back and tell me that everything is going to be okay. You don't realize how much you miss human interaction until it is removed from your life. Simple touches go a long way toward providing comfort.

I've tried to get a dog online but haven't found a way to make that happen yet. You can order dogs through the Internet and have them shipped to you, but you always have to pick them up at the airport. I could find one through Craigslist and have the person leave it tied up in the hall, but that sounds sketchy even to me. Besides, a dog needs to be walked, and that's impossible for me. And I hate cats.

Paul would bring me the puppy. All I'd have to do is ask and he would move heaven and earth to force Whitehorse's delivery, scoop up the puppy, and hop on the first flight to bring it here. Like I said, Paul is too nice. Too helpful, too sweet, too good, to be anywhere within a five-state radius of me.

CHAPTER 50
CAROLYN THOMPSON

POLICE TYPICALLY WAIT twenty-four hours before a child is considered missing, an archaic rule that has led to countless unnecessary deaths. That rule doesn't exist in Bulloch County. In a town with two deputies and one patrol car, where everyone knows everyone, Annie's disappearance was instantly and immediately taken seriously.

Carolyn and Henry Thompson sit in the small office that makes up half of the Brooklet police station—she in a metal chair, he in his wheelchair. Across from them is Deputy John Watkins, a man who went to high school with Henry, sat in church next to Carolyn, and held Annie's hand as she crossed Brooklet's Main Street. His face is long, the lines enhanced by years of tobacco use and sun, aged even further by the morning's events.

Carolyn had called their station at seven thirty-five a.m., speaking with Maribel, the department's secretary. Maribel had radioed John, who had been across the street at the Old Post Office Café, having coffee with Hank, the department's other deputy. Hank is now sweeping the Thompsons' house, along with a few uniforms from the sheriff's department. The radio on John's desk, set to channel 8, keeps them abreast of their findings—which have been absolutely nothing. There is no sign of forced entry, no sign of foul play, no blood, no strange items, and no tire tracks or witnesses. The window leading to Annie's room is too small for anyone to fit through, and the flimsy desk beneath it shows no signs of being disturbed. She either vanished into thin air or got out of bed and just walked right out.

"I am certain I locked the front door when we went to bed last night." Carolyn's voice is steely, though her face looks as if it will crack at any moment.

"Carolyn often worries about the door," Henry says. "She'll usually get up and check it. She worries, you know, about us living out there all alone." *With a defenseless husband.* The thought hangs, unspoken, in the air.

"You think Annie could have walked to the Bakers?" John leans back, looking at the couple over the pen in his mouth.

"Annie could have walked to town if she wanted to. You know that girl—she's got enough determination to accomplish whatever she puts her mind to." His raspy voice wobbles slightly but remains fierce in his pride. "But she is terrified of the dark. She wouldn't have left the house in the middle of the night to walk down that dark road. And Carolyn checked her shoes; they're all at the house. So she was barefoot."

John nods, understanding the unspoken thought process. "I'm going to call the Feds. Have them go through the process of issuing an AMBER Alert. Can't be too cautious."

Carolyn stands, gripping her husband's shoulder. "I'm

going to call the store. Let them know I'm not coming in."
He nods, looking up at her, their tight eyes meeting.

"She's gonna be okay, Carolyn," he whispers. "I promise
you, she's gonna be okay."

She blinks rapidly, smoothing down her dress. "I'm gonna
call the store."

CHAPTER 51

IT'S BEEN SO long since I've lived a normal life that I don't know if I could do it again. If all of my dark fantasies—*poof!*—went away, could I function in normal society? I say that I want a normal life, but everything now is just the way I like it. I eat when I want and how I want, assuming that I want to eat nuked chicken pasta primavera the rest of my life. I have my own space, nine hundred square feet without the annoying trappings of another person, their shoes on my floor, their body in my bed. I have friends, of sorts, ones who are willing to pay top dollar for my attention, ones who hang on my every word and will rearrange their day to spend time with me. Plus, there's Jeremy. He likes me because I am an oddity, a mystery. And the five-foot-eight body of perfect proportions can't hurt. But would he even want me if I was a normal girl? The kind who visited the mall on Saturday afternoons, giggled on the phone with friends? The kind he could live with, be with, know enough to find out there is no mystery at all? It doesn't make sense for him to like me for me. Not when me is a twisted, sick individual. So it must be the mysteriousness that attracts him. If I was able to return to normal life, to go to parties, and movies, and take trips and interact with people... I might gain all that only to lose him in my normality.

I am content, in these four walls, without normality. Lonely? Yes. Miserable? At times. But that is what being content is. Comfortable enough with the situation not to prompt change.

Thinking about a return to society is as dangerous as holding on to that scrapbook. Hope, in general, is dangerous. Hope can be the loose thread that pulls apart your sanity.

❖

The AMBER Alert is issued on Monday at 9:14 a.m. The notification is sent instantly to all broadcasters and state transportation officials. It interrupts all regular television and radio programming. The message is displayed instantly on highway signage in Georgia, Florida, Alabama, and South Carolina. In that single minute, more than eighty thousand text messages are sent out with the alert, and banner ads pop up on Internet sites everywhere.

I cam, unaware, for five hours. At 2:21 p.m. I sit on the floor, lean against my door, and pull up my e-mail as I peel back the top of a Savory Chicken with Wild Rice meal. I am midchew when the sidebar headline catches my eye and I click on the link, opening the alert.

Annie Cordele Thompson

AMBER Alert: Georgia

Last updated: Monday, April 23 09:14:08

An AMBER Alert has been issued in Georgia for 6-year-old Annie Cordele Thompson. Officers say Annie was last seen when she was put to bed at approximately 8:15 p.m. Sunday night. Annie is approximately 37 inches tall, with blond hair and blue eyes. Investigators have no leads at this time, but expect her to be in the vicinity of Savannah, Georgia. We need your help in finding Annie.

There is a toll-free number listed at the bottom of the e-mail, along with a plea to call if you have any information regarding her whereabouts. I stare at the screen for a long time. Then I reach for my cell and dial the number.

It rings five times before someone answers—a man, his voice clipped and unfriendly.

"I'm calling about Annie Thompson."

"Yes. Please state your name."

I hesitate. "Jessica Reilly."

"And the number you are calling from?"

I give it to him, certain it is showing up on his screen already. My stomach feels sick, tight. This is a bad idea, a threat to my bubble, my carefully cut ties.

"What is your information?" The man's voice is cold, expressionless.

"You need to look at Ralph Atkins. He is a plumber that lives in Brooklet, Georgia."

"What is his relationship to Annie?"

"I don't know that he has a relationship to her."

"What is the connection between them?"

"I...don't know." This conversation is going nowhere, tumbling downhill like an out-of-control skier gathering speed. I hear the weakness in my voice and hate it.

"Why don't you explain what you *do* know?" I sense a touch of kindness behind the efficient steel.

"I know that I have had multiple conversations with Ralph Atkins, in which he has been obsessive in his desire to have sexual relationships with a young girl named Annie."

"Did he provide a last name for Annie?"

I grind my teeth. "No."

"Why didn't you report this to the authorities?"

"I've been trying to get more information—about Annie— who she is, if she even exists."

"How long have you known Ralph?"

"I don't know him really. He's a client. I'm an Internet sex operator. I have cybersex with men for money."

"And it was in one of these sex sessions that he mentioned Annie?" *I've lost him.* I can hear it in the tone of his voice, the disbelief that coats his words.

"Yes."

"Do you have his address?"

I give it to him, both hope and regret flooding my body. Hope that she will be found and regret that I won't be able to kill the monster myself.

We end the call, and I sit on the floor and think. Long ago, I lost any respect for the police, for their inability to find the truth, even when it is thrust, front and center, in their faces. My call might lead them to Ralph; it might even lead them to the rescue of Annie. But in anticipation of their failure, I need to take action.

I reopen the file Mike sent three hours earlier and start to search the depravity of RalphMA35's computer and mind. It doesn't take long to find what I am searching for.

I receive confirmation of Ralph's sickness in his movie and photo files. In his e-mail, I find subscription con-firmations, forum postings, and e-mail correspondence in all things pedophile. It is in his web history that I hit the jackpot. Craigslist searches for rentals. Two postings he returned to more than five times. I go back to his e-mail account, looking for correspondence on either listing, and find a two-week-long e-mail trail and what looks like a final conclusion—a six-month lease, written in some bogus-ass name. Deposit was mailed in the form of a cashier's check, and the lease began on April 1.

Bingo.

❖

Staring at that lease, looking at an address that could possibly hold Annie, I feel woefully unprepared. It is almost laughable when I look back at the last three years. Three years of thinking about death, about me taking the life of another. And now, when the time to act arrives, I don't have the faintest idea how to properly go about it. My failure with Jeremy, his body easily overtaking mine, my weakness against his strength, is too fresh in my mind. Maybe I can't do it. Maybe I will fail. But it is there, that word that has been held off for so long, in my mind as clearly as its *Wait* predecessor. GO.

GO.

CHAPTER 52

KNIFE: *CHECK*. I push all my books off the old, faded suitcase they sit on. After unzipping it, I pull out the sole item it holds: a black stiletto knife. Depressing the button on its front snaps out a long, thin, ridiculously sharp blade. I had bought it in a moment of weakness—or rather, four hours of weakness—in which I had meticulously researched different knives and switchblades, looking for the most effective and efficient killing tool. My fantasies center mostly on death by blade. Knives result in more blood, more suffering by the victim, and a slower death if you stab the right places and avoid main arteries. Not that I was going to restrict myself on this mission. I stuff the knife in my sweatshirt's pocket.

Gun: *Check*. When I moved out of my grandparents' house, a pawnshop was one of my first stops. I applied for a permit and now own a Smith & Wesson 317. I carry my desk chair over to the fridge and stand on it, reaching back till I feel the space between the wall and the appliance. My fingers brush the edge of duct tape, gritty and peeling at the edges. I reach farther, gripping the cloth bag that the tape holds to the fridge. Yanking on the cloth, I rip off the duct tape and pull the bag over the edge, then cradle it to my chest and step carefully off the chair. When I first got this gun, I made cleaning it a full-time job. I loved the feel and weight of it in my hand, loved examining the mechanisms that made it deadly. Back then, I visited the gun range two or three times a week, my fantasies having a field day with the targets in my scope. If anyone at the range found it strange that I used lifelike target cutouts, they didn't say anything to me about it. I haven't cleaned or touched the gun in over two years. It is a bittersweet reunion.

Car: *No check*. I need a vehicle. I log online, trying to find the closest rental company. Enterprise's site indicates that they will pick me up, so I call them first. It is almost five o'clock. The rep who answers the phone says that they won't be able to get me until the morning. I start looking up taxi companies.

A knock sounds on the door—two quick raps.

Jeremy.

❖

He holds flowers, a ridiculous gesture now that he thinks about it. He sweats in front of her door, the wilted daisies looking sad after sitting all day in his hot truck. This is his last stop of the day. He pushed her to the end of his route, hoping that she reconsidered his note and that today will be the day she will let him in.

The door swings open, startling him in its unexpected movement, and she stands there, smaller than he remembers, dressed in black. She reaches forward, grabs his shirt, and pulls him inside.

His fantasies pop their heads up, ready for a reunion of orgasmic proportions, maybe a deep kiss leading to ripping of clothing and a fuckfest right here on the worn-out floor. She leaves him standing in the middle of her apartment, in between the two bedroom areas, the stupid flowers weighing down his arms. His fantasies wilt slightly, his cock taking a detour toward soft. She paces to a desk, leans over a laptop, and types furiously into it, tossing words over her shoulder at him. "Do you have a car?"

"A car?"

"Yes. A car."

"Yeah—but I'm driving the delivery truck right now. I brought you flowers."

"Toss them. Trash can is in the kitchen." She finishes typing, then reaches behind the laptop and unplugs it, coiling the cord around her hand in a quick, hurried motion. "Thank you," she says suddenly, turning to meet his eyes, the words an afterthought. "Trash. Kitchen."

"Right." He walks over to the kitchen and pushes the rejected daisies into the trash, squashing TV dinner boxes in the process. *So much for that gesture.* Come to think of it, maybe she isn't a hearts-and-flowers kind of girl. He turns to watch her, her feet moving quickly as she opens a black backpack and slides her laptop inside, the cord along with it.

"Are you done with your route?"

"Yes. Are you allergic to flowers?"

"Where is your car?"

"It's a truck. It's at the distribution center."

"How far is that from here?"

"Umm…like ten minutes. Are you going somewhere?" It is a ridiculous question to ask, but she seems to be going through the normal activities of someone who would actually step outside. Leave the apartment. She even has shoes on.

"We."

"We what?"

She stops, turning to him, an irritated expression on her face. "*We* are going somewhere. I need a car. Take me to yours, and I will pay for you to take a taxi home. I'll bring your car back to you tomorrow." She turns back to her bag, shoving in a thick black object and a bound stack of cash. His eyes follow the cash, his mind questioning his vision even as it focuses on the cash's wrapper: *$10,000?*

"Uh…no."

"No?" She turns, her eyes flashing at him—dark and confident. Wherever the crazy, I'll-stab-you-to-death persona is, it has taken a break and is sipping coffee somewhere else in this girl's mind. "We'll talk in your truck. Let's go." She grabs a ring of keys, shrugs into the backpack, and heads for the door. With no clear option in sight, Jeremy follows.

She avoids the elevator, hesitating briefly before banging open the stairwell door at the end of the hall and jogging down the steps. She takes the six flights of stairs quickly, time seeming to be a valuable commodity. He follows closely, trying to figure out what is going on and if he should toss his box cutters into the closest trash can. At the bottom she pauses, takes a deep breath, and presses open the exit door, stepping into the light.

Vampire. His niece's diagnosis pops into Jeremy's mind when he sees her reaction to the sun. She sways briefly, her feet glued to the ground, and squints into the sun—seeming to notice and avoid everything in one brief moment. Looking around urgently, her eyes lock on his truck, and she moves toward it, her feet stumbling slightly.

CHAPTER 53

IT SOUNDS RIDICULOUS, but I am scared to press that stairwell exit handle. Scared that my dark side will go apeshit when presented with the unlimited opportunities the outside world offers. Scared that a little girl will have to listen to the words I've heard for the past two weeks. Scared that she will be afraid and alone while I am out killing strangers, mutilating the body of the gorgeous delivery driver who now stands just a few feet away. I don't even crack the exterior vent in my apartment, worried about the triggers that might exist, the sounds and smells of normalcy that might awaken my psychosis or, even worse, my memories of what normal feels like. And that is my biggest fear when I step out this stairwell door. That I will taste normal, step on its street, ride in a truck and smile on its face, and not be able to resist. That I will psychologically paint over my situation and convince myself that I can handle it. Lie to myself because I want so badly to return to the world. And then, *snap*.

After I appropriately freak myself out, I push on the exit handle and step into the light.

The sensation of being outdoors surprises me, even with my mental preparation. You don't realize how much damn activity there is, all the noise and smells that assault your senses when you do something as simple as stand on a public street. *I have been shut away too long.* The gritty feel of pavement beneath my shoes, the weight of actually wearing shoes—my feet feel heavy and hot. My nose recoils from the smell of car exhaust, my skin prickles from the feeling of warmth and nonartificial light from the sun, harsh and powerful to my raw senses. My eyes squint and I look around, wanting the cover and protection of a vehicle. Jeremy's truck is at the curb, and I step unsteadily toward it.

He beats me to the passenger side, pushing a jacket and box off the seat, flashing me an embarrassed grin. I move past him, climbing onto the truck, and sit on the warm vinyl seat. The outdoor world distracts me briefly, a rainbow of colors and sights before me as the beauty of everyday life beckons. Images and memories—*rolling on the grass with Summer*—hit me, a wave of nostalgia interrupting my focus. Jeremy climbs into the driver's seat, starts the truck, and a roar fills the air, the truck shaking briefly before settling into a constant vibration. The lack of protection in the truck unnerves me; the missing doors and loud engine are strange to my sheltered senses. I focus, pulling out my laptop and logging into Ralph's hard drive to look for anything that I might have missed. Jeremy is saying something, a garble of words in the background that I tune out. All of my thoughts and focus center on finding Annie and getting to her as soon as I can. I feel something jabbing me, and I look at my shoulder, following the finger, to the hand, to Jeremy's irritated face.

"Pay attention—I'm trying to talk to you."

"Don't touch me," I snap, scrolling through files, opening occasional documents.

"Where are you going?"

"I need to visit someone. It is very important that I get there as soon as possible."

"Why don't you have your own car?"

"I don't leave the apartment. A car is an unneeded expense."

"Why don't you leave the apartment?"

"This is all a waste of time. Please focus on driving to your car as quickly as possible."

"I'm not letting you take my truck."

My eyes snap away from the laptop, alighting on his face. *Fuck. This might be a problem.* "Why not?"

"Can you even drive?"

"Yes. I'm an excellent driver. I haven't had a ticket or accident in over three years." I say the words with a straight face, while my mind rolls hysterically with laughter, patting myself on the back for my wit. "What do you want?"

"Want?"

God, it was like talking to a parrot. "What do you *want* in exchange for letting me use your truck?"

His face twists in frustration. "I want to know what's going on!"

"I don't have time to explain what's going on; I *can* tell you that I need your help. If you won't let me use your truck, then drop me off at a car rental place. I'll pull one up on my phone."

"Let me come with you."

"Absolutely not. It's hard enough for me to sit next to you right now."

The wide smile that crosses his face makes me realize the error of my words. "Not for that reason, Fabio."

"Oh." His face falls. "You're still on that kick about hurting me?"

I grin, despite my irritation. "Yeah. I'm still on 'that kick.'"

"I can defend myself."

"Whether that is the truth or not, I don't have the time or the energy to fight you. I have something else I need to take care of."

"A date."

"What date?" I find a folder titled "Annie" and open it, seeing hundreds of photos, the most recent candid ones of a blond girl who in one image wears a pink boa and crown and sits in front of a cake. *Annie.* My joy at finding her is instantly dampened by the idea that someone would want to hurt this perfect little individual.

"You asked what I wanted. If you take my truck, I want to take you on a date."

"Not gonna happen."

We pull into an empty parking lot, clones of our UPS vehicle lining spots to our right. Jeremy focuses on driving, pulling forward and then backing into a spot on the far right. He shuts off the engine and turns to me, his eyes studying mine.

I fight the urge to fidget, my eyes flitting from his to his keys. GO. The command pounds in my head. "Please," I manage, the word awkward on my lips. It is a word frequented in my cam chats but neglected entirely when the camera is off.

"A kiss."

I scowl, understanding the negotiation behind the words. A kiss is the last thing I want to do right now. "Four hundred dollars. That should more than cover the use of your truck."

"No," he says softly, his eyes on mine—pale green eyes that remind me of a dress I wore in high school. My gaze travels down from those eyes and rests on his mouth, remembering him above me, mouth on mine, hands on my naked skin. GO. I lean forward and sigh, closing my eyes and pursing my lips stiffly.

He clears the hurdle that is my resistance with the first touch of his lips. My body melts, forgetting everything but the feel of his hand on my neck, gripping my hair and pulling my mouth tight on his—his mouth taking everything in smooth, perfect movements. He disorients my world, captures my spirit, and heals a little of my soul, all in the course of seconds—my mouth responding to his, hands releasing my bag and traveling into his hair, greedily pulling and grasping, unable to get enough.

GO. I push him away, my hands lingering on his strong shoulders as we separate, his cloudy eyes concerned. I breathe hard, my eyes fighting to not look at his mouth. "Please," I whisper. "I have to go."

He nods, stretching out his legs, pulling out a key ring, and holding it out to me.

"My truck is the gray Ford, in the back of this building."

A wave of relief floods me, and I smile, reaching out and grabbing his keys. "Thanks. I owe you one." I grab my bag and turn, my escape stopped by his firm hand on my knee. I turn questioningly.

He holds out a business card. "The date. Think about it. My cell is on the card."

I hesitate and then nod, grabbing the card and hopping out. I round the bumper of the truck, flash a quick smile to Jeremy, then take off at a run toward the back of the building.

❖

Jeremy watches her go, her stumbling steps of before gone — urgency now making them strong. His initial diagnosis echoes in his head. *She's hiding from something.* It doesn't look as if she's hiding. It looks as if she's running full force to tackle confrontation and eat it for dinner.

He shouldn't have given in, shouldn't have handed over his vehicle in exchange for, of all things, a kiss. But she needed it, the urgency spilling out of her, panic interlaced with determination in her eyes. Wherever she is headed, if it is from someone, or to something, it is important. It is certainly more important than the inconvenience of him finding a ride home.

He frowns, thinking about their initial meeting, the madness in her eyes, her attempt at violence. In the course of the last hour, he has overlooked that part of her, pushing it to the side in his excitement at being near her, being acknowledged, included. She had seemed, in this inter-action, normal. Sane. Was it a trick? A new take on the sexual deception that she had tried at their first meeting?

There is the sound of his truck engine, the rip of tread against asphalt as she leaves the parking lot and turns east, headed to parts unknown. And he hopes, a knot of dread growing in his stomach, that he hasn't just enabled a madwoman.

CHAPTER 54

THE LAST RELATIONSHIP I had was with Jesse Howell. I met him when I was eighteen, at Taco Bell, when he offered to pay for my eighty-nine-cent taco. He had shaggy hair under a backward cap and a loose Abercrombie tank top over lean, tan muscles. We dated for four weeks, enough time for him to realize I wasn't gonna put out, then he moved on. It was for the best: we weren't going to work out. He didn't understand my obsession with slasher movies, and I liked how his skin fit so perfectly on his face. It seemed like a waste to rearrange his features, to ruin a perfectly good face in the name of bloodshed. He woke up one night and found me above him, my hands wrapped around a knife I had taken from the kitchen. I was in the middle of trying to decide where to stab him first, in the neck or the chest, when his eyes flipped open. It was easier when his eyes were closed, when I couldn't see into his soul. When he was just a blank canvas, ready for the splatter of wet blood.

I froze when I saw his open eyes, confusion present as his brain tried to wade through the layers of sleep and decipher what was before him. In the dark room, I wasn't sure what he could see, and I tossed the knife to the ground, leaning forward and trying to distract him with a kiss. He pushed me off, accusing me of trying to cut off his luscious locks.

I stuck my toothbrush in my purse the next morning, deciding that sleepovers were something I obviously couldn't handle. Thank God he woke up. His face was too beautiful to be mutilated.

❖

Carolyn stands in the hall of the station, filling a plastic cup with water from the fountain. She watches the flow of clear liquid, the cup getting heavier and heavier. Something enters her peripheral vision, and a hand reaches out, takes the cup from her.

"Carolyn. Let me take that for you."

She looks up, meeting John Watkins's eyes. "John. Thank you."

He leans in, lowering his voice. "I called around this morning. Spoke to Screven and Evans County. They've both had a girl disappear that was around Annie's age, Screven seven years ago, Evans three. The girls were never found. I'm waiting on a callback from Effingham County to see if they've had any similar disappearances in the last decade. We may be looking at a serial—"

"John. Please don't use that word with me. I just…can't take it right now."

His eyes soften. "Shit, Carolyn. I'm sorry. I wasn't thinking." He pauses, looking at the floor. "I'm just not used to this sort of thing around here. You know us—we normally go after missing cows and abusive husbands." His southern drawl is soothing, bringing back so many memories of easier times. "Carolyn, can we step outside? I'm dying for a cigarette and could use the company."

She looks over at the office that has been their prison for the last six hours, the edges of Henry's wheelchair visible. "Just for a bit. I could use some fresh air, but I don't want to leave Henry too long."

He smiles, the gesture not reaching his eyes. "Great." He pushes on the exit bar and opens the door, holding it for her. She steps out, the sun harsh on her unprotected eyes.

The police station sits on an unassuming corner of Brooklet, at the far end of Main Street. The small size of the town means that only a handful of stores line the one-block street, and she can see a number of people on the town's only street of commerce. Out here, life is ordinary; people are going about their everyday business, seemingly oblivious to her situation. To a woman who has every aspect of her life crumbling, the proof of normal life seems painfully unfair. She leans against the building, folding her arms and turning her face to John. "What is it? Did they find her?"

He looks over, surprised. "What?"

"You quit smoking six years ago. Bitched and moaned enough that folks in Savannah probably heard the news. So you brought me out here, away from my husband, for something. What is it?"

"I almost don't even want to mention it..." He looks down at the dirt, spits a wad of something to the side. "The Feds called. They've gotten a bunch of calls on the hotline number. Most of them are useless, but one of them, a young girl, she called about Michael."

Carolyn stiffens, her back leaving the white brick. "Michael? My brother?"

"Yeah. Only this girl didn't call him Michael—she called him Ralph. The AMBER Alert doesn't say where Annie disappeared from, just says the vicinity of Savannah. So for this girl to call and mention Michael, it's strange, you know?" He studies her face, sitting back against the hood of the closest car, an old black-and-white cruiser.

She clenches and unclenches her hands, taking measured breaths. "What did this girl say?"

"That he's had a bunch of phone calls with her—sexual ones. That the calls always center on fantasies he has with a young girl. One named Annie."

The world closes in on her with one black swoop that darkens her vision and has her legs collapsing beneath her. He steps forward, catches her arms, and pulls her to her feet. "Carolyn, Carolyn. Be strong. Stand up. I need you with me."

She pushes against him, moving to the car and sitting on the hood, her hands shaking and gripping her dress, scrunching the fabric and then smoothing it out. "Jesus. Did you ask Junior about this? He's Michael's son, he might…" she raises a hand to cover her mouth, the words dying on her lips. Junior, a nineteen-year-old kid…images of him as a child flash before her. She closes her eyes and sends a small prayer upward.

"I haven't asked anyone about this. You know this kind of thing, Carolyn. Once you throw it out there, the thoughts, the suspicion, never goes away. The call might be bogus. Could be some girl with a grudge. Do you think…do you know anything about him that we need to know? About his sexual preferences?"

She shakes her head rapidly. "I don't know. I was older… he never…not that I ever knew. No. I would never suspect Michael of that. Never. Christ, he's spent time with her. Alone! It can't—"

"Carolyn." His voice is strong, and she holds on to it with all of her remaining sanity. "It could be nothing. Don't worry just yet. But we have to check it out. You know that. It's nothing against you or your family—"

"Enough!" She jerks to her feet, surprising him, and he takes a step back. She holds up a hand. "Don't insult me, John. Annie is the focus here. I could give two shits about any inconvenience or offense that is put on my family. If Michael is responsible for this, I'll be the only person you'll need to arrest, because I will kill him myself. And I mean that, with every fiber of my being."

CHAPTER 55

JEREMY'S TRUCK IS an F-150 single-cab that is meticulously clean and smells faintly of air freshener. It has GPS, and I pull over at the first gas station I find and plug in the address for Ralph's rented trailer. It calculates that I am twelve hours and twenty-four minutes from my destination.

I fill up the tank while I am there, the feel of the gas nozzle strange in my hands. My hands sweat on the metal handle, the flow of liquid causing a vibrating sensation against my palms. I glance at my watch: 5:47 p.m. More than a half hour spent outside of my apartment, and no one is dead and no uncontrollable urges have racked my body. I think briefly of the cam appointments I am missing, the men who are constantly refreshing their screens, waiting for sexy Jessica, who would not appear. The order came again. GO.

I steel myself for disaster and head for the convenience store—rough, gritty pavement underfoot, I breathe deeply, focusing. I need food for the road and to use the restroom. There is one car parked in front of the store and one in a gas bay next to me. Two cars. One or two employees. *Blood spray hitting the glass cooler doors. Bodies thudding against tile floors.* I leave my bag in the car and head for the store unarmed. Trying to block out other thoughts, I center my mind on Annie. *Save Annie. Save Annie. Ignore everything else.*

The door to the store swings open easily, exposing me to bright fluorescent lights, the smell of hot dogs and other food. My eyes meet rows and rows of food I have been deprived of for three long years. *Soda.* I think my body has forgotten the power of crisp-from-the-can carbonation. *Chocolate.* Real, nondiet chocolate in the form of fifty-plus options. *Chips, nuts, Twinkies. Alcohol.* My lust for death disappears in the presence of such abundant decadence. I grab items from the shelves like a woman possessed, filling my arms with anything and everything I can hold. I dump an armful of sugary perfection on the counter, and the dark-skinned man behind it shoots me an odd look. I move to the coolers, grabbing Fanta, Cherry Coke, a Monster Energy drink, and a Dr Pepper. This is easily one of the greatest moments I have had in recent memory. I set the drinks on the floor, snag a white Styrofoam cooler from a shelf and move the drinks into that, then add a few more from the refrigerated bays. With a huge smile on my face, I move to the register. "I'll need a bag of ice, also. Please."

He glares at me, strangely irritated by the swell of business I bring to his store. There is a flurry of fingers, clicking, and register sounds. "Thirty-two eighty-six," he announces. I pull out two twenties and hand them to him, waiting while he counts out the change and slides it across the counter before bagging my loot and shoving the items toward me.

"Thanks." I beam at him. *The gun would be the best route to taking his life. My knife wouldn't reach across the wide counter.* "Have a nice day."

GO. Annie.

❖

I call Mike from the road, dialing a number I've used for him in the past, hoping it is still active. I cradle the phone in the crook of my neck as I drive, hands at ten and two. I'm nervous at being on the open road and in this strange vehicle. I have only ever driven my high school car—a ten-year-old Honda Accord that had belonged to my mother. This truck feels huge in comparison, taking up more than its fair share of the road.

Mike answers on the third ring. "Yo."

"It's Jessica."

"What up, chica?"

"I need to employ you for the next day. How much will it cost me?"

"Damn, girl. Lately you've been like the fucking lottery. What do you need done? It won't take me all day, I'm sure."

"An assortment of things. I need you committed to whatever shit I ask for, so yes, it will need to be all day. Nothing else, just me for twelve hours, maybe more."

"Starting when?"

"Now."

"Now, now?"

"Yeah."

"For twelve hours? I guess I can cancel my hot plans. Given your excellent payment history." I can hear his grin through the receiver and fight to keep irritation out of my voice.

"Fine. How much?"

"A thousand. I'm giving you a break on this, but if you go too far outside of the legal realm with your requests, there may be surcharges."

"Everything you do is out of the legal realm."

He laughs. "Whatever. Clock's ticking. What do you need?"

"First, turn on a television. Keep it glued to CNN or some other news outlet. If there are any updates on a missing child named Annie Thompson, call me and let me know. Second, you know Ralph Atkins?"

"Of course."

"Pull him up. I want to know if there are any guns registered to him. Also, see if you can track his cell."

"What's his cell number?"

I think for a moment. "Fuck. I didn't send it to you?"

"No. Do you have it?"

"Yeah. I'll have to look through my cells and see which one he calls. I would have saved his number on that phone. Give me five minutes; I'll find somewhere to pull over, and I'll text it to you."

"I don't know what exactly you think my capabilities are, but the best I'll be able to do, if he is using his phone, is get a general idea of where he is."

"That's fine. I just need to know if he is at home or somewhere else."

"Jess, what's going on? I can help you out a lot more if I know what you are trying to accomplish."

I watch the centerline, my vehicle moving closer and closer to oncoming traffic, fighting to keep the big vehicle in line and under control. "I think Ralph Atkins has Annie Thompson. I think he kidnapped her. I'm trying to find him…or them."

"And do what?"

"Play fucking hopscotch, Mike. Why does it matter? Now you know what I'm trying to do, so just help me."

"Why don't you call the police? No offense, but you suck fake dick for a living, you're not a secret agent."

Because I want to kill the piece of shit myself. "I already called them. I don't think they're doing anything with the information, but that's why I need you to keep an eye on the news."

"I'll log into a forum I'm part of, have someone tie me in to the police scanner for that area—see what we can pick up."

"That would be great. Good thought."

"It's what I'm here for, babe."

"I'll text you Ralph's cell in a few minutes."

"Ciao." There is a click, and then I am alone in the truck again. I toss the cell down on the seat and press the gas harder, until the speedometer reads sixty-eight, eight scary miles per hour above the speed limit. *God, I need to grow a pair of balls.*

CHAPTER 56

I DRIVE, SCARFING down crunchy Cheetos, Twix bars, Twinkies, and sodas. I begin to feel nauseated after I've finished about half of the gas station haul. It's as if all of the junk food has molded together in my stomach and become a rolling knot of carbonation, preservatives, and high-fructose corn syrup, sending my stomach into irritated spasms. I vow to stick to water and fruit at the next pit stop. I remind myself that there is a greater purpose for this trip than my own junk food debauchery. The last thing I need, in the midst of a lethal, perfectly orchestrated attack, is an attack of diarrhea.

My opinion of Jeremy continues its upward ascent when I realize he has satellite radio—a technological wonder that has apparently gained in popularity since I last owned a car. I find a Georgia news station and keep the radio on it. Their reports on Annie are few and far between. If I go off the limited information in their reports, the police have no leads and no clear idea where Annie could be. I call Mike again.

"What's up, my evil-avenging angel?" I hear music in the background, a clash of guitars and screaming.

"What is the scanner saying?"

"They went to Ralph's house. Searched the premises for Annie, but she's not there and they'll need a warrant to look through his stuff, though they did take a computer with them. The cops are keeping a cruiser parked down the street to watch his house all night."

"Good. So my tip was taken seriously. Did you get the cell number I texted you?"

"Yep. It shows him in the general vicinity of his home address—so it corroborates the police statement that he is at home."

"So Annie must be at the other house."

"What other house?"

"I assume you have a copy of his computer clone—the one you sent me."

"Duh."

"Scroll through his search history. There are two Craigslist properties that he viewed a bunch of times about a month ago. One of them—the trailer, not the house—he signed a lease on. I think that's where he has her. No other reason to have it."

"I see it. I've been going through his shit for the last hour. Unless he hunts."

"What?" I approach a car and put on my blinker, flying past them in the opposing lane. My stress and trepidation over driving took a flying leap out of the truck seventy miles ago.

"You said there was no reason for him to have this second place. That's true, unless he hunts. This place is smack-dab in the middle of a four-hundred-acre hunting preserve.

That's the only reason the owner can get five hundred bucks a month for this piece of shit. It's actually a pretty cool piece of property—it has a gutting barn and deer hang, as well as a shitload of blinds."

"So, we're talking about an isolated location, with no one around for miles, that is designed for killing and disposing of bodies."

"Deer bodies. But yeah, when you put it that way, it sounds all psychotic."

I push harder on the pedal, watching the shaky needle climb past eighty-five. "What came back on guns registered to Ralph?"

"Nothing showed up. But this is Georgia, baby. If someone needs a gun that's off the books, all you have to do is know someone who knows someone who's part of the system."

"What's the law on hunting guns—rifles, shotguns—do those require registration?"

"In Georgia? I don't know."

"Find out. And let me know if anything comes across that scanner. I don't care if it's a discussion about Jessica Simpson's tits. I want to know about it."

"You're a lot more fun when you're naked."

I grin into the darkness of the empty truck. "No doubt."

"Talk soon."

I hang up, fighting the urge to open the Snickers bar I can see lying in the plastic bag on my passenger seat. I glance at the GPS's clock: 7:15 p.m. Ten hours and fifty-two minutes from Annie. It seems so far, almost a thousand miles stretching between her home and mine. But in actuality, I am lucky. What if she had lived in California? Or Alaska? There wouldn't have been time to reach her, not unless I hopped on a plane. And while I am reckless enough to leave my apartment, to risk harm to others in my hunt for Ralph, I know that I would not be able to handle an airport. Not be able to handle a red-eye flight surrounded by peaceful, sleeping bodies. I'd probably try to strangle my seatmate with the seat belt, my arsenal of weapons locked away in the checked baggage. Plus, I'd have to deal with the litany of questions about said arsenal. Yeah. Total disaster.

I lean forward, watching the road, and press harder on the gas pedal.

CHAPTER 57

THE POLICE KNOCKED on Michael Atkins's door at 6:12 p.m. on Monday night. He and his wife, Becky, had just sat down to a meal of overcooked beef stroganoff. When the knock sounded, Becky threw down her napkin and rose with an annoyed sigh. Michael stayed in his polished dining chair, tilted his head, and listened. Then she was back, her lilac perfume competing with the smell of beef. "Michael? The police are here. About Annie."

They questioned them together in the formal living room. Becky's hand grasped Michael's and on certain questions squeezed it almost to the breaking point. Their answers had been quick and concise.

No, they had no idea where Annie could be.

No, they hadn't seen her, not since her birthday party.

No, neither of them had any criminal history.

Last night they were both here, all evening. Both of them can attest to that.

Yes, they will stay in the area and be available for future questions.

No, they can't imagine who would want to hurt poor Annie.

No, they own only one computer.

The police searched their home thoroughly, then asked to view their computer. Becky led them to the study and to the ancient PC that sat there. They stated that they would need to take it with them, and she agreed, signing a receipt that they provided, saying nothing to them about the laptop that she knew Michael possessed. After that, the police left, and they returned to their cold meal.

It was a meal eaten in silence, forks and knives scraping heavy plates, ice cubes settling into tea. Only a single sentence was uttered.

"I don't know what you've done, Michael, but you are staying *here* tonight. All night."

CHAPTER 58

THIS DRIVE SHOULD be difficult for me. The open road, nothing to distract my mind. It's a twelve-hour stretch of emptiness, which should be dangerous as hell for my inner demons. At home, in my apartment, I struggle with the half hour between my last cam session and sleep—that dead time is when my horrific fantasies grow wings and fly. Tonight's long length of time, nothing to distract me, at the time of day when I am at my weakest...it is a perfect storm of disaster. I should be frothing at the mouth, my knife ready in my hand, this truck turning off at every exit until I find a victim. But my mind is behaving, focusing on the photo I had found on Ralph's hard drive. Annie. She is what's important, and my mind seems to understand that.

I think about calling Dr. Derek but don't trust myself. Sometimes words come out before I can contain them. Certain things I can't share with him. Doctor-patient confidentiality goes only so far, and my research has let me know exactly where those lines lie. I can share past crimes, but only if the reason is to help treat my current illness.

There the rules are blurry—giving the doctor free rein to decide whether the information I am sharing is helpful in treatment or if he feels it should be reported. But crimes that have not yet occurred? Definite cause for reporting to the authorities. And knowing the staunch moral code Derek seems to live by, I realize that sharing anything above and beyond the bare minimum will get him on the phone to the police. He has the ability to end my secret life, to turn me in. The knock will come, the suits will appear, and they will cart me off. I will not go gently. I will go kicking and screaming, my knife poised and in my hand, ready to cut and spill whatever blood I can. There may be a day when I turn myself in, but this isn't that day. As I said before, prison is no place for a girl like me.

I call Dr. Brian instead, glancing at the clock as the phone rings. In California it should be seven or eight, too late for him to be at the office, but he may still answer his cell.

"Hello, my sexual demon." His sly voice makes me smile, the nickname more accurate than he will ever know.

"Hey, yourself. Am I interrupting a hot date?"

He sighs heavily into the receiver. "Unfortunately, no. Lately the well's been a little dry in that area. You're the closest thing I've had to sex in almost a month."

"Ouch. That's sad."

"Anyway, you don't pay me the big bucks to bitch about my love life. Whatcha got cooking? Any new and kinky clients?"

I grin. "Let's see…got an offer of thirty grand for a blow job in Manhattan. What's your expert opinion? Should I take him up on it?" I slow the truck down, stuck between two semis, jockeying into place as one of them brakes.

"Fuck no," he says emphatically. "You should pass his number on to me and let me suck it. I'll make him forget the name Jessica Reilly in about four swallows."

I laugh, the sound bursting out, and I fight to control myself, my smile so wide that it hurts. "I'll tell him I'm sending a comparable replacement, see how he reacts. I'm sure he'll love the idea."

"If he doesn't, tell him I'll knock down the rate. Cut him a discount at twenty-nine thou."

Monetary offers for sex are something I deal with on a daily basis. I don't know how many of them are legitimate and how many are just some guy wanting to know what my personal threshold for prostitution is. Thirty thousand is a pretty high offer for just head; oral sex offers normally hover closer to three or four grand.

My regulars know my limits. Know that any attempt to set up a physical meeting is futile. Except for Paul. Paul holds out hope that we will marry and have babies. He wants to rescue me from this life. He has given me vouchers on three different airlines and begs me to cash them in, to come to him so that he can take care of me. I should just tell him the truth, rip off the Band-Aid with one short explanation of what would occur if I visit. How I would start at his feet with my blade and work my way up. But I don't want to traumatize the poor guy, to ruin his rose-colored view of the world.

"You still there?"

"Yeah," I respond. "I'm here."

"That pedophile ever get back online?"

I lose any trace of the grin that might still be lingering on my face. "Yeah. Two nights ago."

"He do the same shit?"

I tighten my hands on the steering wheel. "Yeah. We did a role-play."

He is quiet for a moment. "How much of his fantasy involves pain?"

"Not much. It's almost all focused on sex."

"I asked because a lot of people who fantasize about death or administering pain . . . they often fantasize about children. Not because the children are young, or innocent, but because it is the easiest victim for them to target. Children can't fight back, children trust. Children are the best chance they have at success."

"Not all of them."

"Not all what? Children?"

"No. People who fantasize about pain. They don't all fantasize about children."

"Well, shit no. The only rule is that there is no rule. There is no preset formula for any form of mental anomaly. I was just asking because I was trying to figure out if he is thinking about her because of the violence or the sex. Next time you cam with him, try and move the conversation—"

"There won't be a next time," I interrupt him.

"You block him?" I've blocked clients before, some at Dr. Brian's suggestion, some because $6.99 a minute isn't worth dealing with certain levels of stupid.

"No. But I don't think he's going to be getting back on." It will be difficult for him to once he's dead.

"Jess…" Brian's voice is wary. "I know you hate dealing with him, but I worry. If he's not online…"

We've talked about this. A lot. I am Ralph's outlet. I could be how he releases the pressure of his fantasies, similar to how I envision macabre death rampages when the urge to kill strikes. Brian worries that without me, without Ralph's ability to air his thoughts, he might turn to action instead. Action that might involve the object of his obsession.

"I know. You've told me your thoughts on the matter. I've also told you that I might be feeding his obsession, and you agreed."

"Barely agreed. I said it was a possibility."

"I don't want to help him hurt her."

"We don't know that's what you're doing. It is a much greater possibility that you are helping her."

I exhale. "It's a moot point. I don't think he's getting back online."

After that, there isn't much for us to discuss, and I hang up the phone, my eyes and thoughts returning to the highway blacktop, and I try to find a new way to entertain my brain.

CHAPTER 59

HE SHOULD BE there with her right now. Exploring the fantasies that have bombarded his mind for the past few months. He should be with her, not stuck in this house, looking at his ugly wife, listening to her drone on about quilting bees and next week's canned-food drive. He nods in her direction, bringing the cup to his mouth, letting the warmth of coffee and whiskey sear down his throat.

Tonight, when she is asleep and the house is quiet, he will retrieve his laptop and log onto the Internet. The police didn't find his laptop or his box of souvenirs. Tomorrow morning, he will carry everything out to the truck, will sneak the items to the trailer and leave them there for safekeeping. In a few days, everything will calm down. He will have more freedom, fewer eyes on his actions, the small local police force will be focused on other leads, different possibilities.

Tonight, in lieu of Annie, he will use Jessica. He will use Jessica for one last night, and then tomorrow he will go to Annie.

CHAPTER 60

IT IS HOUR five, and Mike is calling me, for apparently no other reason than that he is bored. It takes me a good three minutes to discover this fact, my questions all leading to a status report of "no new news." I settle in, content to chat because I'm pretty bored off my ass and my mind is starting to play hopscotch with the idea of vehicular homicide.

"So, you got a boyfriend?" He talks while typing, the clatter of keys indicating an impressive wpm rate.

I hesitate, unsure of the correct answer, not sure if Jeremy's and my awkward courtship classifies as any type of relationship. I always tell clients I am single. We are all single, all four thousand of us on the site. Beautiful, sexual, single ladies. But there is no need to lie to Mike. I think it's safe to say we are past that.

He takes my silence as hesitation. "You know I can hack into your phone records, right? Look at who you call at least once a day? Or if any purchases were made on your credit card on February fourteenth?"

"I have clients I talk to at least once a day."

"Damn. Those jokers must be loaded."

"Or lonely," I muse.

"Or lonely. Good point. So, do you?"

"I don't think so. There's this guy…but we are a long way from being in a relationship."

"You guys fucking yet?"

I laugh. "No. Definitely not. We haven't even been on a date."

"He a client?"

"No. I met him outside of work. I do have a normal life, you know." The lie slides off my lips easily, but it should. I say the same lie over and over, hundreds of times a week. If I can't convince my clients of that, how can I expect them to believe that I find their five-inch cock a gift from God?

"You *ever* date a client?" He is smiling, I can hear it in his voice.

"No. And no, I don't plan to start with you."

"Ouch! And here I am, giving you an all-nighter."

"Oh, so it's a gift. Thank God, I thought I was paying you some exorbitant fee." I grin, my eyes noticing a passing billboard, a juicy Big Mac decorating its surface. Mmm…My mouth waters. I would kill for a Big Mac and a strawberry milkshake, complemented by a large side of salty, crispy fries. My stomach picks that moment to protest, churning its way through some of my earlier feast. Probably the pork rinds; those were unnaturally chewy.

"Got any crazy cam stories to tell me? I bet you get some freaks on that site."

"Actually, most of the guys are pretty normal. There is this one guy who freaks me out…" I let my voice trail off, hooking him easily and without effort.

The typing stops. "Really? What's he into?"

"I shouldn't say."

"Come *on*, Jess. Share."

I lower my voice seductively. "As soon as he takes me private, he makes me change, he only likes seeing me one way."

"What's that?"

I sigh. "It's really sick. I don't want to tell you. You'll think he's too weird."

His voice was suddenly close to the mike, the words slightly scratchy. "No, I won't. Really. What's he into?"

I pause dramatically. "Catholic schoolgirls. He makes me wear the plaid skirt, white tights, and everything."

There is silence for a minute before he gets it. "That's bullshit, Jess. Total bullshit. You got me all excited, thinking that you were gonna share something good."

I drop my voice to a dramatic whisper. "I am the keeper of all secrets. I don't share your secret fantasies with others and I protect those that confide in me."

He snorts. "Well, that's boring."

I grin. "Boring isn't always a bad thing. Trust me."

He is silent for a moment. "Jess, when you get there… what's your plan?"

It's the second time he has asked me this, and our brand-new buddy status isn't enough to bring him into my world. "To save her."

"That's all well and good if she is alone, but what if he is there?" The concern in his voice is touching, if misguided.

"Let me worry about that. I'll be fine."

"I'm just worried that if…if you're *not* fine, how am I going to get paid?"

The laughter bubbles out, the line delivered perfectly, lightening our conversation's mood by about five shades. "I'll make sure my estate covers your cheap ass," I shoot back. "Now let me get back to driving."

"Fine. Drive safe. I'll call you if anything changes."

I hang up with a smile and realize, with a start, that it was the first personal phone conversation I've had in three years, Dr. Brian and Dr. Derek conversations excluded.

❖

I cut off all contact with my grandparents when I moved into the apartment. At community college, I called them weekly, then monthly, then bimonthly, before I realized that it was a waste of effort. Their lives had died with my family. My calls were a drop into a bucket of darkness, the words unheard and immediately forgotten.

So many lives were affected that day by my mother's actions. I can only hope that I never have such a devastating effect on the world.

CHAPTER 61
ANNIE

IT IS DARK, no lights on in the small room where she sits. Not pitch black, though: the slow fall of night allows her eyes to adjust, to see the basic footholds of her prison. She tugs at the ropes that hold her, the rough thread painful against her delicate skin.

There is a scratch against the door, a scratch that reminds her of every monster that ever hid in her closet, every scary branch that ever knocked at her window. Then the scratch comes again, and she can hear breath, a snort, a blow. The monster has claws. The monster has teeth. The monster is real.

She whimpers, covering her ears with her hands and closing her eyes tight. There she stays, for a long time, until the monster moves away and she feels brave enough to open her eyes.

❧

I killed a cat once. It's funny how that bothered me more than anything else. I had serious guilt after that incident, scrubbing my hands furiously even though no trace of blood remained. I buried its body, spending almost an hour on the hole, wanting to be sure to dig deep enough that no scavengers would smell and come for its body. I cried when I laid it in the hole, lines of ants already present on its open eyes, their blood thirst greater than my own.

That was during my misdirection phase—when I was trying to channel my need in some direction other than murder. When I tried to placate it in a way that didn't involve human flesh. After the cat, I stayed away from animals. I hate cats, hated them even more back then. To think that I had all that mental anguish over killing one was ridiculous. I was pissed at myself, my level of self-hatred hitting an all-time high, frustration at my psychological limitations crippling me.

It was such a waste. Not just the cat, but my entire life back then—the year I spent between my grandparents' house and here. Twelve months of fighting my impulses, a year of building memories and expectations that I would never be able to revisit. You can't miss what you've never known. All that year did was give me a whole lot to miss. The higher you build up that personal expectation level, the further the fall. And that first week of being locked in 6E? I fell a hell of a long way.

The first week was painful, my built-in impulses accustomed to answering the door when someone knocked, going outside to get the mail, hitting the sidewalk when the view outside promised a gorgeous day. At that time, I didn't have boxed food yet; I had gone to the grocery store the day I moved in, packing every square inch of my car with dry and canned goods. I sat at the window and watched my car in the lot, wondering how long it would last before the tires rotted away or it was towed. It lasted three weeks, and its disappearance came in the form of a crowbar and two thugs. I heard the alarm sound, paused my cam, and watched from the window as my car came to life and drove away. I was jealous of my car in that instance, jealous of its ability to leave its prison, to ride to a new life, even if that new life involved disfigurement and death. I spent most of that first week staring at my door and convincing myself that I wasn't strong enough. Not strong enough to resist the pull of outside life, not strong enough to control my urges, not strong enough to live off delivered meals and apartment 6E's stale air.

But I *was* strong enough. I made it through the misery, until misery became normality. I find it ironic that when I finally became okay with the life I created inside 6E—that is when I ended up leaving it. Driving on this road, hours and hundreds of miles now separating me and the sanctuary I created.

My eyes find the clock as a road sign goes by, welcoming me to Alabama: 10:50 p.m. My chest constricts, the familiarity of the situation suddenly hitting me hard. Me, driving late at night, on a road not far from where I am now.

I have been in this situation before.

CHAPTER 62

Four years earlier
10:50 p.m.

After an hour of driving from country roads to suburban streets, I parked two houses down from ours, in front of a neighbor's house, and cut the engine. Keys in hand, I got out and closed the car door softly. I wore workout shorts, a T-shirt, and flip-flops. Our street was well developed, the lots spread far apart, stately homes separated by pavered drives and detached garages. I walked quickly down the sidewalk, past the dark homes of our neighbors, and turned down our driveway, headed for the exterior door of our garage. I glanced up at our house, seeing lights on. I frowned. Mom was a stickler about Trent and Summer going to sleep by nine. Everyone should be upstairs, asleep or getting into bed. I crouched over, jogged softly down the sidewalk that ran by our back door, and turned the knob to the garage, opening the door and slipping into the dark space.

I hit my shin on something and bit my lip to keep from crying out. The pain was intense, throbbing, and I reached down and rubbed the spot, praying that it wouldn't blossom into a bruise. I felt around with my hands until I found Mom's car—always parked in the left spot—and walked down its side until I reached the back door. Opening it activated the dome light, and I saw the turquoise bag on the floorboard, sharing the space with a Dunkin' Donuts box. I reached out and grabbed the bag, sliding my hand inside and double-checking that the dress was still there. Yep. Good, now I just needed to get the hell out. My heart beating loudly against my chest, I pressed the car door shut, bumping it with my hip until the interior light went out. Then I felt my way to the garage door and opened it, slipping back out into the night air. I was hunched over again, making my way past our home's back door, when I heard the muffled but distinct sound of a scream.

The scream came from inside our home—a horrible, gut-wrenching sound that started out powerful and terrifying and then died, winding its way down to a gurgle that was muffled completely by the house. I froze midcrouch and turned my head toward the door. The bag dropped at my feet. Something was wrong.

We were a lighthearted family, always playing tricks on one another, always horsing around if there was the slightest opportunity. But that sound, that scream—it changed everything in an instant. It was, as nondescriptive as the word may be, real. Every ounce of hope, peace, and normalcy left my body in that one sound. I straightened to my full height and walked to the back door, breathing hard, and looked through the glass window of the door.

My first thought was that Mom had redecorated. Put up a horrible wallpaper of sorts, some kind of feng shui nonsense that had paint splatters as a pattern. Then I saw Summer, her body slumped over the table, her dark hair—just like mine—stuck in the pool of blood that surrounded her head. Not paint. Blood. Summer's blood. I moved my head, slow with incomprehension, to the right. Trent. Sitting next to Summer at the table, his hand still resting on his place mat, a white plate with two cookies in front of him. Half of his head was missing—fragments of skin ending in nothing. I grabbed the back doorknob, turned it listlessly, my head in a fog, my subconscious screaming a long, slow howl of death.

The knob, which should have been locked—everything was wrong—turned smoothly in my hand and the door swung open. I walked forward, moving around the door so that I could see the rest of the end of my life.

She straddled him as he sat at the head of the table—his normal place—the place that society always dictates a father should sit. I couldn't see his face, couldn't see past the curls of her hair, the hair that always framed her face. She was busy, her head shaking, words being muttered, her arms jerking and moving incessantly. Busy with whatever she was doing to him. I walked, my fingers reaching out as I passed Summer's chair, then Trent's. My hands itched to hold them, touch them, make them live again. I was at the angle where I could see my father's face, see it dull and lifeless, gray with death, when she screamed.

I then realized it was her scream I had heard from outside. She tilted back her head, her skirt scrunched around her waist, her white button-up shirt drenched in red, and screamed—an agonized sound filled with despair and madness—a release of pure hell that continued until her lungs were empty and her breath was gone. Then her head snapped down, and she resumed her action. My eyes fell to her hands, a knife in each. These were knives I recognized: an Eversharp set that we had given her for Christmas the year before. They stabbed and twisted, repeated jerk actions, into my father's chest, dotting the expanse of his shirt with open wounds, worthless wounds given the fact that half of his neck was blown off. An unintelligible string of words poured from her mouth in an almost jolly cadence.

"Mom." I didn't recognize my voice when it spoke. It wasn't me; it was that of an old woman, someone who had lost all vitality long ago. It was a dead voice. She froze, one knife in, one halfway out, and turned, her eyes searching until they found mine.

My mother was a beautiful woman—statuesque, with perfect china doll features that combined in absolute harmony on her face. I was not looking at my mother. This thing on my father, this thing—with my mother's nose, eyes, and hair—had no soul. Its face was splattered with drops of blood, dark in their dried state. Its hair was a cocoon of curls, sticking out in every direction. A mouth hung open, its eyes pierced me with maddening *clarity, tears pouring out of their edges, painting black mascara rivers down pale cheeks.*

"Deanna? You. You weren't invited to this party." She stood, swinging her leg over my father, yanking the knife out of his chest. She frowned at me, a look I recognized as disappointed. "Get me a paper towel."

I swayed, watching in a cloud of delirium as she turned to the table and reached over Trent's dead body to grab the silver platter that still held a few cookies. I had just looked back at my father when she whirled around, swinging her arm out and smashing the platter with full force against the side of my head.

The pain dropped me to my knees, a reverberating sound filling my head and not shutting the fuck up, no matter what I did. The platter had hit my ear, and I felt my world blacken and tilt as my equilibrium tried to figure out what the fuck was going on. I grabbed the side of my head and moaned, just as my mother screamed again.

I couldn't take it. I couldn't take the black spots in my vision, the piercing pain from my ear, the death and blood all around me, and my damned mother screaming—kneeling on the floor beside me, tears pouring from her eyes—the room echoing from her madness.

Then I heard her voice change, incoherent babbles replacing her screams. I turned and saw a knife in her hand, her eyes hungry on me. She growled, low and deep, and opened her mouth to scream, lunging at me with the weapon raised high. React. I grabbed the closest knife, the floor practically decorated with every blade from our set, and swung it out, burying it in her chest.

It didn't slide in easily. I had expected it to ease in, smooth and fluidly, but I caught a bone, or an organ, or something that stopped it short. I yanked and stabbed again, harder, my body filled with the intense desire to end this all, stop her insanity. Her scream stopped short, and she looked at me with confusion. I moved, ignoring my ear, ignoring the spots in my vision that were gaining in size, and turned, facing her fully, consumed with the need to bury my knife where it counted, where she would gush and moan and cry and be in agony—some form of agony that was comparable to the madness I now existed in. I used both hands and jammed it into her stomach, into an area where there were no bones, nothing to stop the blade from sliding, sharp and fast, all the way into her body. She gasped, pain filling her eyes, madness leaving them for a quick second, and then she was Mom. Sitting there, on the kitchen floor, looking at her daughter, who had just stabbed her.

I sobbed, fully broken, staring into her eyes, too ashamed to meet them but too desperate to look away, needing my mother now more than ever. Our eyes locked, twin brown irises; I reached forward and grabbed her tightly, sobbing into her neck. She slumped against my body, unresponsive to my touch. Then the only screams filling the room were my own.

CHAPTER 63

SHE IS NOT online. It is ten thirty p.m., and JessReilly19 should be here. She is always here. He doesn't always chat with her, she is often too popular, the grayed-out screen over her window indicating a private session, other men occupying her time. But she is always there, like clockwork, regardless of the day.

He flips screens incessantly, between her private website and the camsite, looking for a sign, any sign, of her location. She should be here. On a night like tonight, when he really needs a release, she should be here.

His fingers shake atop the mouse, anxiety taking over, heaviness pushing upon his chest. He paces to the window, glances through the blinds at the police cruiser. Maybe he should go to Annie. Find some way around the police and go to the property. He didn't have time with her last night, didn't do anything more than tie her down and listen to her cries. And now the temptation is too great, knowing she is his. Secured. Waiting.

And her replacement is nowhere to be found. He clenches his fist and refreshes his screen. Looks for her face. He needs a release.

CHAPTER 64

MY FATHER WAS a police officer during one four-year period in his life. His department made cutbacks, and as a new officer, he was moved to the Department of Corrections, working twelve-hour jail-duty shifts among rapists, murderers, and drug dealers. After four years of hell, he quit the force and went into real estate, quickly earning more in one month than he had earned in a year as a public servant. He always said he learned more about human behavior and conflict resolution in those four years than in all of his other work experience combined. He preached that I could accomplish more with voice inflections and body language than with a weapon. He taught me that if I was ever confronted, I should hold my ground, meet the eyes of my attacker, and use firm, authoritative language. It is a lesson I have never forgotten.

More than a cop, or a father, he was my friend—someone I could always count on for advice, help, and support. There aren't enough words in the world to describe how much I miss him.

Now, driving down the dark highway with a gun beside me, I wish he were here. It would have been really great to have a friend in all of this.

My mind wanders to jail, to the knowledge that what I am planning on doing will earn me the right to belong in jail. My mother was one thing. A good attorney would categorize that as self-defense or temporary insanity. No one could walk into that situation and be expected to act in a reasonable manner.

But this is something far different. This is premeditated. Planned. I am driving along this road with every intent to kill this man. The jury will realize that my trip gave me twelve hours to change my mind, plenty of time to call the police and let justice handle Ralph in a proper manner. All signs point to murder one. Maybe I won't get jail time. Maybe I'll get the death penalty and this whole mess will disappear, my murderous inclinations gone in one lethal injection. There are worse ways to die, and then I could join my family on the other side. I am not afraid of justice. Justice is a good thing, even if I am on the losing end of it.

CHAPTER 65

JEREMY IS ABOVE me, *his face intense, worshipping me with his eyes. I arch my back, offering myself, and he groans, lowering his head. He takes me into his mouth. His rough hands caress and squeeze my breasts, pushing them up and into his mouth as he moves from side to side, breast to breast, driving me crazy with his soft lips and tongue.*

I am wet, incredibly ready and wanting, the need throbbing between my legs so strongly—morget me e than I have ever experienced. His touch, masculinity, the breath on my skin— all sensations my body has forgotten, every experience magnified by my time alone. I moan, pulling him to me, his hand traveling down. The incredible sound of a zipper reaches my ears.

I wake up, real life bombarding my senses all at once. I gasp, shocked into reality, my subconscious trying to understand the strange setting, sideways, dark truck, a rest stop parking lot.

Asleep. My head nodding, I had fought sleep for over

twenty miles, blaring music and rolling down the windows. It hadn't worked; the truck veered off the highway twice before I pulled into a rest stop and set my phone timer to fifteen minutes, hoping to recharge in that short length of time. Sleep had come instantly, my eyes closing as soon as I had pressed "start" on the timer. And dreamed of Jeremy. It was my first dream in a long time that hadn't involved mayhem and blood. *Dr. Derek will be pleased.* I roll my neck and start the truck, watching the dash as it comes to life.

The first thing I notice is that Jeremy's truck is low on gas: the fuel warning light is illuminated. I glance at the dashboard clock: 11:46 p.m. I have slept for about fifteen minutes. I look at the GPS, doing calculations in my head. Getting back on the road now, I will arrive at about six in the morning. According to all of Mike's updates, and the limited chatter on the police scanner, Ralph is down for the evening, and they are going to watch him all night. I assume he'll head for Annie in the morning, if he hasn't killed her already. If I can get there quickly enough, I can have her out of harm's way in time. I press on the GPS's screen, looking for the next exit with gas. There is only one option, a gas station seventeen miles away. I cross my fingers and hope that it will still be open.

❖

The station is pathetic and run-down, sitting alone at the exit, the flickering white lights announcing its availability. I pay at the pump, swiping my card and reaching for the handle, suddenly aware of the emptiness surrounding me. I look over my shoulder to find the clerk eyeing me through dirty glass, acne-covered skin surrounding beady eyes and a grinning mouth. *Great.* I hear the gas topping off and loosen my hold on the handle, watching the number slide past twenty-four gallons before the pump clicks in my hand. I squeeze a little more into the tank, hearing the slosh of petroleum topping off, then withdraw the nozzle. I open the truck and hit the lock button, my eyes on the black bag that contains the gun and my cash. I have a moment of indecision, then shut the door and stride for the convenience store, my eyes conscious of the surrounding emptiness, my good ear tuning to the ominous quiet of the lot. My tennis shoes crunch loudly on rough pavement.

I open the advertisement-riddled door, revealing a small, crowded store, the floors sticky and dark, the air stale. I glance at the fruit basket next to the lotto counter, the bananas browning and oranges hardened. I grab an apple, the skin too soft to be good, and move down the first aisle, snagging some peanuts and bottles of juice. I avoid the eyes of the clerk, feeling his presence even in the farthest reaches of the store. I duck into the bathroom after first setting my items on the floor outside; but having found no good place to put the apple, I carry it into the restroom with me and chuck it in the trash. I shut the door and lock it, squatting over the filthy toilet and trying not to pee on too much of the seat. I relax, the pressure on my bladder lessening, the relief wonderful.

My eyes catch movement and focus, watching the handle twitch slightly, just once, and then return to its place. It takes me a moment, my mind slow, incredulous when it finally understands what is occurring. *The bastard is trying the door.* I rip off a wad of tissue, wipe, and yank my pants up, my mind realizing the next step before my thoughts do. *A key. He'd have a—*

The door shoves open, and he is there, inside the small enclosure, shutting the door behind him with a metallic click, grinning at me with disturbing confidence. "Well, well. And I was just getting bored with my evening. What's a tight little thing like you doing out this late?"

I meet his grin, my own stretching easily across my face, my hands sliding into my sweatshirt pockets. I wrap a hand around the handle of the stiletto knife, rubbing its grip, finding and fingering the release. *Wait.* If only he knew that he is prey and I am the hunter. And he has made it so damn convenient for me. This time, I will succeed. This time I will not falter, will learn from the mistakes with Jeremy. I will not go to the ground, I will kill him on my feet.

My grin confuses him. I see the hesitation, the pause in his movement, and the flicker of uncertainty in his stare.

"Don't stop," I say. "Please. Whatever you had in your mind to do, I welcome you to try it."

He starts forward, then stops. He moves again, then pauses, his hesitation growing at my tone and lack of fear. I laugh, a sound he doesn't like, and his fists ball while the dark look in his eyes returns. *Hunger. Hate.*

"Drop your pants," he rasps, his eyes falling to my waist and the open pants. "I want to see the little snatch I am about to—"

My hands reach out, my forearm against his throat; the speed of the motion catches him off-balance, pushing him back against the closed door. The stiletto is freed, the flash of blade catching his eyes. His body freezes in response. I bring it to his cheek, my eyes on his. I smile wider, cracking my face in two. I try to picture his death, to welcome the gruesome visions that battle constantly for entry into my mind, but can see only her—the tiny blonde, grinning into the camera, white-iced cake before her. *Annie. GO.*

I battle my inner demon, not wanting to let this moment pass, a victim finally in my grasp, one worthy of killing, my timed attack perfectly executed. But I have to think about her. The reason I left the apartment. To do something right with the twisted cards I have been dealt. A dead body might slow my progress, might get me to a jail cell instead of to Annie. I grit my teeth, grounding out words as I stare into his eyes. "There's nothing I'd love more than to carve into that ugly shit that you call a face and leave you bleeding and helpless on this filthy floor, scrambling to stand, your eyeballs cut out and squishing beneath my feet. But I am *fucking* late, and I don't have time for this bullshit right now." I press the blade into the thin skin under his eyes, feeling the easy slide of it, blood swelling around the tip. His eyes flit from the blade to me in a panicked jerk. My eyes drink in the red liquid, unable to move from the drip, my fingers unresponsive to my desire to stop the pressure and keep the blade from slicing deeper. I yank back, the blade catching a bit on his skin, and his hand jumps up to press against the cut, his face shocked.

Blood. I want it. I need it. My hands shake, barely controlled. "Get the fuck out of my way," I spit out.

He reaches backward, stumbling till he finds the door

handle, his red hands slipping on it, then turns the knob, falling backward into the store, his hand returning to his face. I lean over, take my items, and walk through the store. I hesitate briefly by the counter, grab a plastic-wrapped prepaid cell phone, and walk out the door to the parked truck. The words come again, louder. GO. *Annie.*

CHAPTER 66

THAT NIGHT, IN my childhood kitchen, surrounded by carnage—my mother dying in front of me—the screams that came from my mouth weren't cries of mourning. They were because when I stabbed her, when I shoved that knife in, again and again, when her blood soaked my hands and hit my clothes, I had experienced relief. I had taken her soul, extinguished her life. My mother, the person whose shoulder I had leaned on, who had packed my lunches, kissed my cuts, and been my inspiration, was dead. I had killed her.

That long, agonized scream was for the life I had taken, both hers and mine. It was a scream for what, in that instant, I had become.

❖

It is 6:04 a.m. when I pull off the highway, turning down the two-lane road. The road curves around on itself, taking me back parallel to the highway. The GPS indicates that I turn left, and I look in vain for a quarter mile till I see a thin dirt road. I turn down the road, the ruts causing a vibration throughout the cab. Fog is heavy, blanketing the fields in white clouds, all but obscuring my view of anything beyond the clay road with deep ditches on either side. I almost miss my destination, slamming on the brakes beside a white metal gate that is chained closed with a shiny new combination lock. A NO TRESPASSING sign is visible, hanging from rungs on the gate. *Bingo.*

I get out of the truck, leaving the door open, and look around: nothing but fog, trees, and empty road. The closest house is about a half mile behind me, a small clapboard frame set flush against the road, acres of fields surrounding it. I need to leave the truck somewhere and advance on foot. I get back behind the wheel and call Mike.

"God, I'll be glad when this shit is over."

"Yeah, earning money's a bitch. Pull up a map, and tell me how Ralph would get from his house to this place. I need to know which direction he'll drive down this road."

"What road?"

"The fucking road I'm on!" I fumble with buttons on the GPS, pressing the wrong thing and zooming out to a map of the world. "Jesus Christ!"

"Damn, you are bitchy in the morning. Are you on the road that the trailer is on?"

"Yeah. I'm looking at a white gate right now."

"Okay, I am pulling you up on GPS also. Just an update, lights are on in Ralph's house, but no one has left yet. The cops watching the house are leaving at seven."

"Going where?"

"Getting off shift. They're not watching him today."

"Fuck. His cell still puts him in the house?"

"Yeah, unless he's sleeping at the neighbors'. He's in the area of the house, so yes."

"A simple yes will do."

"Again, bitchy." He breathes loudly into the phone. "Okay. If he heads to the rental, and follows any type of normal thought process in driving there, he'll take the quickest way, which would have him traveling west down that street."

"I don't have a fucking compass, Mike. I don't know which way is west."

He laughs, ridiculously chipper for being up all night. "You came from the east."

"Okay." I put the truck in drive, backing up, my taillights illuminating only fog. Then I hit the brakes. "How do you know which direction I came from?"

"Uh…what?"

I speak slowly, making certain that my anger seeps through each word. "How. Do. You. Know. Which. Direction. I. Came. From?"

"Just assumed."

"Bullshit. You know where I live?"

"Uh…yeah. You think I can track Ralph's cell but not yours?"

I try to control my panic, not comfortable with where this is going. I glance over at the gas station attendant's phone, which I turned off six hours ago. "Do you know *who* I am?"

"Uh…yeah." In those two words he is able to communicate both wariness and pride.

"How easy was it to find out?"

"Not easy. I followed your—"

"Stop. I'll bitch you out about it later. Fix whatever gap you crawled through so no one else can follow suit. *Now.* And keep an eye on Ralph's cell."

"Will do, boss. You know that bullshit security package you paid for doesn't cover shit. A few months ago I hacked in and amped up your firewalls. But there's still more I can do. I—"

"Mike," I interrupt him, "just fix it. You can upsell me on more services later."

"Sheesh. Just letting you know. You're *welcome* for the free security upgrade. Don't forget, you know I gotta leave soon. Like in an hour."

"Protect my privacy. Watch Ralph. *Please.*" I end the call and look over my shoulder, putting the truck into reverse and accelerating backward.

I find a place to pull over and park the truck, then grab my backpack and lock the vehicle behind me. The parking spot hugs a curve of trees, far enough off the road to avoid unwanted attention. If someone comes from the west, it'll be hidden. If someone comes from the east, the gray truck will stick out like a sore thumb. I say a quick prayer as I trudge through thick dirt toward the locked gate and, hopefully, toward Annie.

As I walk, I think, trying to prepare for what is ahead. I have only ever thought of my demons as constricting—heavy chains that I drag around, trying constantly to wrestle myself free of—their cumbersome weight restricting me in daily movement, stopping me if I try to reach too high or go too far. The thought that I could actually put this personality quirk to good use—to help someone instead of hurt them—has put a glimmer of hope into my heart. A glimmer that I am trying my best to ignore. Hope is dangerous. Hope leads to expectations, which lead to disappointment. Disappointment in others is tough. But disappointment in yourself is far worse. I'm not expecting others to disappoint me. No—I am my own dream killer. That hope, that spark of expectation that I might aspire to something greater than evil? That hope will learn the taste of disappointment. Others letting you down is ice cream and cookies compared with the rejection of your own soul. I don't know what is sadder, expecting myself to fail or being too scared to dream of success.

CHAPTER 67

THE GATE'S SOLE purpose seems to be keeping out cars: there is a two-foot gap on either side of it. I walk through, starting to jog as soon as I hit the drive, a curving, rutted path—cutting a tight hole through the heavy woods. Google Earth had shown the trailer about two hundred yards down. With the sun already peeking through the trees, I need to move quickly. My feet work their way over the ruts, visions of a twisted ankle sashaying mockingly through my mind. My legs tire quickly, not used to cardio, and I have a stitch in my side by the time the trailer finally comes into view. I slow, ducking into the woods. Crouching over my backpack, I unzip it.

I pull the gun out first, switching off the safety and setting it softly on the ground beside me. I check my sweatshirt pocket, closing my hand briefly around the stiletto knife, reassuring myself of its presence. I finger the ski mask I had packed but decide not to use it. *I want him to see me.* I want him to recognize me, to know that he is the cause of his own demise. My cell buzzes, quiet against the fabric. I answer it and speak quietly into the receiver.

"Yes."

"Police escort just left Ralph's."

"It's early!" I fumble for my sleeve and pull it back to reveal the watch face: 6:16 a.m.

"There was a report of kids spraying graffiti at the local high school. They needed someone to check it out. You're talking about a small town here. There's only one deputy out right now."

"Fuck."

"I can hack into his financial grid, which will tell me if he uses his credit cards, but that has a bit of a delay. I got no eyes on his vehicle, just his phone. But he won't leave the house without that. And you know I gotta—"

"Yeah. You gotta leave soon. I know." I hang up the cell and stuff it in my pocket, carrying the gun in my hand. I leave the pack and step out of the woods, staring at the sad excuse for a trailer.

All trees have been cleared from the patch of land it sits on. It's a shame, really, because it makes the shabbiness of the trailer even more apparent. It just slumps there, dingy and neglected, damaged flashing around its base. It had originally been white but is now a yellowed gray, either from pollen or mildew; it's essentially one long box with only one window visible. Two concrete blocks sit beneath the metal front door, a diamond peephole at eye level. No cars are in sight, but there are fresh tire tracks on the dirt.

Crunch. My steps, taken as gingerly as possible, make the noise of an entire marching band on dead pine straw. I avoid the tire tracks and walk around the side, my steps quickening as I move to the back of the trailer.

The doors are locked, and I knock on the back—hoping,

wishing that for once it will be easy. That Annie will come bounding to the door, put her hand trustingly in mine, and we will go skipping out to Jeremy's truck together—my mind free of murderous thoughts—her innocence intact, spirit unbroken. No one answers the door, so I move to the first window and use my knife to pop the screen, then try to pull up the uncooperative glass.

The third and last window to the trailer is my salvation. It slides up stiffly, dirt in its tracks, and my gut clenches in excitement and anticipation. I place both hands on the sill and heave my body up and into the dark space.

The interior of the trailer smells of emptiness, stale old cigarettes, and wet towels. I know, standing in the empty bedroom, pale green wallpaper peeling off the walls, that the trailer is empty. The structure is too still, too quiet. Nevertheless I move, stepping into a hall, through another bedroom, a bath, living room, and finally a kitchen.

I search the trailer twice, first with careful trepidation, then in desperation, but the minimal furniture makes the task depressingly simple. No one. There is no blood, no signs of a little girl. No Annie.

I sink onto the couch, an orange floral disaster that practically bends in half under my weight. Could I have been wrong? I had never made a physical connection between Annie and Ralph. I had found this rental in his computer, verified his depravity in his computer, and assumed that his fantasy Annie was the same girl as the missing Annie. What if he just fucking hunts? Has no little girl tucked away? What if he satisfies his sickness with our Internet chats? What if I had killed him and he had been, in terms of Annie, an innocent man? The stress and adrenaline of the last twenty-four hours come hurtling down on me, hard stones on my fragile sanity, and I sway from the gravity of the situation. A second possibility enters my mind, one I have fought to ignore the entire drive. *I might be too late.* I stand, looking at the window through which I had entered, facing the fact that I might be leaving empty-handed.

I do another sweep of the trailer, looking for bloodstains or splatter, a pair of pink jelly sandals, or a glitter bow, or a big fucking ANNIE WAS HERE sign. Then I leave, ignoring the window, unlocking the front door, and stomping down the stairs, despair filling every step. I stand against the mildewed side of the trailer, trying to figure out my next course of action, when I hear an engine.

My eyes flip open as I crouch, a ridiculous action when there is nothing to crouch behind. I run, around the back of the trailer, my eyes searching the surrounding woods, looking for cover, listening to the sound growing louder, closer. It has to be close to the gate. It would take a moment for him to stop, unlock the gate, and come in. My feet trip, stuttering in their step when my eyes catch on the outbuildings, on the wooden framework that is probably a deer hang, a small shed behind it.

It's actually a pretty cool piece of property—it has a gutting barn and deer hang, as well as a shitload of blinds.

So, we're talking about an isolated location, with no one around for miles, that is designed for killing and disposing of bodies.

I run for the shed, cursing my stupidity with every step, excitement growing as the engine roars.

CHAPTER 68
CAROLYN THOMPSON

CAROLYN THOMPSON WAKES up alone in bed, the first time this has happened in more than three years. She lies still in a moment of quiet solitude before reality hits and the tears come. She closes her eyes tightly, swallowing sobs and suppressing the emotions that threaten her sanity. She needs to be strong: for Henry, for Annie, and for herself. Annie is still alive. She knows that, needs to believe that. She feels that if Annie has passed, she would feel it. Surely a mother would know. For now, she prays that wherever she is, whomever she is with, she is not in pain, and she is not scared.

Finished with her prayers, she rises and pulls on her bathrobe. She walks down the empty hall to the living room, then pauses at the entrance, watching her husband. His neck slumps at an odd angle; he has slept in his chair, his hand resting on the phone in hopeful anticipation. She knows without waking him that a call has not come. She moves forward, grabs a small pillow from the couch, and places it gently underneath his head, moving his neck into a more comfortable position.

She steps quietly through the kitchen, wanting Henry to sleep as long as possible, prolong his peace. Once she has a cup of coffee in hand, she returns to the bedroom, picks up the corded phone, and dials the police station.

Five minutes later, she hangs up the phone and makes her way back to the living room, cradling the warm coffee cup in both hands. There are no updates. Michael stayed home all night, and their interest in him is now waning. The most likely scenario is that Annie has been taken out of town, possibly out of state. Calls had come through on the AMBER Alert hotline reporting sightings of her as far as six hours north. But the calls always came too late—the police were always fifteen minutes behind, the trail cold by the time they arrived. Her hand trembles around the coffee cup, her mind filled with horrific images of the possibilities. If Annie's abductor is on the run, if they're moving north, maybe that is better than her being locked away somewhere, alone with a madman.

Michael. Her thoughts focus on the possibility that she has tossed and turned all night over. She has examined every piece of their upbringing and cannot find a hint in those memories of anything sinister. If only she could talk to this girl who had called the hotline. She had pressed John for more information, but he had only repeated the same things over and over. Sexual conversations. Centered on a young girl named Annie. She had told John that it must be a mistake—the girl had called him Ralph, after all. No one referred to Michael by his first name. But John had stayed firm. The girl had provided his address. It was Michael. She watches her husband sleeping, his chest rising and falling in uneasy breaths. He is an extension of her soul, a partner in life as well as by law. And they share, more than anything, a love for their little girl. Her mind returns to Michael, and she has a sudden thought. She sets down her coffee and hurries to the bedroom, shedding her robe and yanking open the dresser drawer.

Becky. If anyone will know this about Michael, it will be his wife.

CHAPTER 69

THE GUTTING BARN has a huge new padlock on it. It is the first observation that gives me any hope. I press my eye and then my good ear to the crack between the doors, hoping for any sign of what is inside. I'm met with darkness...silence. I turn, listening as the engine in the distance continues, without pause, past the front of the property, its grumble fading as it moves farther away. My phone vibrates, the movement startling me, and I crouch, tugging at my pocket until I get the phone in hand, then sliding my finger along the screen when I see Mike's name.

"This better be important," I breathe.

"Problem. Ralph's credit card dinged three minutes ago at a BP station eight miles north of you. I don't know the delay in posting...it could be anywhere from thirty seconds to fifteen minutes. But Jess, you need to get out of there *now*." Mike's voice is breathless, strain evident in his words, the rapid click of keyboard strokes sounding in the background.

"Fuck. What's his cell phone say? Why didn't you see him leave?"

"It's still pinging at his house." He blows out a frustrated breath. "He must have left it at home. It's a stroke of luck the prick used his credit card."

Urgency now coats my movement. I end the call and stuff the cell in my pocket, feeling a drip of sweat run down the side of my face. I tug at the lock in vain, then move to the window, trying it and then stepping back, measuring the distance before striding forward and kicking the glass. Visions of it splintering beneath my foot, an explosion of power, are overimagined—the only result of my kick is a spiderweb crack. I step back and try again, putting everything I have into it. My foot goes cleanly through, jagged edges of glass catching my leg as I pull my foot back. I tug my sweatshirt sleeve over my fist and knock out the sharp pieces, then hoist my body up and into the dark hole.

Fear.

It is a strange feeling, one I haven't experienced since that night in my family's kitchen. It invades me now, cutting off my breathing and finding its way into my heart, its grip reaching around and squeezing it tightly. Fear of the perversion inside that man. Fear of failure to protect Annie. Fear of wasting the homicidal rage within me.

I hang for a minute—half in the window, half out—my eyes trying to adjust to the room. There is a low counter beneath me, and I bring one foot up to the sill and crawl down, stepping gingerly on the surface until I am sure it can hold my weight. The room smells of death, a smell that brings me instantly back to my childhood kitchen. The flashback causes an uneasy curl in my stomach, and I try to table the emotion, to save the desire for a time when it will be best served. I hear something and freeze, trying to pinpoint the source of the sound. I hear it again. A whimper—small and muffled. And it is in the room with me. *Annie*.

CHAPTER 70
CAROLYN THOMPSON

CAROLYN RINGS MICHAEL'S doorbell, looking at the wilted geranium that sits on the stoop. She hears the chimes fading through the home, then the door opens and Becky stands before her.

Becky: a woman she has never liked, never welcomed, never made a friendly effort with. An oversight of manners that might cost her dearly. The woman had once been beautiful, but pinched skin, a perpetual frown, and worried eyes have aged her early. Becky seems always to fret, a habit that is in full force as she stands before Carolyn, twisting a rag in her hands, swaying gently on uneasy feet.

"Carolyn," she says shortly. "What are you doing here?" No concern for her situation, no worry expressed for Annie. There is a reason that Carolyn has never cared for her, a reason that is showing its teeth now.

"I need to talk to you about Michael. May I come in?"

"I'm busy. And, as you probably know, the police were here last night. Interrupted us during dinner. You can find any answers that you need from them." She starts to close the door, but Carolyn steps forward, pushing the door open and moving into the foyer.

"No, Becky. As rude as this may seem, I need to talk to you."

Becky gapes at her, glaring at Carolyn's feet as if she is shocked to find them there, inside her home, invading her personal space. She finally raises her gaze to Carolyn's, frowning at her and shutting the door.

"Fine. Sit in the dining room, if you refuse to leave. What do you want to know?"

CHAPTER 71

I JUMP OFF the table quickly, cursing myself for not bringing a flashlight, especially since the window is placed on the wrong side of the building to receive any sunlight.

"Annie?" I speak quietly, in the friendliest voice I can manage. "My name is Deanna. I am here to help you. Can you tell me where you are?"

Silence meets my question. A moment stretches into two, and my hands begin to clench and unclench in panic at the time lapse. "Annie, I know you don't know me. But I want to get you out of here. I want to return you to your mommy. Can you please help me?"

I hear a sniff and spin, trying to place its origin. My left. I move in that direction, blinking rapidly, trying to see in the dark, second-guessing the direction of the sound. I freeze when I hear her speak. "I want my mommy."

I find her before she finishes speaking, my hands reaching out, closing over soft skin and flannel. I instinctively pull her to me, my arms closing around her in a hug, the first hug I have given in a very, very long time. The smell of her brings back memories of my sister, of Christmas mornings and bedtime stories. I almost sob at the memories but instead plant a quick kiss on her head and release her. My hands pat gently over her, following her limbs until I discover the rough rope, knotted tightly around her wrists and feet. I tug at the knots but give up quickly, the complicated bindings too tight. "Stay still," I say quietly. I pull out my knife and flip open the blade to cut the ropes, not bothering to see where they lead. She behaves, sitting perfectly still until I pull her to her feet. Then she resists, tugging back against my hand and flattening against the dirty wall of the shed. I can feel her fear, the seesaw of her desire to leave the shed and her wariness of me.

"I'm going to need you to listen very closely to me, okay?" I crouch, touching her shoulder gently, feeling her nod.

"I will not hurt you. I only want to return you to your parents. If you come with me, you can be with your mommy and daddy very soon." I keep my voice light and happy and feel her relax, her small shoulders dropping slightly.

"Okay. Is Uncle Michael coming back?" she whispers.

I freeze at the question, wishing that I could see her face, could know the emotion between the quiet words. Uncle *Michael*. Ralph Michael Atkins.

"Was he here?" I asked, holding out my hands, asking for her permission before picking up her light body and placing her on the counter.

"He brought me here. I'm supposed to wait for the kitten, but he never came back, and it got dark." Her voice shakes, the barely contained hysteria evident.

I climb onto the table next to her. "Annie. I need you

to be really grown-up for me for about ten minutes, okay? Be strong, sweetie. It's really important. I'm going to crawl through the window, and then I'm going to help you out. Do you understand?"

I can see her faintly now, dawn having fully arrived. She nods, her face tightening into a determined frown. I smile at her. "Good girl." I move through the window and jump easily down to the dirt. Then I move back to the sill, reaching out with my arms and feeling her eager body, her bare feet stepping up. In the next moment, I have her cradled in my arms and out of the shed. My cell buzzes in my pocket, and I reach for it, my other hand clasped firmly around Annie's.

"Hey."

"Jess, I've got to go. I just wanted to check in with you first."

"No more activity on his credit card?"

"What do you expect? A shopping spree on the way to see her?"

"A girl can hope," I mutter, whispering to Annie to hurry, my hand tugging hers. Then I realize, as we move, that her feet are bare, and I slow down slightly to allow her to pick her way through the rocky dirt. "I got her, Mike. We're heading to the truck now."

"That's awesome, Jess. Really fucking awesome." I can hear the smile in his voice, stretching his words, and I smile despite my fear. *I have her.* I have saved this girl, without fantasizing about harming her in any way. Now I just need to get away before he arrives. Mike's next words mimic my thoughts. "Now get out of there."

I can hear him moving, the rustle of keys, a few taps on a computer, and I speak quickly. "I am. Thanks, Mike. See you online sometime."

He laughs in my ear. "Definitely, babe. Glad to help."

I hang up, smiling down at Annie. "Ready to go home?"

She nods, hesitancy in her face, fear mixing with hope, the faint glow of trust in her eyes. The look breaks my heart, reminding me so much of Summer. Children are the quickest to trust because they have no concept of the depravity of our species. Summer trusted, as I once did. Before I knew what existed in the world. Before I found that darkness residing in my own soul.

We run together, finally reaching soft dirt, allowing her bare feet to fly, my backpack bouncing against my back. The run distracts her, and a small laugh spills from her mouth, the simple act of bare feet digging into dirt entertaining. Worry, the pressure that any moment we could see the cloud of dirt road smoke that will follow Ralph's truck, could hear the roar of his engine, grips me. But I still feel giddy, blown away by the insane possibility that my rescue attempt may work, that she is beside me and we are almost to safety. We squeeze back through the gate, jump into the ruts of the baked dirt road, and race to the truck, and I let her win. I buckle her in the passenger side, the familiar movement painful in its normalcy. Putting the truck in reverse, I experience one heart-stopping moment when the tires spin, but then they catch traction and we move, flying backward onto the dirt road, no other vehicles in sight, freedom in our grasp. I head left, for Brooklet, my mind thinking through the best way to return her as I drive. I am distracted, high on our escape, and almost don't notice the vehicle that turns right as we prepare to turn left. A dark blue Ford Explorer. My mind follows a moment after my vision, and I slam on the brakes as I watch it disappear in a cloud of red dust. *Ralph Atkins. Georgia tags—X42FF—navy blue Ford Explorer.*

Decision time. Ralph is *here*. I breathe hard, emotions shooting through me like heroin, every nerve in my body twitching, focusing on the need to destroy. Through the roaring in my head, I hear a voice and turn in my seat, trying to focus on her. *Annie.* Sweet and innocent, her mouth moving, words saying something. I frown, fighting a losing battle in my seat, concentrating on her lips. My mind clears briefly, and I hear her voice.

"—are we stopping?"

I grip the steering wheel, trying to sort out the madness from the logical—what I should do versus what I want to do. I should keep driving, ensuring that she will remain safe. I should get her home. I should give the information I have uncovered to the police.

I shut my eyes tightly, trying to breathe, trying to think, but they flip open of their own accord. I press the gas and yank the steering wheel roughly, jerking out into highway traffic and skidding into a tight turn before accelerating back down the dirt road.

❖

I pull into the first farmhouse we come to, driving around to the back. The yard is empty, no cars in the drive. I park and turn to Annie, my eyes focusing and finding her. I grip the steering wheel, trying to concentrate on her face, trying to attempt to inject some normalcy in my voice. But I see from her eyes that she can sense something is wrong.

"Annie. I need you to go and wait on this porch. I will be right back. Do you know your parents' phone number?" *Please say no, please say no.* My evil subconscious chants the words, ready to leave this girl and follow that Explorer.

She shakes her head, and I breathe a sigh of relief. "Okay. I'm going to leave you a cell phone and set a timer on it. If the timer goes off without me being back here, I want you to use it to call 911. Do you know how to call 911?"

She looks at me soberly. "Momma says I shouldn't call 911 unless it's an emergency."

"And you shouldn't. I don't want you to call it unless the timer goes off. I should be back here before then, so you probably won't need to call them at all."

Her eyebrows pinch together, the expression so sweet, so full of concern, that I just want to hold her in my arms and kiss her head. "You're leaving me? Alone?" Her eyes grow large, moisture making them shine. "I don't want to be alone again."

I try to breathe normally, to speak clearly and in a calm manner. "I'll only be gone for a bit. Fifteen minutes. I need you to wait here, on the porch. Then I'm going to take you home, to your parents."

She looks down, fingering the nylon of her seat belt. "I don't want to be locked in the dark again." She sniffs, her voice shaking a bit. "I was scared, in that place. Uncle Michael was different...not like he is at Momma's."

I have got to go *now*, I can feel the urgency pulling at me. Ralph is at the house now, will have discovered her gone. What if he leaves? What if I miss my opportunity? What if he escapes?

I fight to keep my voice calm, a smile on my face. "I know, sweetie. I'm taking you away from there, away from him, I just need you to do this one thing for me, okay? Do you feel safe here? Can you wait on this porch for me?"

She looks at the porch, sun filling its deep surface, big pots on either side of the back door overflowing with bright red zinnias. Her fingers grip the seat belt, and her voice is small when she answers. "Yeah."

With shaky fingers, I pull out my phone and set the timer on it. I hold it out to her, showing her how to silence the alarm and how to dial the emergency call. Then I hand it to her, fighting to keep my face calm and my eyes on hers. "Stay on the porch, and don't make that call until the alarm goes off. I plan on being back here before it goes off, okay?"

She nods, her face solemn.

"Go on, Annie. Sit on the porch and wait."

I watch with twitchy fingers as she sits, waving to me with her small palm. Then I swing the truck around and floor it toward the dirt road.

GO.

CHAPTER 72

IT IS RETURNING, the rush of intense need, flooding my veins and traveling through my limbs, causing my hands to shake and my breath to come in short, tense pants. For the first time in my life, I am grateful for its presence. Being with Annie stunted my mind, the fear of losing her crippling my body's ability to travel to this point, my thoughts centered on her and getting her to safety. It is the first time, in as far as I can remember, feeling fear. When you are the darkest presence in the room, there is very little to fear. An opportunity to interact with evil would only justify any violent actions my body might take. But when I was account-able for her, when her innocent life was in my hands and I was relied upon for protection…my demonic urges failed, withered and suffocated by the mothering instinct that was concern. Concern for her safety, concern that I, if engaged in a confrontation with Ralph, might fail her.

Now that she is safe, now that he is in my sights—that fear is gone, replaced with the uncontrollable urge that is my obsession. *I want to kill, I need to kill, I have a target before me.* It is the first time I haven't fought the feeling, haven't tried to control it with closed eyes or a redirection of my mind. Instead I embrace it, flexing my hands around the shaking steering wheel, celebrating the release of dark energy as it spreads through my body.

The gate is now open, the chain hanging loosely from metal piping, and I swing the truck in, all concerns of stealth gone. A battle is before me, and I almost moan at the excitement of it. After four years of waiting, I feel beyond ready, tensing at the thought of it.

The Ford Explorer is parked at an odd angle, his approach probably as hurried as mine. The door to the shed stands open, and he appears in the doorway at the same moment that I step out of the truck, my hands tucked into my sweatshirt, one palming the knife, the other my gun.

It is amazing that with all the chats, the multiple times that I have heard his cruel voice, I have never seen his face. No smiling photos in the documents I received from Mike. No identification or screenshot to prepare me for his likeness.

I have imagined him in my mind for so long, my imagination creating a monster of grotesque features and proportions. But standing in the opening of the shed, his head tilted and eyes sharp, is just a man. Slightly balding, twenty pounds too heavy, whose mouth is turning into a sneer. Whose eyes are narrowing, stance strong, the combined effect sinister. This man, this balding, thick man, has whispered in my ear, poured out the disgusting thoughts of his soul, showed me the dark evil in his heart. And now he is stepping closer, the excitement radiating from his body like a foul smell.

Come on...baby. Come on. Closer, you sick fuck. I want to smile, giddiness spreading through my body at the joyous task before me. I am about to kill. About to take a life, feel live flesh, and carve its breath in a burst of blood. I am almost overcome with excitement, the concept of dropping my barriers strange, my push to contain these demons so ingrained that it feels odd to open that latch, odd to let myself think, feel, and act without censorship or control. But I must be smart. I must be quick. I must punish this man and get back to Annie. I must remember what happened with Jeremy, his overtaking of my body. How quickly I was brought under control, how the tables were reversed and he was on top and holding me still.

The gun. The gun is the best chance. I should pull it now, stop his forward advance. Then fire a shot that will kill. Done. Mission accomplished. No chance of error. It is also fucking boring. I have fantasized for four years over this moment, envisioned countless killing scenarios, 90 percent of which involved close contact, a blade, and an intimate encounter of the killing kind. Not a gun, ten feet away from the target, one trigger pull and a human body's flop to the ground. *Anticlimactic. Disappointing.*

I contain my smile, wanting to put him at ease, wanting him to think that he is in control, that he is the aggressor in this battle. He steps fully out of the shed into the morning light, and my hand releases the gun, leaving it in my pocket as I step forward and wonder if he will recognize me.

I can feel his panic. Not at me, not at this young girl before him in a sweatshirt and sneakers. His eyes have already glanced over me, running up and down my body, dismissing me as a threat. No, his panic is over Annie. Wondering where she is. Wondering what happened to his plans, his restraints. Wondering how far she has traveled and how long she has been gone. I am a distraction, a waste of time that should be dealt with quickly so he can move forward and secure his prize.

I can't stop it, can't stop the grin from stretching across my face, the glee at this possibility spreading through my body. He hesitates, the friendly expression confusing him, his eyes squinting at me as he moves forward, our bodies within two steps.

His beady eyes examine my face, hesitantly and then boldly, his face hardening as recognition slowly dawns. Incredulity, then anger gleams in his eyes.

"What are *you* doing here?"

He is unarmed—his soft body stiffens only with his newfound anger. He has no need for a weapon; his victim is a helpless six-year-old girl. My confidence grows at the same time that his brain processes the possible reasons for my presence. He steps back, looking toward the shed, his eyes studying the broken window, the empty shell. I stand there, wondering at the intelligence level of the man before me, so much about him unknown, and wait for him to make the connection.

I can see the moment it happens, the slow draw of his gaze from point A to point B. My presence. Annie missing. My knowledge of his carnal desires. Understanding hits, and his head whips back to me, his eyes blazing with raw fury.

"You. Little. Bitch," he grounds out, stepping toward me. I move quickly in response—learning from my mistakes with

Jeremy. I cannot let him grab me, must catch him off guard and unprepared. I yank out my right hand, the stiletto blade tight in its grip, and press the release button while moving. The sharp blade shoots into place, the sharp jerk beneath my palm making my legs clench and stomach curl. *This* is the moment. *This* is my time. The guilt—that giant boulder that suffocates my shoulders, telling me that my thoughts are wrong, my intentions twisted—is gone, and my conscience is light, doing nothing to impede the rush of energy flowing through my body. The knife shakes slightly as my hands tremble from excitement, and I eye his neck, my sharp gaze examining the curves and valleys I will soon puncture. He sees my knife and pauses, stopped momentarily by the reflective flash of a weapon in my hand.

In movies, they always refer to the jugular: "Go for the jugular." But the jugular is actually a vein located on the outer portion of the neck. Cutting it will cause some bloodshed, but not enough to kill, not unless you do something like hang them upside down and slowly let every drop of their blood drip out of their neck. That's a boring death. I'd probably fall asleep after twenty minutes of listening to the soothing sound of blood drops.

When slicing a throat, you actually want to go for the carotid arteries, located in the small indentations on either side of the windpipe. You don't have to *slice* the arteries: simply applying pressure on the artery will stop the flow of blood to the brain, causing your victim to pass out and—if pressure is continued—eventually die. But that's no fucking fun. Strangling them for five additional minutes after they pass out? You might as well sing a lullaby and rock them gently into the great beyond. Ralph doesn't deserve a soft sink into death, his mind blocking out the pain and allowing him a slow and graceful sink into oblivion. Fuck that. This man deserves to bleed. I need him to bleed, I need to provide my dark obsessions with some sort of reprieve after four years of neglect.

The best way to slice his neck is straight across the tracheal area, one quick swipe that will destroy both the windpipe and the carotid arteries simultaneously. This method will remove his ability to speak or scream, plus his gasp for breath will pull the blood in, preventing a spray of blood from covering me.

The problem is, I want his screams. I want to hear his pain, howls of agony that won't stop until he dies. Screams are always my favorite part of the fantasies; they are the evidence that I have the power, that I am in control and they are scared and at my mercy. I also want the blood, want it to spray everywhere, covering my hands and body, my dark needs wanting the proof of their devastation, the proof that we, as a unit, took the life of this man.

But there is Annie to think of. A girl too close, who might hear his screams, who might be scared. A girl who has already been through too much. A girl who doesn't need me, a stranger, to return covered in the fresh blood of her relative.

For a moment I imagine what I want to do, how I want to decorate his body with my knife, cut off fingers and toes and listen to him scream, to beg me for mercy, for me to hear the strength of my power through spurting blood and gasps of agony. Then my fantasies shut down, pausing when Ralph rushes forward and grabs the fabric of my shirt, slamming his fist into my face.

Blackness.

❖

I have new recognition of the level of my inadequacies. I am weak, my muscles worked enough for cellulite reduction and little else. I am puny, easily overcome by a man who is nothing other than naturally strong. One firm punch into the delicate bones of my face and I am stunned, destroyed, every reflex in my body wanting to curl up and scream my mother's name. But my mother will not save me. She cannot; I killed her. That perverse recognition causes me to fight the pain, to stretch the muscles in my face and open my eyes, blinking weakly as my ruined nerves try to focus.

I am weaker. I am inferior. But I am also a killer, and that sickness may be the only thing to bring me strength.

My vision comes into focus and I look up, my grip tightening on my knife, and stare into the silhouette that is Ralph. He is breathing hard, kneeling alongside my body, leaning down and resting on his hand, which pins my arm into the dirt, the knife useless against 190 pounds of weight.

I grunt, struggling beneath him, trying to move away as he leans over me. "Where. Is. She?"

This is a disaster. It is Jeremy all over again, but instead of a smoking hot man who wants my body, I have the man of my nightmares, have risked Annie in the process, and will be lucky if I live. I need my gun. Fuck the blood, fuck my enjoyment of the fucking process, my once-in-a-lifetime-justified-opportunity-to-kill. I just need him dead, and my inner demons will have to get over the fact that it won't be picture postcard perfect.

I mask the sound of my movement with a scream, a long, tortured howl, something I pray Annie will not hear. The sound causes him to jerk back, his hand tight on my arm. As my brain reverberates from the noise, I slide my free hand into the pocket of my sweatshirt, grab the gun, pull it out, point and fire. Let the double-action do the work, no cocking needed. One hard squeeze that blows fire from its depths.

I would have loved to hold the gun to his face, talk some serious smack, and wait for him to release my arm and back away. But that'd be stupid. Give him time to knock it from my hand and punish me for every smartass comment I made. I already made my stupid mistake for the day. I had wanted intimate bloodshed so badly that I'd allowed him to walk right up and pulverize my face.

So I shoot him, not really paying attention to where, my hand pulling the trigger at a target two feet away. I can't miss. He starts, his eyes dropping to my gun, then traveling back to my face, anger mixed with pain in his expression. He sits back, holding his side, where it appears my bullet has hit. I don't know what organs lie in the right side of someone's rib cage, but my fevered mind doesn't come up with anything important, and I sit up quickly, scooting my legs underneath me and kneeling before him. Having regained my grip on the knife, I bring it forward through the air in a smooth arc that instantly satisfies every wet dream I've ever had, moving across and sinking the sharp blade into his skin just under his left ear.

I yank left, cutting the throat as I have imagined countless, fevered times, the blade jerking in a wet sweep across his neck until it breaks loose of the skin. The movement is sluggish but clean, the blade barely slowing, my mind surprised at how easily it slices, how little effort is required.

Time pauses, a heart-stopping second when I worry that I didn't cut deep enough, that the knife slid too easily, a superficial wound that will do nothing but infuriate my adversary. His eyes meet mine, fury against fury, strength against weakness.

Then he slumps.

He falls forward, a hand reaching up to the cut, some blood gurgling through his fingers as he tries to speak, tries to communicate the hatred and frustration that blazes through his eyes. I catch him with my hand, holding him upright, my hand twitching around the blade.

Then I bring it up again, and his eyes follow. His other hand reaches out and grabs my shoulder, gripping it tightly, the force behind his grasp surprising me. *I can finish him.* I *can* stab, twist, mutilate his body, follow the actions of my countless fantasies. This is finally my moment, my opportunity. But my hand betrays me, falling harmlessly, and I stare at it, useless and quickly going limp around the knife. I reach down into my overfull reservoir that I always avoid, the one perpetually full of bloodlust, the one that scares the ever-loving crap out of me. But it is empty. Drained. I look at him, the despair in his eyes mirroring mine. His for his future, mine for my inability to fulfill my fantasy. His hand goes limp on my arm and he slumps backward, a few thin streams of blood running down his neck and pooling on the dirt and pavement beneath him.

Maybe I am not my mother. Maybe my need of bloodshed stops at the point of mutilation and dismemberment.

I stand, trying to retain my grip on the knife, and stride to Ralph's car, yank open the door, and grab the keys from the ignition. Then I pull off my bloody sweatshirt, jog to Jeremy's truck, and toss it behind the driver's seat, the only thought in my head being Annie. *I need to get back to her.*

CHAPTER 73
ANNIE

HER MOTHER HAS always told Annie that angels exist. Angels who watch over and keep us safe. Annie had prayed for an angel in the dark space of the shed, and now she prays for her angel to return. She frets, her hands turning the phone over and over, the display flashing in the light. She has never used a cell phone; their family doesn't own one. Once, she had been given a pink plastic cell phone, its buttons squishy, the faceplate a sticker that displayed all zeros. She had coveted it, feeling oh-so-important when she would pull it out in public, making a pretend call and speaking excitedly into its plastic receiver.

She strains to remember the phone number to their house. Her mother often recited it to her, preaching the importance of knowing it by heart. It starts with a nine. That is all she knows, and she opens the phone, pressing the nine button and trying to remember more. Nine. Nothing else comes. Her stomach growls.

The angel had said to wait until the alarm went off and then dial 911. That number is easy to remember. That she can handle.

She hears an engine growl and looks up, seeing the brown-haired girl pull up in her gray truck when there is still five minutes left on the timer. Annie stands, waving excitedly, seeing the smile on the girl's face through the truck's windshield. The girl responds, gesturing Annie to come, and she jumps down the stairs, running up to the truck and climbing in.

"You came back!" The words burst from her, relief flowing through her body. Soon she will be home. Soon she will be with her parents. Yanking on the car handle, she pulls open the door, struggling with the weight of it, and climbs into the truck.

The girl smiles, her face scratched, black marks on parts of her skin. "You bet, sweetie. Thanks for following directions. Ready to go home?"

Annie nods, tugging on the seat belt and pulling it over her body. "Yes!"

The girl puts the truck into drive and pulls backward, the truck rolling over the soft dirt. "I know your family is ready for you to come home."

Annie wraps her arms tightly around her body and looks out the window.

❖

It takes ten minutes to find civilization and a parking lot to pull into. I grab the disposable cell, activated by Mike three hours ago, the same cell that had flipped through Annie's hands, and reach into the floorboard, digging around until my hands close over my iPad. As I pull it out, I notice Annie's eyes locked on my bag of gas station fare. "You hungry?"

She nods quickly, and I reach over, pulling the bag up and depositing it into her lap. The plastic bag opens to reveal a plethora of chocolate and candy. She shoots me a questioning look and I wave my hand dismissively. "Whatever you want. It's all yours."

There is a squeal of excitement, and the sound brings a smile to my face. My fingers dart quickly over the tablet's surface, and then my search finds an answer, one home phone number for Henry and Carolyn Thompson. I perform a second search, looking for a location close to their home, its area a good twenty minutes from our current location. I take a deep breath, lean my head back on the seat, and try to think, try to figure out the best way to go about this. Then I open the phone, block my number, and dial Annie's home.

CHAPTER 74
HENRY THOMPSON

HENRY THOMPSON SITS in the living room, his hands tented in front of his face, tears soaking his unshaven cheeks. He had woken up to an empty house, Carolyn having left a note on the counter stating that she had "gone to Becky's." Why she would be wasting time visiting family now is beside him. He called the police station twice, both times learning nothing. They knew nothing; the cops are all idiots as far as he is concerned. He has never felt so useless and curses his legs and his inability to drive down to the station himself. The phone rings next to him, and he stares at the receiver. He has waited all night and all morning for the phone to ring. And now that it finally has, he is terrified of the news that it brings. He finally picks up the phone, his voice gravelly when it works. "Hello."

"Mr. Thompson?" It is a young girl's voice, one he doesn't recognize.

"Yes."

"I have Annie with me. She is safe."

He sits up, gripping the phone tightly. "Who is this?" he demands harshly.

"Who I am doesn't matter. I will bring her to you, but only if there is just you and your wife present. Is your wife there now?"

"No. She's at her sister-in-law's. May I speak to Annie?"

"Yes, but I need to arrange things with you first. Are you comfortable with meeting me alone, without police?"

"What do you want from us? We don't have any money," he responds quickly, worried at the words he speaks, worried that they will affect Annie's return.

"Mr. Thompson, I am not the one who took Annie. I am just the one returning her. I have no interest in anything other than bringing her back to you."

He releases a breath, fresh tears running down his face. "Yes, we will meet you alone. Where?"

"I have an address if you will write it down. We can meet you there in thirty minutes. Will that give you time to get in touch with your wife?"

He nods frantically, wiping at his eyes. "Yes. Please let me speak to Annie."

There is a pause and whispered words that he can't catch. Then there is a breath into the phone and Annie speaks, and it is the most beautiful sound he has ever heard.

CHAPTER 75
CAROLYN THOMPSON

CAROLYN STARES INTO the woman's face, sweet tea and wilted napkins between them on the dining room table. In the background a phone rings, and Becky's eyes flicker to it.

"You're not getting that phone, Becky. You're going to answer my damn question. This is my daughter we are talking about!" Carolyn stands, leaning over and looking into the woman's watery blue eyes. "Do you think that Michael had anything to do with this?" The phone stops ringing, and the sudden silence hangs stagnant in the room.

"You've been asking me the same question for thirty minutes!" Becky's voice breaks and she pushes to her feet, stepping away from the table and to the front window, looking out the blinds. Looking at the place where the police cruiser sat last night. "He's your blood," she finally says, her back rigid, a hardness coming over her face, the words broken and dead. "You should know how he is. Secrets... he's always had secrets. And he hasn't been interested in me for a long time. We're not like you and Henry. We live together. Not much else." She turns to Carolyn, stubborn pride mixed with indecision in her eyes. Her hands knot together and Carolyn waits for more, the woman before her hesitating, thinking through her next words. Then the phone starts up again, a demanding shrill, and she moves quickly, hurrying to the wall, away from Carolyn, and snatches up the receiver. "Hello?"

There is a pause, and then she turns, her eyes large. "It's Henry. He says he has news about Annie."

❖

I have one final item to take care of and glance over at Annie, who is fiddling with the radio, flipping through pop stations. She smiles hesitantly, and I return her smile, seeing her eyes light up when she finds a song she likes. I quickly create a bogus e-mail address and send an e-mail to John Watkins, one of two deputies listed on the Brooklet Police Department's online roster. It is a brief e-mail, stating the address where Ralph lies, stating that he may or may not still be alive and that he was the responsible party in the Annie disappearance. I press "send" and then set down the tablet.

"Okay, sweetie. Let's go meet your parents."

CHAPTER 76
CAROLYN THOMPSON

ANNIE'S REUNION WITH her parents is held at a church parking lot ten miles outside of Brooklet. The marquee is faded, the building poorly maintained, but Carolyn Thompson doesn't notice anything but the empty parking lot. She had quizzed Henry from the moment she had walked in the trailer door, asking questions she knew he didn't have the answers to, speaking just to speak, nerves frying every receptor in her body. She doesn't trust it, this strange girl calling to return Annie, someone they don't know, her intentions unclear. It is too good to be true. And meeting here, without police, smells like a trap. She wanted to call John, wanted to involve the police or the FBI—who have so far been utterly useless—but Henry had been adamant about following the stranger's instructions to a T. So here they wait, alone and exposed, their sanity as much at risk as their safety. She doesn't know if either one of them can handle disappointment at this stage.

She unloads Henry's chair from their van, and he sits in the sun, his eyes closed, a small smile on his face. He seems utterly at ease, a condition that infuriates her. How he can be calm baffles her. If only she had been home, had spoken to Annie, heard the words that could have been her last. Henry has that moment, and she feels cheated—an unfair sentiment, but present all the same.

"It's late, Henry," she says tightly, looking at her watch. "She said eight, right? You told me she said eight."

"Relax, Carolyn. It's only a minute past. Give them some time."

And then there is a sound, an engine, and Carolyn almost cries, her heart breaking as she turns, afraid to give credence to her hope. A flash of blond reflects from the passenger side of a truck, and her throat constricts. The truck comes to a stop in front of them, the sun's glare obscuring the windshield, and she runs, oblivious to anything but the thought of Annie. She flies to the passenger side, scrambling for the handle, ripping it open, and catching Annie when she tumbles out, gripping her tightly and sobbing into her curls, her hands squeezing the small body, which squirms in her grasp. "Oh, Annie!" she gasps. There is a squeal of metal on metal and she turns, seeing Henry struggling in his chair, trying to roll over the root-filled dirt, his eyes catching her, and his hands releasing the wheels, straining outward, reaching toward her.

Cursing her inconsideration, she runs with Annie in her arms to Henry, falling into his embrace, Annie tumbling into his lap, her giggles reaching their ears. Henry's eyes meet hers, tears spilling from them, his mouth shaking as he reaches down, cradles Annie's face, choking on his sobs. His arms grab her tight, and the three of them embrace for a very long time.

I watch them, my throat tight, the love that they share evident. They are an older couple, Annie obviously a miracle in their life. I am surprised to see her father in a wheelchair, a scenario I had never considered and one that hadn't been mentioned in the news reports. I hadn't really thought of them at all. My own greed had consumed me, my need to kill giddy at the justifiable opportunity that had been presented. Annie's giggle reaches me, and I cover my mouth, her childish innocence breaking my heart in two. I feel like an intruder in their private reunion, and I clear my throat, stepping forward.

"I'm going to leave." I gesture to the truck. "I have to get on the road." The mother turns, her eyes meeting mine for the first moment. She pats Annie as if reassuring herself of her existence and then turns away, taking steps forward until she stands in front of me.

When she speaks, her words are clear, her head held high. "I don't know your part in all of this, but my husband says you helped Annie, and for that I am forever in your debt."

I smile, meeting the little girl's eyes. She flashes me a winning smile. "I was happy to do what I could to help. But I do have a favor to ask, if I may."

Her eyes sharpen, suspicion present in their depths. "I figured as much. What is it?"

"My anonymity. I couldn't think of an easy way to return Annie, I didn't want to leave her somewhere with people who I'd be unfamiliar with. Your husband was kind enough to meet me here without involving the police, but if you could keep details about me private, I would greatly appreciate it."

She waits, her eyes locked on mine, but then finally speaks. "That's it? Anonymity is all that you're asking for?"

I grimace, torn. "Certain actions I took in the rescue of Annie you might not appreciate later. You will understand more in a few hours. I apologize in advance for any pain that I have caused your family. Please know that I, for the most part, acted with Annie's welfare in mind." I pause. "I don't want to put you in an uncomfortable situation or ask you to lie. But again, if there is a way to avoid sharing details of my involvement, I would certainly appreciate it."

The mother looks back at her daughter, cradled in her husband's arms. "I appreciate your actions in a way that can never be repaid. If that is all you want, I can certainly honor those requests."

I smile at her, the action catching her off guard, and she is hesitant in returning the gesture. Annie interrupts our exchange, jumping off her father's lap and running to me, holding her hands up and reaching for me. I lean down, and her arms wrap easily around my neck.

"Thank you," she whispers in my ear.

I grip her, trying to ignore the memories of Summer that push at my psyche, memories of her smell, her kisses, her tugs on my clothing, messy cheeks, tangled hair. I forced myself to stand, to separate myself from her. "I need to go. She is an incredible child. You have done a wonderful job of raising her." I nod at both of them; the father holds out his hands to me, and I walk over to him. Bending over, I accept the hug he offers, surprised at the strength with which he grips me.

"Thank you," he whispers. "We will forever be in your debt."

I straighten, run a gentle hand over Annie's hair, then turn and head back to the truck, open the door, and climb in. I watch them for a moment, the mother crouched next to the wheelchair, the three of them talking excitedly. Then I put the truck in reverse and back up. I am pulling forward when I hear a shout. I look up to see the woman running to the truck. I roll down my window, worried that something is wrong.

"Were you the girl? The one who called the hotline?"

I pause, my indecision answering her question. Her mouth tightens and her eyes narrow. "So, it was Michael? My Michael?"

"Yes. But I don't think he did anything to her. She was tied up when I found her. Unharmed."

"But you told the police...you think he was planning..." Her voice falters, and she grips the truck window tightly.

"If he planned on doing what he discussed with me...that is why I came for her. Why I did what I did." I close my eyes, squeezing the steering wheel tightly. "I'm sorry." I open my eyes, hating to look into hers, hating the disbelief and judgment I will see there.

She sways, the pain in her eyes sharp. "I can't...there was never any sign," she whispers, glancing over her shoulder at Annie. "To think that someone who carries my blood would hurt her..." Her mouth tightens and she straightens, strength returning to her eyes.

"I don't know what you did to him, and I don't care," she spits out. "Blood doesn't excuse taking a child. You stopped what needed to be stopped." She shakes her head tightly, her bottom lip quivering before she pushes them together. "Our police say that there are other girls. Like Annie, who've disappeared in this area." She reaches through the window and grips my wrist tightly. "Don't you feel one bit of guilt for anything you did to him." She stares firmly at me, waiting for a response, and I finally nod, not sure how else to react. Then she sniffs, releases my wrist, and steps back, walking back to her family and swinging Annie up onto her hip. They turn toward me and wave, and I wave back and pull out, hitting the highway and heading toward home, if my one-room prison can be called that.

Don't you feel one bit of guilt... Guilt? I search myself for it but find no trace, no emotion over what I have done. What I do feel is a lack of closure. When I stabbed my mother, I saw her die. Saw the moment when her eyes became still and her breath stopped. With Ralph, I should have stayed. Should have used the knife a few times more, ensured that the job was done correctly, waited for that final huff of breath, the dry wheeze of death.

CHAPTER 77

AT MILE MARKER 84, on Alabama Highway 78, I put on my blinker, moving to the slow lane as I prepared to turn. Heading to Annie, I didn't have time for personal errands, for walks down memory lane.

But now, with six hours ahead of me and no excuse other than fatigue, I need to stop. I need to see my family.

I get off on the exit, traveling twelve miles north till I enter familiar territory. Memories of my past seize me, causing a lump in my throat, and my hands grip the wheel tightly as I turn through the gates of the cemetery, bright red flowers framing my entrance.

I haven't been here since the day of the funeral, but I will never forget the path, never forget the large tree that hangs over their graves. Trent would have loved that tree, its low branches perfect for climbing and jumping. I picked these plots because of that tree.

I park and step out into the sun, surprised at the weather. It should be gloomy, misty, sad weather for a sad occasion. But the weather is downright cheerful, fluffy clouds dotting a brilliant blue sky, birds chirping, frogs jumping from underfoot as I move through the thick grass.

I sit before their graves, four perfect spots with an empty spot on the side. After pulling off my tennis shoes, I dig my toes into the grass, appreciating the tickle of blades, the warmth of the sun.

I have avoided this for so long, the guilt at their deaths weighing heavily on my heart. Not because I feel responsible for them, but because I am alive and they are not. I have life, and they have only death.

I sit there for twenty minutes, speaking to each of them in turn, my conversation with my mother the longest. I tell her that I forgive her. And I realize, as I speak the words, that I mean it.

Twenty minutes later, I return to the truck and shut the door, staring for a long moment out the window at their plots. Then, feeling slightly lighter than when I arrived, I return to the road.

❖

I complete the rest of the drive in a daze, running on pure adrenaline and caffeine, stopping every few hours and catnapping at rest stops. When I finally stumble down the sixth-floor hallway, Jeremy is outside my door, sitting on the nasty orange carpet. I stop a few steps away, my bones exhausted and eyes drooping. He stands when he sees me, his strong arms reaching for me and crushing me into a hug—a hug that I don't want and don't need, until the moment I am touched. I sink into his grasp, the strength of his embrace fortifying me, the affection so foreign, so forgotten, that I almost cry from the sheer beauty of it. I have been alone so long, scared of myself and for myself, deprived of so many freedoms. His hug breaks me, breaks every wall I have built, dam I have constructed, and weight I carry. He supports me, lifting me up with his arms, propping me against the wall as his eyes find my face, worry and concern in them, his gaze narrowing at what must be bruises from Ralph's punch.

"Are you okay?" he asks, his eyes sweeping over the rest of my body, checking and reassuring him that I am in one piece.

"Please, hold me." The words spill from me, uncontrolled— a tidal wave of emotion pushing in every direction out of my body, tears plummeting down my face.

He stares at me wordlessly and then leans over, lifting me easily, and carries me inside.

❖

Jeremy helps me to undress, his eyes respectfully looking the other way as I pull on sweatpants and a T-shirt. Then he tucks me into bed, holding me in strong arms as I curl to one side, my body tucked perfectly into his. I have never been held in this way, and the last thought, as my mind sinks into slumber, is that I never want to leave this spot again.

I wake once during the night. Staring at the ceiling, his arm resting across my belly, I wait for the urge to come. For my brain to explode with ideas for mayhem. But it stays quiet, exhausted. It allows me to sleep in his arms without consequence.

I sleep for two days, awakened occasionally by my bladder or stomach. Jeremy is always there, his strong presence filling the void left by my weak one. He feeds me, he brings me ice water and aspirin and chats with me until my eyes droop and I fall back asleep. And then, on day three, I am back.

CHAPTER 78

I OPEN MY eyes to a bag that I have never seen. I blink, trying to place the object; it comes in and out of focus as I awaken fully. It's a backpack, gray and black, a carabiner hanging from the top handle. *Jeremy.* It must be his, which means he is still here. I sit up, squinting against the bright sun, and see him sitting against the front door, a laptop open before him. My eyes narrow on it, then relax when I recognize that it is not mine.

He glances over, a smile stretching across his face when he sees me. "You're awake," he says, setting aside the laptop and hopping to his feet.

"What time is it?" I say quietly. I feel drugged, too much sleep making my brain slow and sluggish.

"It's nine thirty. On Friday."

I nod, thinking of all the cam appointments that I have been a no-show for, of Dr. Derek and what he must be making of a missed Wednesday appointment. That has never happened; my schedule is precise in its lack of conflicting events. The cammers will forgive me. Dr. Derek will probably want to increase my meds.

"Want me to leave?" He picks up a bottle of water off the floor, drains it, and takes it to the trash. My eyes follow his movements, picking up on the sparkling kitchen counter, the clean floors, the foreign, faint smell of lemon.

"Did you *clean*?"

He grins sheepishly. "Just the areas I used. I didn't want you having to pick up after me."

I tilt my head toward my pink bedroom. "And what about over there?"

He widens his eyes, holding up his hands. "I didn't even step on that...side of the apartment."

I laugh, waving my hand dismissively as I stand. "I'm joking." I notice my clothes, pale pink striped pajamas that I don't own. I frown, looking at him.

"They're my sister's. I borrowed them. I didn't want to go through your stuff..." He stops the sentence awkwardly. "Yesterday, during the night you went to the bathroom and came back naked. I couldn't...it was hard for me to be around you when you sleep like that. I felt like I was violating your privacy."

"*Hard?*" I run my tongue lightly over my teeth, giving him a mischievous smile, laughing when he blushes. "Chill, I'm not judging you. Thank your sister for the PJs. I'll give them back once I do a load of wash." I stretch, my back popping, and roll my neck.

"Do you want me to go?" He repeats the question I ignored earlier, the one that I got too distracted to answer. I stop midstretch, dipping into the dark bowels of my mind, looking for a red flag, a flicker of something dark and disturbing.

I shrug. "No. It's okay. You can stay for a bit." *Friday morning.* The day suddenly alerts me of its presence, smack-dab on a workday. I squint at him. "Shouldn't you be at work?"

"I called in. I have some vacation time accrued, so I took a few days off." He sits back down, watching me as I move to my dresser, pulling open drawers and rummaging for panties and clothes. "You talk a lot. In your sleep."

I slow my movements, my mind racing. "Really? What do I say?"

"A lot of nonsense. Mostly words that don't exist. You mentioned summer a few times, and something about a trench."

I shut the drawer, panties, jeans, and a T-shirt in hand. *Summer. Trent.* The loves of my life. I unbutton the top of the sleep shirt and tug it over my head, then finger the waistband of the pants, pulling them over my hips and dropping them to the floor. I am trying to think of a plausible explanation for the words of my sleep when I glance over and see him, his mouth open, his eyes locked on my body.

I'm naked. The thought suddenly occurs to me. For me, it is second nature—this apartment is a place in which no one else exists, my own private sanctuary. My online world has conditioned me to being nude, my body on full, high-definition display to anyone who is willing to part with a measly seven bucks. I forget that for other people, a glimpse of skin is coveted—something to be withheld until the proper moment, once the correct hoops have been jumped and relationship boundaries established. "Sorry," I mutter, sliding my arms through the sleeves of my shirt and ducking into it before stepping into my panties.

"No. I'm sorry for looking. I should have..." He closes his eyes briefly, shaking his head before opening them and looking at me. "God, you are beautiful."

Beautiful. It is a word I don't hear often, which is odd considering the days stacked upon weeks upon months upon years that men have spent ogling my body. Sexy. Hot. Gorgeous. Fine. Bitchin'. Pretty, when the man is short on words or unfamiliar with the English language. But beautiful is not a word often used. "Thank you. I should have gone into the bathroom, but I'm so used to being naked that I forget normal social protocols."

"You don't have to apologize. Trust me. And I remember." I shoot him a questioning look. "The first time I came in, you were naked." He gestures to the left side of the apartment. "On the bed, lit by the lights."

I nod, remember the moment well, my admiration at his looks interrupted by the bloodthirsty lust I had for his box cutters. Just the memory of it causes a shiver of darkness to shoot through me, and I shift uncomfortably.

He laughs uncomfortably. "So, what? You do porn?"

I smile, shaking my head. "No."

"I'm sorry. I didn't mean to offend you. It's just the lights, the cameras, the toys..."

"I'm not offended. You might consider what I do porn, so I probably shouldn't have answered so quickly. I webcam. Those cameras are hooked to my computer, and I broadcast the videos online, in private chat rooms. Men, and sometimes women, pay me to have cybersex with them." I pull my hair into a ponytail and turn to him, watching his face, curious about his reaction.

"Cybersex? Like what people used to do in Yahoo! chat rooms?"

"No. Not like that. That was just typing. My clients type, but I communicate through a video feed. It has audio, so it is more like a FaceTime call, but my system is about ten times more sophisticated than an iPhone."

His eyes travel over my equipment, the lights, the wires and connections, and the toys, which cover two dresser surfaces. "It's a lot of equipment."

It is a useless response, one that doesn't give me any hint into his thoughts. "Yep."

He laughs. "It's not as bad as I expected. I don't know what I expected. You do this for money?"

I nod.

"So the guys...they don't actually come here."

Oh, they definitely cum. I smile. "No. The sex is all virtual."

I don't necessarily expect him to be okay with my work. But it is a non-negotiable, at least if we are discussing the possibility of a relationship. Which we're not. Especially since my mind just wandered away from my superexciting inner dialogue and is envisioning his backpack straps wrapped tight around that gorgeous, hasn't-been-shaved-in-three-days neck. I blink, bringing myself back to the present. "It's what I do. How I support myself. I don't expect you to understand."

He holds up his hands. "Trust me, in the arena of odd, your Internet webchats are at the bottom of the stack as far as you are concerned. It doesn't bother me."

I try to frown, to look hurt, but "odd" is about the nicest word someone could pick to describe me.

He tilts his head slightly. "Well, maybe it bothers me a bit, but I don't have the right to dictate what you do with your body." He glances around the apartment. "It does seem like a lot of work for little pay. This building...one day it's just gonna cave in around you. There's got to be something else you can do for more money."

I bite my lower lip, keeping a grin from slipping out, his concern over my finances laughable. "Like stuffing envelopes?" It was a joke, but something that I seriously considered my first week in 6E. Searching "work from home jobs" in Google brings up a plethora of choices, from telemarketing to taking surveys to working in technical support. I picked camming for two reasons: money and the desire to not be yelled at or hung up on. Online, I do the yelling, traditionally while brandishing a riding crop or seven-inch dildo. And when I do get hung up on, the cash register chings, signaling another successful orgasm-for-funds transaction.

"Like stuffing envelopes," he says with a smile. "That'd probably give me more packages to deliver. More opportunities to stare at your closed door."

"Maybe I'll start opening it for you. Just to stop your hand from making any more girly signatures."

He grins at me, and I grin at him, and there is a spark of possibility in our exchange. *Maybe.* Maybe there is a chance for happiness after all, despite my online slutdom and psychopathic urges.

Then there is a different flicker inside of me, my dark demons reminding me of their power, and I meet Jeremy's eyes. "You should probably go."

Maybe. Maybe not. I have to remember what I am.

CHAPTER 79

"YOU SHOULD PROBABLY go." I repeat the phrase unnecessarily, testing the words on my tongue while my heart argues with the logic.

"Okay." He stands and walks to his bag, slides the laptop in, and zips it closed.

I haven't had physical interaction in a long time, haven't ever shared this space with another body. I'm out of practice in relationships, courtesies, and social norms. So maybe this is normal, this casual acceptance of my directive. "Okay? You don't mind?"

He turns, grins. "I was here because I thought you might need someone. You seem to be back on your feet. Plus," he adds with a wink, "I needed my truck back. Wanted to make sure you didn't run to the border with it."

I laugh, an awkward sound that my throat is still getting used to. Giggling it knows. I've giggled more in the past three years than four preteen girls at a Justin Bieber concert. Men seem to love a girlish giggle, especially when it's in response to some bit of wit they have conjured up.

I hesitate as he moves closer, then allow him to wrap his arms around me, a sigh slipping out of me as he nuzzles and then gently kisses my neck, breathing in the scent of me before letting go.

"I'm gonna hold you to that date," he warns. "I want a full evening—dinner, movie, the whole works." He does that thing again, that casual grin that my heart finds irresistible.

I scowl despite the pattering of my heart. "I never verbally agreed to that."

"You accepted my keys. It's kind of a physical acceptance."

I follow him to the door, then pull it open with a pointed look. He leans in, hovering above my lips, asking for permission, and then moves forward when I don't pull away, placing one soft kiss on me, a moment that is way too short, my lips begging for more as he pulls away. "You know, I can always hold your packages hostage," he whispers, before straightening and stepping out into the hall.

I narrow my eyes, sticking my head out into the hall. "You wouldn't dare!" I call to his departing back.

"Two weeks from tonight. A date. I'll call first to confirm."

I shut the door with a smile. A smile that darkens, the jitters of my soul reminding me of who I am, what I consist of. What I am capable of. I hear the squeal of metal as the elevator descends and walk to the window, watching as he climbs into his truck and shuts the door.

I have to remind myself that "out there" is normality. Something that I am not. Just because I left this apartment, walked down that street, and got into a car doesn't mean that I am normal. I am locked away for a reason. I have to remember that. I don't need a first-date disaster, a drive home with that beautiful man dead in the passenger seat, his head hanging loosely from tendrils of skin, blood staining that soft gray leather. I know what I am. I know what I have done. That is what I need to remember.

I pull off my jeans and T-shirt, slip on lace thongs and a push-up bra. Then I power up the computer, turn on the spotlights, and return to life.

CHAPTER 80

LIFE AFTER DEATH is a strange thing. I have forbidden myself to follow Annie, to meddle in her life any more than I already have. It is a selfish mandate, fueled mainly by my desire not to know how the other half lives. To see the media storm that is no doubt surrounding her return, the images of her and her parents, her normal happy life...it will remind me too much of Summer and Trent—of the life they should have lived—of the pieces of life I am missing out on now. It is easier for me not to look, for me to concentrate on another thing: the eye of the camera. I need to continue surviving as I did before: eighteen-hour days spent with clients, wearing out my body and soul, so I have little to think about at the end of the day except sleep.

But I am different now. The step into the outside world has poured fresh blood into my veins. I feel like Simon—the need for more more more tugging at me. At night, when I lie down on the bed, my thoughts move to loneliness before bloodshed, the yearning for arms wrapped around me stronger than death before me. It was a mistake, having Jeremy stay over those nights. I can't stop thinking about it—his easy grin in the morning, his utter lack of anything sinister—just carefree kisses placed softly on my neck. Not even a push for sex, his moves restricted to comforting touches. A hand trailing over my neck when I opened my eyes. An arm encircling my waist and pulling me to his hard, warm body. Soft lips pressed to mine, slow kisses until my drugged mouth responded, letting him in to explore further. The heat of his breath against my hair as we spooned in my bed, his leg wrapped around me, holding my body captive in his arms.

It's been eight days since he left my apartment. I have spoken to him through the closed door every day since then—his deliveries resuming their steady and dependable schedule. He hasn't pushed, hasn't argued, hasn't done anything but accept my regular response, his mouth twitching that gorgeous smile through my peephole view. I don't know why I won't open the door. I am fairly sure, in the middle of the day, with this man I have lain with, that I could control myself. He is aware of my weakness, has already shown an aptitude for defeating me in the game of combat. Plus, as evidenced by a cheerful yellow Post-it note left three days ago on one of my packages, he no longer carries box cutters. It'd be difficult for me to kill him with my bare hands. So maybe I keep the door shut to protect my heart and not his body. Whatever the reason, I haven't opened the door and I now yearn for his touch.

CHAPTER 81
ANNIE

ANNIE SITS IN a small room, her mother and father on either side. Across the desk are a woman and a man, both in dark suits, their faces unfamiliar. She can feel the tension in the room, coming from her parents, their nerves radiating in waves from their body. They shouldn't be nervous. She knows what to say, remembers everything she has been told.

"Annie, we only have a few questions for you, but it is important that you tell the truth. Do you understand?" The man speaks slowly, in a tone that is normally used with babies.

She nods solemnly, keeping her expression quiet, her eyes big.

"You've told us about Uncle Michael and the shed. But you haven't told us how you got out. How you got to the church that your parents found you at."

"I don't remember." She speaks clearly, looking the man in the eyes.

"Did someone threaten you? Tell you not to tell?"

She feels her mother tighten beside her and speaks

quickly. "Uncle Michael made me drink the soda, and then I fell asleep. I woke up at the church."

The man stares at her, then at his partner, the two of them exhaling in frustration.

"I think Annie's been through enough," her mother says, standing and tugging Annie to her feet. "I'm taking her home now. Where she belongs."

CHAPTER 82

IT'S A SAD world when I am bored by the sight of a grizzly-bearded trucker modeling lace panties. I fight a yawn, move briefly upward, out of sight of the camera, and let the yawn out. Once I recompose, I settle back down, an impressed smile on my features.

"Oh...," I purr. "The sight of your ass in that lace is *so* fucking hot. You like that, don't you?"

Mistyone62 looks over his shoulder, at the cam—his dirty face a mess of want and arousal. "Oh God, yes..." He giggles, the sound contrasting with his gruff features.

I bite my bottom lip, widening my eyes in a show of amazement. Then I hear something. *Shit.* I straighten, looking toward my door. I look at the cam and hold up a finger to my lips in a shushing motion.

The sound repeats—a knock. It is so out of place at this time of night that I almost second-guess the sound. I glance at my computer screen, at the clock in the upper right-hand corner: 10:46 p.m. I lean forward, speaking quickly. "Misty, I'm sorry, but I have to go. My roommate just got home."

His screen quickly goes dark. The threat of exposure is always their greatest fear. God bless my imaginary roommate, who has gotten me out of more ridiculous situations than my stun gun or knife ever will. He types a few sentences of text, promising to be on tomorrow, then he is gone, the END CHAT message filling the screen. I am already moving, stepping across the room and placing my eye to the peephole, taking a deep breath before looking through.

It's Jeremy, his body showcased in a sleeveless shirt and what looks like running shorts, his hair damp, earbuds pulled out and hanging around his neck. I swallow the drool that is threatening to drip from my mouth. I can almost smell the masculine scent of his sweat, the glisten on his muscles visible even through the warped view of the peephole.

"Leave it. Thank you." I speak the words of our script, a smile stretching across my face.

He laughs, his head tilting backward, the carefree movement catching my heart through the peephole. He rests a hand on the door, leaning closer in a way that allows me to hear him more clearly. "You're up. I was worried you'd be sleeping."

"What, and leave half of the men in America hanging?" I say dryly, eliciting another chuckle from him, his grin widening when he hears my voice.

"I didn't mean to bother you." He runs a hand through his hair, my eyes drinking in every inch of the movement. "I just needed to hear your voice. I—" He curses under his breath. "Fuck, I don't know. I just wanted to hear your voice."

I bite the side of my cheek, trying to keep from smiling. "You just come from the gym?" *Sweat. Sweat tastes good.*

You can lick it off of him. Maybe nibble on his skin. Draw a little blood. Then a little more. Fuck, maybe he's a masochist. Just let him in and let us work on him. Tie him up. The voices inside my head titter, greedy with excitement and the possibility of blood. I push them to the side. I have missed his voice, his casual air that accepts the twisted woman that I am.

He glances down at his outfit. "No. I mean, I was out on a run when I decided to stop by. Sorry it's so late."

I don't bother responding to that apology. He can stop by at four a.m. if he wants to. Five a.m. if he takes that shirt off and lets me see his sweaty chest, heaving with the evidence of his exertion. I want to touch that chest, want to run my fingers over the cut of his muscles. When he was here with me, spending those days…sex was the last thing on my mind, Jeremy acting the perfect gentleman. But now I have recovered from my trip outside, now I am back into my world, away from the breeze and the sounds and the experience of sharing air, vehicles, space, with others…and contact is an experience I miss. The unpredictability of real life, outside of this apartment. In 6E, I control everything, no variables present to fuck with my normal. Out there are people. People like him doing things that affect every thought, action, and emotion that exists.

"May I come in?"

My breath hitches, the push and pull inside of me too strong to ignore. "I don't know," I say slowly, running my hand along the seam of the door, my ear pressing expectantly against it, hoping he will continue speaking, my body craving another bit of his voice.

"Is it because you worry about hurting me?"

I nod, forgetting for a moment that he can't see me. "Yeah."

"I could hold you down. Straddle your body. Like we did the first time we met."

"You mean when I was naked?"

He looks up at the peephole, flashing me another smile. "Yeah. You naked now?"

I laugh, looking down at my sheer bra-and-panty set. "Not quite."

He *can* control me. He's shown that before, when my attempt to take his life was thwarted by his strength and agility. This time he will be prepared, will be more capable, especially if I move into a position of restraint willingly, before the urge to kill strikes. I toy with the notion of letting him in, the dark desires in the back of my mind sitting up and taking notice. *I shouldn't.* It is too dangerous, too risky.

He sits on the floor by my door, leaving my field of vision, the door moving slightly as if he is leaning his weight against it. I follow suit, sliding down the steel surface until my butt hits the floor, my ear pressed against the cold metal.

"You didn't try to kill me when I stayed with you." His voice is quieter, and I have to strain to hear it.

"I know. I think my body was recovering. For a minute, I thought that maybe..." My words fade and I feel him shift.

"Maybe what?"

"I had hoped that maybe I was better. Back to normal." And I had hoped. I had allowed myself, during those three days with Jeremy, to dream of normality. I had been at peace, my demons quiet, my psyche granting me the gift of touching him, kissing him, without thinking about how good his head would look decapitated from his body. It had been almost cruelty, getting those days, a glimpse into a life I will never have.

"You used to be normal?" He sounds so surprised that I laugh, a real laugh, one that bubbles out of me and feels incredible.

"Yeah," I whisper. "I used to be totally normal. Till I was seventeen. That's when things changed."

He doesn't push the conversation further, a fact I am grateful for. I don't want to ruin this moment by bringing up my past, don't want to appear any more freakish than I already am. We sit in silence.

"It's okay, though, right?" His voice breaks the silence. "This is your normal now. And you're happy, right?"

"Yeah," I say softly. "I'm happy." And I am. Right now, with him, I am happy. In that realization, I decide to open the door.

I move quickly, before my brain has a chance to react—to tell me that what I'm doing is foolish. I stand, running my hands over my body, adjusting, pushing into place, and putting the lines of my lingerie where they should go. I fluff my hair, wet my lips, and reach for the handle, my heart beating a rapid pulse in my chest.

CHAPTER 83

THE KNOB TURNS and I yank, a smile on my face, my heart dropping when the door doesn't move. Doesn't budge. The crack of metal on metal reminds me of the dead bolt that holds me in, a dead bolt I have forgotten about in my excitement at having a visitor. I laugh despite my frustration. There is humor in the fact that when I am finally ready to open the damn door to my life, it is locked, and from my own directive.

Jeremy's voice has risen, and I look through the peephole to see him standing. "It's locked," he says.

I roll my eyes. "Thanks. I know that."

"So unlock it."

I groan, leaning against the door. "I can't. I don't have a key."

"What?" He sounds alarmed, and I look through the small bulb of glass, to see his fists clenched. "What if you get hurt? Or need help?"

"It's kind of hard for me to get hurt in here. And if I was in a situation where I needed help, I'd just wait for the morning. That's when he unlocks me."

"Who?" The word is vehement, angry. As if he will rip

apart the keeper of the key, all in an attempt to protect my independence.

"Jeremy..." I try to pacify him with my voice. "Calm down. It's for my own good. At night..." I pause. "At night is when I am the most dangerous. A lot of times I can't control myself, and I want to leave the apartment—to go out and hurt someone. I need this lock. It is what keeps me inside. The day is easier. I can control the day, can survive without the lock."

"I don't want you caged in like an animal. That is bullshit!" He pounds the door with his fist, the strong impact creating only a dull thud of sound, every dollar spent on its construction showing its worth.

I shake my head, stepping closer to the door. "You don't understand, Jeremy. What I am, how I think...it isn't like you, or like others. I have survived this long because of how I live. Because of the rules that keep my sanity, and my urges, in place."

There is silence, and I wait. I do not begrudge the lock. The only times I hate the lock are when it is needed most—when I am blind with need and it is the only thing keeping me inside. At those times I scream and pound against the door, cursing Simon, cursing myself. But right now, when my mind is clear? I don't care if there is 180 pounds of yummy on the other side. I know what I need. And I need and appreciate the restraint.

"Mind if I talk to you a little longer?"

I grin. "I'm good with that."

I sit back down, hearing his voice move as he does the same, and we talk, our conversation passing back and forth through the steel door for almost an hour. Until my eyes droop and my voice slurs. Then he says good night, giving me one last peephole glance at his beautiful body before he walks down the hall.

"Be careful running home," I call out, watching him step slowly backward, away from my door. "There are a lot of crazies out there."

He grins, a cocky smile that lights up the dim hallway. "I like crazies. Me and them...we have a little bit of a thing."

A *little bit of a thing*. It is a glimmer, a crack, a chance of something more, and it is what I focus on as I drag myself into bed, my eyes drifting closed before I even have a chance to pull my blanket up.

I don't know what is going to happen with Jeremy. I don't know whether he is my "happily ever after" or not. But I know he makes me smile, and I know he accepts me—the "fucked-up, I'll kill you with your own box cutters" me. And with that revelation, I fall deep, my demons letting me be, my body sinking into the peaceful oblivion that is sleep.

❖

One week later, Mike forwards me an article that was printed in the *Statesboro Times*. It describes Annie's rescue by an "unknown person" and states that the police thoroughly searched the trailer and grounds, finding a box with photos and souvenirs from more than eight missing girls, all around Annie's age. They also found a laptop, the original that Mike had cloned. With the information found on the laptop, they hoped to solve the cases of the missing girls and bring some closure to their families.

I respond to his e-mail, asking him to get me the Thompsons' bank account number. When he replies, I have him set up an untraceable wire and transfer two hundred grand into their account.

My eyes had picked up on the details. Their van, sagging in the church's parking lot, duct tape holding the side mirror in place. The faded wear of their thrift store clothing. The shake in Henry Thompson's voice when he expressed their lack of ransom funds. I had the money, no reason not to share it. It was a small price to pay for the experience. I had left this apartment, wandered among the living. I had helped someone. As much as I may have rescued Annie, she rescued me even more. She made me feel that in all of the rotten of my soul, there still existed goodness, light.

Hope.

There is a knock at the door and I look up, checking my reflection one last time in the mirror, the Betsey Johnson dress fitting perfectly, my hair curling gently over my shoulder, a sparkle in my eyes that I hope is excitement and not insanity.

Today is Friday, and I am doing it. Going on a date with Jeremy. It is ridiculously early, four p.m., and he has promised to have me home by seven. It is dangerous, it is risky. He has strict orders to tackle me to the ground if I start acting odd. But I think, in some small way, this is possible. And I want it. I need it. So, so badly.

Hope.

Hope is dangerous. Hope can be the loose thread that pulls apart your sanity.

NOTE FROM THE AUTHOR

Writing this book was so intriguing because it allowed me to dive into the world of camming. In my research, I immersed myself in the industry and was amazed at the women I encountered — ones from all walks of life, many of whom are highly educated and independent, and led previous lives as business professionals. Some turned to camming by choice, others by situation, but all share one overwhelming characteristic: confidence. These women are not ashamed of their profession, they are proud of it.

Although the characters in this book are fictional, the situations and setup of Deanna's webcam operation are as accurate as I could portray them, and the clients are modeled after different fetishists that frequent the webcam community.

If you are interested in learning more about this industry, you can visit www.webcammingfaq.com for more information.

NOTES

1. Dan Savage, Savage Love, *The Stranger*, June 21, 2001, http://www.thestranger.com/seattle/SavageLove?oid=7730.

2. Robin Bell, "Homosexual Men and Women," ABC of Sexual Health, *British Medical Journal* 318, no. 7181 (February 1999): 452–55; http://www.ncbi.nlm.nih.gov/pmc/articles/PMC1114912/.

3. Eric W. Hickey, *Sex Crimes and Paraphilia* (Upper Saddle River, NJ: Pearson Education, 2006), 165, cited in "Foot fetishism," *Wikipedia*, last modified November 1, 2013, http://en.wikipedia.org/wiki/Foot_fetishism.

4. Lucy Moore, "Foot Fetishes: Fun or Freaky?," *Student Life*, November 4, 2009, http://www.studlife.com/scene/2009/11/04/foot-fetishes-fun-or-freaky.

5. Cameron Kippen, "The History of Footwear—Foot Sex," November 2004, http://podiatry.curtin.edu.au/fetish.html, cited in "Foot fetishism," *Wikipedia*, last modified November 1, 2013, http://en.wikipedia.org/wiki/Foot_fetishism.

6. William A. Henkin and Sybil Holiday, *Consensual Sado-masochism: How to Talk About It and How to Do It Safely* (Los Angeles: Daedalus Publishing Company, 1996).

7. Anil Aggrawal, *Forensic and Medico-legal Aspects of Sexual Crimes and Unusual Sexual Practices* (Boca Raton: CRC Press, 2009), page 147.

8. See http://www.psychosissucks.ca/whatispsychosis.cfm#isa.

9. "Erotic humiliation," *Wikipedia*, last modified November 2, 2013, en.wikipedia.org/wiki/Erotic_humiliation#Psychology_of_humiliation.

10. *Diagnostic and Statistical Manual of Mental Disorders*, 5th ed., text revision (Arlington, VA: American Psychiatric Association, 2013), cited in "Pedophilia," *Wikipedia*, last modified October 11, 2013, http://en.wikipedia.org/wiki/Pedophilia.

11. "Pedophilia," *Psychology Today*, September 7, 2006, cited in "Child sexual abuse," Wikipedia, last modified October 24, 2013, http://en.wikipedia.org/wiki/Child_sexual_abuse#Causal_factors.

12. David M. Fergusson, Michael T. Lynskey, L. John Horwood, "Childhood Sexual Abuse and Pychiatric Disorder in Young Adulthood: I. Prevalence of Sexual Abuse and Factors Associated with Sexual Abuse," *Journal of the American Academy of Child and Adolescent Psychiatry* 35, no. 10 (October 1996): 1355–64, cited in "Child sexual abuse," Wikipedia, last modified October 24, 2013, http://en.wikipedia.org/wiki/Child_sexual_abuse#Demographics.

13. E. J. Dickson, "'Do it again or I'm gonna call your wife':
Inside the World of Financial Domination," *Salon*, June 29,
2013, www.salon.com/2013/06/30/do_it_again_or_i'm_gonna
_call_your_wife"_inside_the_world_of_financial_domination/.

14. Aaron Sankin, "Inside the Twisted World of the Internet's
Priciest Fetish," *The Daily Dot*, September 11, 2013,
http://www.dailydot.com/lifestyle/findom-kinky-fetish
domination-extortion-blackmail/.

ACKNOWLEDGMENTS

This book is my wicked baby. It is devious, and naughty, and often completely disobeyed any orders I gave it. It also has a love-hate relationship with many individuals. It takes a certain type of person to "get" it, and I am overwhelmed with love for the group that worked on this book. They all embraced the individuality that was *The Girl in 6E* and made it even better than I ever dreamed it could be.

To Redhook's art, marketing, and publicity teams. You designed a cover I absolutely love and have constantly surprised me with your innovative ideas, creative approaches, and collaborative attitude. You are an incredible group, and it has been a joy to work with you.

To Susan Barnes. You have taken this book to a level that I love. I appreciate your fearlessness in embracing this book, in taking it deeper and darker. Your editorial changes have taken it to the place it needed to go, and I couldn't be prouder of the end result. I can't wait to work with you on the next one. Thank you for your dedication to this book and for appreciating what it is and letting it stay that way.

To Maura Kye-Casella, my agent. Thank you for your hard work with this book and for your passion and fire for it.

You've been with me every step of the way, and I appreciate it immensely. Here's to the next hundred.

And last but not least, the readers. Social media allows me the opportunity to connect with some of you. But I will never get a chance to speak to all of you, and hope that this note reaches those I have not. Thank you for spending time with this book. Please pass it on to your friends and family, please reread it until the pages are worn and the cover is falling off. And please know that I appreciate you.

Sincerely,
Alessandra

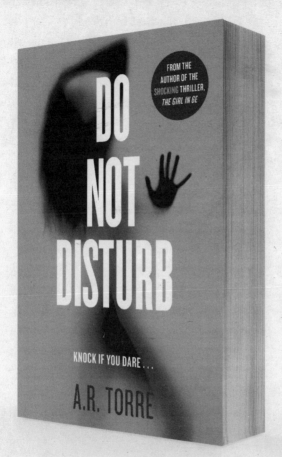